Dearest
For Noah
Ginger

19.09.'11

DRESSING FOR GOD

There's no bout a-doubt
it

[signature]

Library and Archives Canada Cataloguing in Publication

Tallon, J. F., 1944-
Dressing for God : a parable of self-discovery / J.F. Tallon.
ISBN 978-0-88962-924-0
I. Title.
PS8639.A45D74 2010   C813'.6   C2010-906386-4

No part of this book may be reproduced or transmitted in any form, by any means, electronic or mechanical, including photocopying and recording, information storage and retrieval systems, without permission in writing from the publisher, except by a reviewer who may quote brief passages in a review.

Pubished by Mosaic Press, Oakville, Ontario, Canada, 2011. Distributed in Canada by Mosaic Press. Distributed in the United States by Midpoint Trade Books. Distributed in the U.K. by Gazelle Book Services.

MOSAIC PRESS, Publishers
Copyright ©,J.F. Tallon, 2011
ISBN 978-0-88962-928-8

www.mosaic-press.com

Mosaic Press in Canada:
1252 Speers Road, Units 1 & 2
Oakville, Ontario L6L 5N9
Phone/Fax: 905-825-2130
info@mosaic-press.com

Mosaic Press in U.S.A.:
c/o Livingston, 40 Sonwil Dr,
Cheektowaga, NY 14225
Phone/Fax: 905-825-2130
info@mosaic-press.com

www.mosaic-press.com

DRESSING FOR GOD

A Parable of Self Discovery

J.F. Tallon

mosaic press

Contents

Prologue		1
Chapter 1	In the Beginning	3
Chapter 2	As One Door Closes	5
Chapter 3	Six Degrees of Separation	15
Chapter 4	Imagine This …	21
Chapter 5	Déjà vu	32
Chapter 6	Noah's Art	38
Chapter 7	'Thoughts Are Things…'	58
Chapter 8	'Move the Car'	73
Chapter 9	E.F.T.	86
Chapter 10	Upside Down	97
Chapter 11	'It Sticks Where It's Stuck'	114
Chapter 12	Divine Breath	127
Chapter 13	Critical Day!	134
Chapter 14	No Answer	148
Chapter 15	The Play of Life	152
Chapter 16	Act As If…	164
Chapter 17	Me, Myself and I	169
Chapter 18	Breakthrough	176
Chapter 19	Message Received	179
Chapter 20	Deliverance	185
Chapter 21	You Reap As You Sow	190
Chapter 22	Whole In One	197
Epilogue		200
Acknowledgments		202

Prologue

MY TRUST LOGBOOK ENTRY WED. FEB. 4, 2009:
0500 Following received from Port Abundance Radio Control VHF channel twenty four: "Provisional port entry granted—proceed to quarantine anchorage and await port health clearance."

Captain John sat at the wheel of his beloved *My Trust*, a mug of strong tea warming his tanned, weathered fist, his upper body weaving a gentle, almost figure eight motion in tune with the rhythmic action of the boat as it pitched and rolled in a moderate sea. The throb of the eighty horse power Cat diesel purring under his feet was pushing him closer to Abundance with every turn of the screw. A slop of a wave breaking on deck at the port quarter reminded him that the tide was turning and would soon be on the flood and would add another knot to his speed.

"Abundance, oh Abundance of health, wealth and happiness. I love you, God I love you. Thank you, thank you, thank you," he repeated the mantra inwardly as feelings of relief surged through every muscle, nerve, fibre, molecule and atom of his body. He felt exhilaration of a kind he had never before imagined. It was just magnificent.

He reset the autopilot to 360 bringing the bow twenty degrees to starboard, heading straight for the blip of the port entrance buoy—thinking how appropriate that was, *"Indeed I have come full circle this time around."* His salt and pepper beard glowed from the reflection of the radar screen as he scanned the twelve mile radius. Port Abundance lay straight

J.F. Tallon

ahead on a course of true north and at this rate, he noted the log speed—doing just over seven knots, he reckoned he would be at the eastern quarantine anchorage in about forty minutes.

"Abundance Port Control, this is the motor yacht My Trust calling on sixteen—come in please."

"My Trust this is Abundance Port Control go to channel twenty-four please."

"Abundance this is My Trust, I confirm our ETA at the entrance buoy for 0610—Have you any further instructions for me?"

My Trust—this is Abundance Port Control—yes there's a message from the Harbour Master—he says welcome home and what the hell kept you so long?"

Capt John smiled as he answered, "Many thanks Abundance—tell him it's a long story and I look forward to sharing it with him over a drink later. This is My Trust over and out."

"Ok My Trust proceed to the quarantine anchorage and anchor up, we'll get Port Health out at first light. This is Abundance Port Control out."

Chapter 1

In The Beginning...

Adam King stared at his laptop screen, a feeling of inner frustration gnawing in his gut. There was something seriously amiss—there always is when his solar plexus tightened up like this. "What the hell is happening now?" He slowed his breathing and reread the last page. Captain John has been ordered to anchor in the quarantine anchorage instead of being cleared inwards to Port Abundance. He hadn't considered this possibility when he'd started writing this life voyage account of Captain John's journey of exploration across the unseen inner seas of life. He knew there was no way he could ignore the instruction and just sail in and tie up in the yacht marina. It wouldn't work like that. If he couldn't *feel* that it was right for Captain John to enter and take his birthright then he'd have to find out why and sort it, and sort it *quickly*. Now he'd have to get him out on deck clearing away his anchor, ready to let go. Damn. Quarantine could take forever.

He had created two parallel journeys. Captain John in *My Trust* was en route to Port Abundance, his metaphorical home port on the Horn of Plenty, while he, Adam King, Captain John's shadow self, was committed to *discovering* how the law of life worked in the unseen worlds of being *and to simultaneously write about it...*

He'd done his research. He'd fully explored as far as he could. His desk was piled with reference books, papers, journals, notes and files. "But I'm just not getting it right—I've got a gremlin in my self-steering—I'm going round in circles and I can't afford to keep *My Trust* anchored outside Port Abundance for much longer. *I need* to find what's causing this and fix it."

He pushed himself away from the desk, his eyes straying to a poem stuck on his notice board. He had penned it months ago when he'd

J.F. Tallon

changed the boat's name from The Prodigal to the more appropriately named *My Trust*.

>**I am**
>**Sailing**
>**In a boat named**
>**Trust**
>**On an Inner See**
>**Of Being**
>**Knowing that My Pilot**
>**Has my Eye**
>**To bring me Home**
>**Aye**
>**Bring me**
>**Home**

Adam walked into the kitchen, made a mug of tea, added two lumps of sugar, a drop of milk then sat outside on the deck of his house overlooking the Kenmare River, the phrase *I need* ringing in his ears. "If *I need* then that's what I'll get," he thought, "Exactly that—more ***need***. So what to do?"

He sat watching the early morning sky brighten in the east behind him, the birds beginning to chirp the garden awake. He closed his eyes and silently asked, "And just how do I solve this one?" An answer struck home instantly and he quickly returned inside to his office, logged online and found what he was looking for. *Private Eye* online. "They have an '*I Need*' section and *that* seems very appropriate." He started writing his advert.

Writer Seeks Research Assistant….

Chapter 2

As One Door Closes

Eve was staring out the window lost in thought as the train accelerated from Edinburgh's Waverly Station heading south. She was in seat 17A facing forward on the left hand side of the carriage. London was down the track a few hours ahead. The Marine Hotel and the links of North Berwick golf course appeared on the edge of her vision and there, just beyond the beach, she could see the outline of the pink sandstone building The Old Granary, her home for the past seven years. When the train drew abreast she turned in the seat, her head close to the window, straining to keep it in sight. The leaden, grey sky heavy with thick rain clouds blurred the scene as the train took the curve heading south for the border. She sighed, watching her breath mist the window momentarily, "Gone from view but not from memory."

She lay back in the seat, her head to one side, propped against the headrest, looking at the reflection in the windowpane as the East Lothian countryside streamed past outside. Her light blue eyes looked tired, she thought, as she studied the person looking back at her. She ran a hand through her strawberry blonde hair. She liked her low maintenance short crop, and then turned slightly to see the small diamond stud earrings catch the carriage light and twinkle in the glass mirror. The sight made her smile with happy memories. She hadn't enjoyed too many of those in the past few months.

Eve brought her hands into view, slender artistic fingers, nails clear varnished, straight cut, a white circular band noticeable against the light tan on her left ring finger. She flexed her hand open and shut, she massaged the ring space then gave a small bob at her reflection and thought "That's well gone also." Eve pursed her lightly glossed lips, closed her eyes, eased off her shoes and stretched her stockinged feet onto the seat opposite and let herself relax. A knot of tension was lodged between her shoulder blades, and she rolled her shoulders and stretched her neck muscles a few times to ease it. The train's rhythm had steadied when it reached full speed on a straight run to the border. Eve felt, "Yes, it's time to start my exercise."

She'd learned it from her dad. "Spring clean your life," he'd called it." Start in your attic and then clear out the basement." She smiled recalling the graffiti she'd seen on a wall in Leith *Keep Scotland Tidy—Dump Your Rubbish in England*.

"Well no, I won't," she thought. "I'm dumping mine in Scotland."

"All right then and just where will you start?" her inner voice replied.

Her dad's advice came back to mind, "Make a list—make *two* lists," he would have said. "Start with the positives and end with the negatives; bundle the crap into a pile and let it go where it belongs. Cut your ties Eve—if it doesn't serve you, ditch it."

"Ok, the positives first...I suppose I'd better write them out." Remembering her dad's emphasis to write it down on paper and give it a physical presence'. Eve retrieved her journal from her bag then sat for long moments looking at the empty page, understanding the finality of her mental clearing out. She was feeling very alone yet strangely excited, it was as if somehow the balance of life was swinging her way again. She'd had her fill of disappointments and it was time now for some good stuff.

With her eyes closed and her head nestled into the edge of the seat back, Eve let her feelings rise to the surface and as they floated in her mind's eye she sent them into piles. The sad and angry memories went in the bucket and the good ones she smiled at and placed in her happy pile. Satisfied she was getting it right she started her list.

My Happy Pile
I'm healthy
I'm free—divorce hearing imminent!
I'm ok financially
I'm 35 years young—well 36 in two days
I have management experience
I'm reasonably content

Dressing for God

I can use my maiden name again!!
- Hello Eve McQueen

The Garbage Bucket
Goodbye to Leith and the restaurant
North Berwick - our flat
Goodbye James — my ex
My old name Archer — I never liked it
My anger and regrets...too many to name!!

She read it over and then closed the journal to resume the cleanout exercise. Eve breathed easily and concentrated on her task. She bundled all her thoughts of hurt and anger into a big plastic waste bag, tied it firmly below a large blue helium filled balloon and then released it, watching as it floated off into space, carrying with it all the worries and hurt of her past months.

She got a set of shears and started cutting each of the threads connected to her past; the marriage breakup, the betrayal, the lies, the anger, the pain, the end of a life dream. She felt emotions churning in her solar plexus as the cords of attachment were stretched and stretched, resisting the release, and then she felt the balloon snap free and she relaxed, breathing deeply, felt lightness in her gut as the balloon floated up and away, and then dissolved completely in her mind's eye.

"Mustn't make a drama out of it," she reminded herself yet again. "Just see it gone. Don't feed it energy, let the memories fade."

The rhythmic sound of the wheels on the tracks and the slight swaying motion of the carriage lulled her into a light doze and she wondered where the tracks of her own life were leading beyond London.

"A new beginning, that's what I need." Eve let the idea settle in her mind. "A new beginning to a new life...."

"Tickets please, have your tickets ready for inspection please." The conductor stood patiently and brought her back to wakefulness.

Feeling peckish, Eve made her way to the dining car where over a coffee and a sandwich she sat quietly immersed in her life options. She'd spend a few weeks in Guy's place in Rotherhithe while he was away, "But then what? I'd like to do something totally different; something to stretch me, but what?" She was more relaxed, watching the fields rush by, the rain streaking the windows.

The posters on the platform hoardings when Eve entered York station were advertising new book titles, West End shows, pension funds, travel adverts, holidays in the sun.

"Maybe I'll check the web and rent a gite in France or maybe make a start on this book idea. I could do a sort of Scottish Kitchen Confidential," she thought. "Nah, that life is gone in the garbage. No, it'll have to be something totally different."

Eve mulled over the possibilities, "Writing? Maybe travel for a few months and get some sunshine, write some short stories?" She shook her head and shrugged, "Ach, it's all too soon... I really don't *know* what I want to do."

She finished the coffee and made her way back to her seat. A copy of *Private Eye* magazine lay on the seat beside her, discarded by a passenger at York, she figured.

Eve sat and glanced at the cartoon cover. Four pinstripe-suited bankers sat in the dock before an ermine robed and bewigged Quizmaster Judge, as part of a *Bankers Panel Game*. They had conferred on the rhetorical question of 'Why was British banking in such a mess?' and answered with the single caption *'I haven't a clue'*.

"And that's exactly how I feel." Eve smiled at the thought, "I haven't a clue either."

She leafed through the magazine; it wasn't her choice of reading and was about to discard it when an advert caught her eye in the 'I Need' column on the second last page:

> Writer Seeks Research Assistant
> Computer literate / open minded person with spiritual outlook required ASAP. Do you recognise synchronicities for what they are?
> Sole use of cottage in SW Ireland available to suitable candidate. Small monthly remuneration; full board provided.

Dressing for God

Be brief, yet concise in detailing your suitability for this position.
Independent references required
Reply Box 8910 or email AK3@gofree.indigo.ie

Eve read the ad twice.

"Working with a real writer! How about that? I'd get some insight into writing, wouldn't I? But I know zilch about research and even less about Ireland? It doesn't say much but I suppose it could have possibilities."

Eve put the magazine down on the table and gazed at the words for some time and then thought, "Well it is an option I didn't have ten minutes ago. Ah hell, nothing ventured, nothing gained."

"But no," her inner voice argued, " It's probably some cash strapped would-be author looking for a girl Friday. I mean advertising in *Private Eye*, it's not exactly the *Scotsman* or *The Times* is it?"

Stifling a yawn, she sat pondering on the advert, trying to read behind the words.

"'*With spiritual outlook*', what's all that about? Am I spiritually minded?"

Eve settled back in the seat and let her mind wander. She recalled sitting with her mom by the fire in their home in Musselburgh on a cold February morning a few days after her grandma passed away, "Must have been nearly what, twenty years ago?" She mused, seeing the scene clearly in her mind's eye.

Her mom holding her hand and telling the story of how the night after the funeral she awoke in the early hours of the morning to see Grandma standing at the end of her bed, dressed in her favourite sky blue dress with the ruffled neckline, she was surrounded by a pale, luminous light. She just stood there smiling lovingly and then after a few long moments she just gently faded away.

Eve could still see her mom crying with tears of joy as she gently squeezed Eve's hand and said, "It was Grandma's way of showing she was OK—she was safe in heaven and there was no need to worry or grieve for her." The tiny hairs at the back of Eve's neck were prickling as she recalled the story. She watched her smile reflected back from the carriage window as she savoured the memory.

J.F. Tallon

"There's no doubt Mom was very, very spiritual and who knows maybe some of it has rubbed off on me?" She felt an interest stir as she pondered on what it could lead to.

"Well then, if I replied," She wondered, "What questions would I ask?"

She slipped her Blackberry from her bag and deliberated for a while before she wrote:

> Hello 'AK3'
> Re: your advert for a research assistant—I'm an Arts grad., computer literate, open minded and I know that not all spirit comes in a bottle of Scotch.
> If my qualifications and your requirements are coincidental, could that be synchronous...??
> Exactly what type of research is involved?
> Regards
>
> Eve Archer
> email address: EVERcher@freeuk.com

"To send or not to send? That's the question." She realized her action was very out of character and she hesitated to send it. "Good, steady, reliable Eve, acting on a whim like that." She imagined what Guy's reaction would be if she told him.

"You did what? Answered an ad in *Private Eye*, are you off your game little sister?"

Eve hit the send button and watched the message fade into the ether. "Ah, probably nothing'll come of it." A dry smile curled at the edge of her mouth as she savoured a little thrill of adventure in doing something different, something daring.

A black cab deposited Eve outside the porter's office at King and Queen Wharf in Rotherhithe in the midst of London's East End Docklands. The porter remembering her from previous visits escorted her to the rooftop apartment in Blenheim Court.

The apartment was Guy's joy. He'd bought it some years ago and Eve had helped him with the furnishing. Guy favoured the soft, black leather suite and matching recliners, deep blue Axminster carpet, the Danish ash and frosted glass dining table and of course the mood

Dressing for God

lighting. However it was the spectacular river vista that was the star attraction for Eve.

This, she loved. She could spend hours at the window watching the river traffic and the feeling of being above it all, looking down on the passing ships, the tugs and barges, the house boats, the water police patrols, the sounds of the pleasure boats with their office parties heading down river to Greenwich, the visiting navy vessels and the rowers; single skulls and eights, all enjoying their space in the great river. She yearned for the water the way a bird yearns to fly.

There was a note from Guy on the coffee table.

Eve

Make yourself at home, usual room made up for you. I'm due back 2nd March, all going well. The car is in garage if you need it—don't crash it! Look forward to seeing you—take care.

You'll get over him. Chin up!

Best love
Guy

An hour later, after taking a soothing soak in the tub, Eve, wrapped in one of Guy's fluffy white robes, sat by the window checking her email. She had two new messages. One from Shore Porters in Edinburgh, confirming delivery of her personal effects tomorrow and one from her solicitor, confirming the divorce hearing date was fixed for May fifteenth. "Excellent, oh fantastic, yes!" The thought lifted her spirits enormously, 'Things are moving at last.'

While exiting from Outlook Express another email hit the inbox.

'*From: Adam King*', Her mouth opened in a reflex action, a feeling of excitement flushing through her veins. 'Oh, am I ready for this?'

She placed the Blackberry on the arm of the settee and stood rubbing her hands along her forearms feeling a chill in the warm sitting room, asking herself, 'Oh Heavens, what to do, what to do?'

Eve stared at the screen unsure of what to do. "Open it or just delete it?" She was curious about the quick response and then with a whispered, "Ruddy hell," she opened the message.

J.F. Tallon

FROM: Adam King
TO: EVERcher@freeuk.com
Subject: Adam to Eve

Hello Eve
Thanks for your email—I appreciate your interest. I am writing a book on the how of life and seeking an enthusiastic research person with an open mind and an interest in spirituality, so if you fit that description, then I'd like to meet up.

I see you're UK based. I'm in London Thursday 19th for 1 night, and could arrange to meet if convenient. Otherwise we could have a telecon to see if there is mutual interest.

You can get me on this email or contact me at London Bridge Hotel 020 7855 2200 from 2pm tomorrow.

Regards,
Adam King

Eve's mind was in turmoil. "Adam King. Eve McQueen. King and Queen Wharf, and he's staying at the hotel just up the river from here An understanding of synchronicity indeed!"

Her mind was whirling. "Am I mad? What have I started?" Thoughts were piling in on her as she sat at the table reading the email again.

"Just what is 'synchronicity' anyway?" she thought. "Is it not the same as coincidence?"

Eve logged on and Googled 'synchronicity' on Wikipedia.

"So: *synchronicity can be a meaningful coincidence that has a causative source.*"

"Mmm... Well I'm not so sure about that. Or it's: *a mystical event—one that illustrates how, at the same moment that a question arises, the answer too can be found.*"

"Am I any the wiser for all that?" shaking her head,"No, I'm definitely not." She went into the kitchen for a glass of wine, wondering just what she was doing playing with this Ireland idea."Well I'm not

Dressing for God

going to answer him now, that's for sure—I'll best sleep on it and see how I feel in the morning."

The Blackberry was shut down, the message unanswered, the idea percolating in her mind.

She snuggled into the soft leather recliner and switched on the music system.

Katie Melua's voice filled the room, "Life is just a slow train crawling up a hill, never stop to wonder why... so here I am in London town.... life is just a slow train." "Thank you Guy," she said aloud, a wide grin spreading across her face, feeling better than she had for ages. "You read that one perfectly."

She awoke to the sound of tugs manoeuvring a warship in the river outside the bedroom window. She counted three long blasts on the tug's whistle followed by three more blasts from the warship, watching as it swung through 180 degrees, moving stern first upriver towards Tower Bridge. A huge red, white and blue tricolour wrapped itself around the flagstaff, like a Maypole streamer in the very brisk wind. The ship's crew, the matelots, were lining the after deck in their dark navy blue uniforms with red pom-poms on their white caps. One sailor's hat flew over the ship's side and whirled across the river like a French frisbee. "I'll bet he gets a kick in the derriere for that," she smiled and then chuckled at the thought.

Picking up Guy's binoculars, Eve focused on the sleek grey warship, the D621 Chevalier Paul bristling with rocket pods, radar antennae, massive satellite domes and anti-aircraft missile batteries. It slowly rounded the bend of the river heading to her berth beside HMS Belfast on the other side of Tower Bridge.

A small motor boat had put out from the water-police jetty at Wapping just across from King and Queen, and now lay broadside on to the river flow. It had cut its engine and lay wallowing in the chop of the flood tide; she watched the spray break against the hull and splash the occupants. There were five people aboard, one of whom she thought was a priest, a Sikh maybe, judging by his beard and turban. He was holding a large black book and the others, except for the boatman at the tiller, were facing him with their heads bowed in supplication.

J.F. Tallon

The priest had steadied himself in a wide stance as the boat rolled slightly as it breasted the current. He then started reading from the book. A silver urn was handed to him which he held over the leeward side and slowly emptied it into the brown muddy Thames, the dust spreading downwind- a light brown stain against the darker brown of the river. It disappeared within seconds.

Her thoughts floated around her. 'Was that a woman who died? Was it a Mother, a child, a Father? What kind of life did it have? Who was it?' The questions crowded her. 'How fleeting is life? The ashes just touched the waters and were gone.' She stayed immobile watching the river flow, deep in thought.

Her eyes were drawn back to the email on her Blackberry. The words '*The how of life*' stood out, as if magnified. Eve pondered on the why of life, 'What does it all really mean? You live and you die and then what?'

Her attention kept moving from the words in the message to the thought of the vanishing stain of the ashes in the river. The boatman had kicked the engine back to life; the propeller churned a circular wake as he throttled up, heading for the jetty. The passengers huddled, heads together in the stern. Eve somehow felt joined in their grief and wondered at this for a long moment

"*Right,*" she said aloud. "My decision is made. I'll call this Mr. King. Get it over and done with, see if there's anything in it for me."

Chapter 3

Six Degrees of Separation

At sixteen minutes past four, Eve approached the reception desk at the London Bridge Hotel and asked for Mr. Adam King. She was put through to room 238. The phone rang three times, a soft Irish voice answered on the other end.

"Good afternoon, Adam King speaking."

Eve, hesitating for a moment, fought her instinct to put the receiver down and leave, to get out. "Oh, hello Mr. King, this is Eve Archer. We emailed each other. I'm here in the lobby." The words tumbled into the mouthpiece, Eve looking around to see if anyone was watching her.

"You're downstairs? Outstanding!" he said. "Look I'll be right down. Why don't you stay by the phone and then I'll know who to look for. OK?"

Eve went to check herself in a mirror before meeting Mr. Writer. The ladies restroom was across the hall beside the Borough Bar, a quick once over on her hair, a touch of lip gloss and she headed back to the phone booth. A tall, well built man in his mid-forties with longish, dark brown hair, trim salt and pepper beard, dressed in a grey business suit was standing by the phone booth. With his hand on his chin he swivelled his head scanning the lobby.

Eve approached him from the side "Mr. King?"

"Eve Archer?" he enquired, a smile spreading across his open face. His ice blue eyes twinkling as he faced her.

They shook hands, Eve pleased at the exchange. One thing she disliked was a wet fish handshake and so far so good, his handshake was firm and not too macho. Having dressed carefully for the interview she knew that the cream Channel trouser suit and the white silk blouse were perfect. It was just an interview and *Eve* was doing the interviewing.

"It's nice to meet you Mr. King. I was driving by and thought I'd see if you were at home. I hope it's not inconvenient."

"Not at all, not at all," he repeated in a soft brogue. "I'm delighted, a lovely surprise. Call me Adam, please." He smiled at her and indicated with his head in the direction of the café. "Would you like tea, coffee? We can maybe have a chat and a cuppa?"

A pot of Earl Grey tea on the table between them, Eve sat upright, knees together, feet crossed under her chair, hands clasped in her lap, listening attentively as Adam opened up the conversation.

"My book project," he said. "I started it two years ago but what with one thing and another, I had to put it on the back burner I'm afraid." He gave a shrug of his shoulders, "And now I'm gearing myself up to drop everything else and write full time." He looked across at Eve as he opened the lid of the teapot checking the brew, his eyes a pale liquid blue under dark black eyebrows.

He poured the tea for Eve and himself. 'Nice hands, tanned, long fingers, no rings,' she noticed.

Placing a slice of lemon in his cup he took a sip. "I'm quite excited about it really, can't wait to get at it full time. However, I'm looking for someone to be my sounding board. Someone with a modicum of spiritual interest who is open minded enough to want to understand how life works and who'd be willing to play a role in bringing it together. Does that sound ambitious?" He finished with a quiet laugh.

"And do you really *know* how life works?" Eve asked, looking him straight in the eye.

"Well, yes I believe I do," he said, "but the proof of the pudding is, as they say, in the eating and now I just need to *demonstrate* my understanding. That's what the book is all about."

He took another sip of tea before continuing. "I'm writing it as a sailing story. My alter ego, Captain John sails his boat to Port Abundance." He paused to explain, "Port Abundance is a metaphorical place of destiny where there's an abundance of health, wealth and happiness waiting for him. It's where anyone living here on earth would aspire to reach…" His words tailed off as he looked enquiringly at Eve, checking her reaction.

Dressing for God

Eve rubbed her earlobe, her face implacable. She caught his enquiring look and said "OK, go on please," but she was asking inwardly, 'Is this another Treasure Island fantasy—another Robert Louis Stevenson in the making?'

"The book concludes with Captain John being interviewed by a lady I call Finity Muze, a sort of Oprah Winfrey of the inner universe, where he shares the insights he's learned on his journey into Abundance."

He waited for Eve to comment, looking at her keenly, his eyebrows rose almost to his hairline.

"So let me get this straight, if you don't mind," Eve asked leaning forward, her fingertips steepled under her chin, "You are saying that you really understand the laws of life enough to be interviewed by this Finity person and that you can *show* rather than *tell* how life works. Have I got that right?"

"Yes, precisely that—*show* rather than *tell*—I like that," Adam replied, visibly pleased.

"And this research person you're looking for, does she..." Eve's hands making a little wave in the air "Does she have to research the questions you'll be asked on this show?"

"Well yes, I suppose so, but I'm also looking for someone who would participate in learning to *use* the lessons of life in the book, so there is a real life development aspect to it as well. Does that sound of interest to you?"

"Possibly, it all sounds rather, well..." she hesitated, "it's very out of the ordinary and to tell you the truth, I'd need to understand a lot more before I could say if I was really interested or not. Can you tell me more about your set-up in Ireland, you mentioned a separate cottage?"

"I'd be delighted to, sure. Have you ever been to Ireland?" Adam settled back in his chair, stretching his legs out to the side of the table.

"Yes, I've been to Dublin and I went to Galway for the oyster festival a few years back."

"That's good. Well I live on the south west coast outside a small town called Sneem in Kerry, in a place called Oyster Bed Pier and it's really very pretty indeed. We have mountains and lakes behind us and Kenmare Bay and the Atlantic on the doorstep. I can email some photos to you later if you're interested."

"That would be nice, thank you."

"I've two houses, the big house where I live and then the cottage which has just been refurbished, it really is very comfortable. Not what you'd call hardship living by any stretch of the imagination. But what about yourself Eve, what are you up to?"

"As I said in the email I'm an arts graduate from St. Andrews. My forte, I suppose, has been in restaurant management. I'm staying at my brother's place across the river from here, in," she paused, smiling slightly and continued. "In Rotherhithe, it's called King and Queen Wharf."

Adams eyes flickered a few times and he grinned in acknowledgement.

"I was on the train down here from Edinburgh yesterday and someone had left a copy of *Private Eye* on my seat and I saw the ad, and I thought what the hell and answered it." She stopped for a brief moment, "I still find this a bit difficult to talk about." Eve paused and then exhaled a deep breath, "You see my marriage has just finished. I'm in the middle of divorce proceedings and I'm still, well, I'm still feeling a bit raw."

Adam nodded, "Yes, I can well understand that feeling. I've been there myself. It does take time to heal and are you OK now?" He leaned forward, looking solicitous.

Eve smiled at his understanding. "Yes I'm fine thanks. I'm just not used to talking about it yet. You see my ex and I, we ran a restaurant in Leith and I…" Eve reached into her handbag and then handed Adam a business card. "Here, that's what I was up to last month".

TALK OF THE TOWN
The Shore,
Leith

Eve Archer
Restaurant Manager

Holding the card in his right hand with a quizzical tone said, "I worked in Leith some years ago on an engineering project for Forth Ports."

Dressing for God

"Really?" Eve asked brightly, "Do you know our restaurant then?"

"No, I can't say I do. How long have you been open?"

"Five years now, we started in April 2004."

"Ah it's been what, six years since I was there but I know The Shore and the bars and restaurants well. You must know some of the management of Forth Ports then, do you?" He asked with an impish grin, his interest in Eve visibly sparked.

"Of course I do, I catered for them. We did most of their boardroom functions and I know most of the directors."

Adams mouth hung open, words failing him. His eyes fluttered as he took this in.

"Talk about six degrees," he said. "Have you heard of the six degrees of separation?"

"I think so, wasn't there a movie by that name?"

"Yeah there was. It's about how everyone is interconnected. It's like there's supposed to be no more than five other people between any of us and I guess this just about proves that theory correct," he said, rubbing his hands over his beard as if to shed his incredulity. "So I suppose if you do take the job I'll have no problem with your references then."

They laughed, "Well if that's the case, then the same will go for me then, with references for you, I mean."

Adam was quietly grinning, scratching the side of his head.

"So back to your question then, what am I up to just now," Eve said, a more serious tone in her voice. "I'm really at the end of a big chapter in my life. I'm finished with the restaurant business. I left Leith for good yesterday. Lord above was it only yesterday? It seems like a week ago." Straightening in her seat, she felt really good speaking her mind to a stranger. It gave her confidence somehow.

Adam held his hands up, palms open, "Eve, can I make a suggestion please?"

"Of course you can, yes."

He checked his watch, "Look its getting on for five now, I'm a bit pressed for time. Would it be possible to perhaps continue our chat later, maybe over dinner? It's just that I have some really urgent calls to make. I was going to suggest across the river at La Pont de la Tour? Could I tempt you?"

Unable to resist Eve replied before she could bite her tongue, "I thought it was Eve who tempted Adam, and not the other way around."

Adam laughed at the repartee while Eve took a moment to consider, "I'd love dinner, thank you, it sounds great."

"Brilliant. I look forward to it. Would 7:30 suit?"

"Sounds perfect, and thanks."

He proffered his hand to Eve who gave a firm grip, looked him in the eye with just the hint of a smile showing at the corner of her mouth. "Adam, I didn't tell you my maiden name, did I?"

"No. You didn't, why?"

"Adam," she paused for maximum effect and then added, "My maiden name was McQueen."

Turning on her heel she hurried to the front door grinning from ear to ear.

Chapter 4

Imagine This

Adam stood inside the entrance foyer of La Pont de la Tour, admiring the seafood counter with oysters and crabs, clams, lobster, scallops, crevettes, mussels, whelks and winkles all dressed in iodine smelling seaweed on a small mountain of ice. He was lost in admiration mentally savouring the crustaceans and failed to hear the soft footsteps behind him.

"Hello, I'm not late am I? Gosh it's really starting to pee down outside."

Standing behind him in a tan leather Louis Vuitton travel coat, Eve shook the raindrops from her hair, her face moist from the short run from the cab to the restaurant.

"Eve, oh my, it's good to see you. No you're not late. Lord yes, it is nasty outside." Helping her off with her coat, he handed it to the hostess.

"You got me earlier you know, Eve McQueen indeed! Are you really Eve McQueen from King and Queen Wharf?"

"I am, yes, really. But it's my brother who owns the apartment in King and Queen. I'm just a visitor passing through."

"Ah it fair blew my socks off, not to mention the Eve and Adam bit. Are you sure you're not making this up?"

Smiling, he gestured with his head at the fish counter "What do you think of this lot? Pretty good looking isn't it?"

"Mmm yes and look at those scallops—Orkney too—they look great."

"Yeah and the Galway Bay Oysters. I think we just might enjoy this dinner. Shall we?" he said turning towards the maitre'd who was waiting, menus in hand, to show them to their table.

J.F. Tallon

They were seated in the alcove at the discreet end of the restaurant. Their table gave them a panoramic view of the quayside and the River Thames. The scene absorbed Adam for several moments as he sat, hands folded on the white table cloth, soaking in the atmosphere. The shadow of the great bridge spilled over the river edge onto the quayside, its lattice steel work with the turret towers reflecting a filigree backdrop for the shadow show of nature being played in front of them. The white painted bollards dotted along the jetty, the scudding clouds in the night sky, the full moon fleetingly broke through the rolling cumulous and as they watched, the clouds opened with an audible whoosh and it deluged. The rain lashed onto the river bank obliterating the bridge from their view. The background music was drowned by the noise of the torrential rain pelting the quayside, and the wind in a sudden gust sucked some loose patio chairs sending them flying through the air crashing into the car park beyond.

The noise broke their reverie. "Good God, now isn't that something? We were lucky to get in before that." Eve nodded her agreement. They watched mesmerised as the rain hammered down, the double glazed windows visibly pulsing from the wind pressure pounding and pushing outside.

He turned his attention to Eve sitting opposite, her light blue blouse with an open neck, a small diamond choker and matching diamond ear studs. He loved the laughter lines around her almost silky blue-grey eyes which were sparkling bright in the candlelight and her golden reddish hair still damp from the rain. 'Very pleasant indeed,' he thought.

They ordered the oysters with roasted scallops and asparagus to follow and were now sipping a glass of chilled Chablis, as a distant lightning flash split the sky drawing their attention away from the table.

Eve, elbows on the table, chin resting on her hands repeated the question that had been on her mind since leaving the hotel earlier.

"I've been thinking about this book of yours Adam, the 'how of life' as you call it. Excuse me if I'm being a bit forthright, but it seems a huge challenge to be able to explain *how* life works—I mean..." she paused, eyebrows arched, "Just where do you start and finish?"

His head cocked to one side, focusing his eyes on the storm raging outside, "It is a challenge, isn't it?" He turned facing her now. "My

Dressing for God

mother used to say to me, 'never bite off more than you can chew', which is why," he started chewing furiously, "I shouldn't speak with my mouth full."

"OK." She said, trying to keep a straight face, "Good answer. I'll remember my table manners too, but seeing as we're talking about life and food sitting in this fine restaurant in the middle of a hurricane, can you answer me this then—how can I avoid getting indigestion on this spiritual diet of yours?"

Adam mirrored her pose, his chin resting on his hands, eyes focused on the candle, a hint of a smile curling at the corner of his mouth, acknowledging her curiosity.

"I read somewhere the other day that just because someone goes to church regularly it doesn't necessarily mean that they're spiritual, any more than if someone goes to a garage regularly, that it means that they're a mechanic."

"Yes I see that, but that begs the question then doesn't it, just what is a spiritual mechanic?"

"Good one," he said giving her a tick of his finger in the air. "Is it not all about understanding the mechanics of living *consciously to get desired results?* I mean you don't have to be a mechanic to drive a car, any more than you have to know how life works to live a good life. However, you'd have to agree, there's more chance that the driver who appreciates the mechanics of the car will care for it lovingly. He'll fuel it right, maintain it and so on, better than someone who knows nought about engines and performance."

"I suppose so, yes, he'd have a better feel for it."

"Aye, definitely and so a spiritual mechanic, as you chose to call him, would understand that to get the best out of his body he'd pick the best mental and physical diets to keep his body, mind and spirit ticking over at optimum revs—a sort of spiritual formula one driver in a brilliantly designed life vehicle." He looked questioning at Eve, "Does that suffice?" He angled his head as he held an imaginary steering wheel in his hands.

"I'm not sure that it answers my question completely." Eve added, enjoying the banter. "But let me change gears then please. You see the reason I asked about the *why* of life is because I saw something intriguing in the river this morning that got me wondering. Can I tell you about it?"

J.F. Tallon

Eve recounted the scene of the ashes being cast into the river, the remains disappearing in a few seconds. "I found it, well sort of morbidly fascinating for some reason. I had never really looked at life ending like that before and I suppose that's one of the reasons I decided to call you. I wanted to see if you can maybe explain about the *why of life and death* to me. Can you do that in one evening, do you think?"

"I can certainly try. I like your style I must say, you're not shy about coming forward are you? I like that—good stuff." He raised his glass and saluted her as the waiter served their main course and refreshed their glasses. "Can I concentrate on enjoying these little beauties and save the discourse for afters?" he asked.

"I couldn't agree more, they look like they deserve our full attention, bon appetite." Eve replied tucking in.

"You were right about the scallops; they're nearly as good as the ones we get in Kerry."

"I was expecting that from you, but then I suppose they all come from the same ocean don't they?"

Eve's acknowledgement of the scallops' Atlantic heritage won a wide grin from Adam.

Outside the deluge had abated to a steady downpour. The quayside was cleared of everything that wasn't bolted down and Adam thought the river looked dangerously high, its turgid brown surface swollen by the runoff from the streets. There was no traffic moving on it at all. Not a barge or boat to be seen.

Plate clean and her appetite satisfied, Eve feeling more relaxed than she'd been for months, sensed an inquisitiveness perking her up. She toyed with her glass of wine waiting for Adam to start.

"So—am I going to hear your story?"

"Yeah, and why not? OK try this for size," he said. "What I'd like you to do is to use your imagination with me."

Picking up the stainless steel salver on which the bill had been presented, he used it as a mirror reflecting Eves flickering face in the candlelight, as he tilted it in her direction. "Try to imagine the size of a mirror it would take to be able to reflect—to capture in itself, the totality of everything that had ever been created."

Eve's face had a puzzled look, brow wrinkling, she showed real difficulty in grasping the sense of it all.

Dressing for God

"Imagine a mirror of infinite size—a gigantic circular mirror stretching to eternity from the beginning of time in every direction—expanding continuously and on the surface of this mirror is reflected everything that was ever created by God. It's like a snapshot of the creator's mind—a celestial screen grab of all of life that was ever created in the universe."

"I can't really say I can picture that but I think I have the idea of what you are saying."

"OK well now, the mirror is a reflection of every man, woman, child, animal, bird, fish, insect, everything of matter and non matter and they are all captured in this mirror of infinite proportions stretching to eternity in every direction. OK?" he asked.

"I'm with you so far, go on."

"Now imagine that this mirror gets smashed to smithereens. Say one of the zillions of angels holding it in place had a sneeze and dropped it crashing to earth in minute particles in a big bang—wallop—breaking it up into gazillions of tiny, tiny shards of the glass mirror."

As Adam was speaking, a massive thunderclap burst directly overhead; twin bolts of lightning slashed the night sky above the bridge, searing its reflection in the roiling Thames now in full flood. The long windows of the restaurant framed the scene—his hotel was sketched in flashing relief across the river. There was a momentary loss of air in the room, as if sucked out by some giant vacuum cleaner. An eerie orange glow lit up their table for an instant. Adam continued talking through it all, his head forward, the words melding in their fluency.

"Did you notice that nature provided the perfect background to my analogy there? Don't you just love synchronicities?" He smiled and poured the last of the Chablis into Eve's glass, placing the bottle upside down in the wine cooler standing beside him.

"Where was I? Ah yes, so this mirror is shattered into smithereens."

"The whole mirror?" she asked, "Smashed by a sneezing angel?"

Adam chuckled. "Yes, something like that, I can see you're getting the picture." He smiled at her, enjoying the moment. "Now then, do you know anything about holograms?"

"Holograms? No, I can't say that I do, although I did see some once at an exhibition in Edinburgh. Why do you ask?"

"Well, let me offer this brief introduction, because it's pertinent to the story."

J.F. Tallon

Adam held his glass of wine against the white background of his table napkin. "When I project light on to the surface of this glass of wine so that every part of the glass gets an equal intensity of light and then I take a holographic photo of the glass, then the Hologram, the developed picture, will comprise of the glass of wine against a backdrop of the napkin. The glass is about sixty-percent of the picture, the rest is the backdrop, OK? "

"Yes, I follow that. Do go on."

"When the development process is complete, the glass appears in three dimensions—3D—like you can reach out and grasp it."

Feeling as if she was back in college at a physics lesson Eve listened on, giving Adam a small flutter of her eyelids.

"And," he added, his index finger making the point in space, "here's an interesting bit about holograms." He took a drink from his glass before placing it on the table.

"If I take the smallest particle possible, a single pixel from anywhere in the picture—from the middle, an outer edge, from anywhere on the surface—and I project the same light onto any one of these pixels," he emphasised, "I can see the *complete* and *w*hole picture in each and every single one of them. Each pixel, each fragment will display the complete picture of the glass and the background within its own discreet portion."

Eve thought he looked pleased with this explanation and blinked her understanding, tilting her head in an attitude of and so?

"So let me return to the mirror. This mirror reflected the totality of the infinite imagination of everything in the universe from before time to eternity. That was the concept. And just as we needed light to project on to the surface of the glass in the hologram, so we must also have light to view the picture of God's imagination in the big mirror."

Adam put his elbows on the table again, his chin resting on his fist, his voice intimate.

"Are you still with me?"

"I think I can see where you're going with this," she said.

"Excellent, because where I'm going is into any one of the tiny pixels of that big mirror that reflected the creator's imagination. Just as in a hologram, we can see that each fragment of that infinite mirror carries within it an image of the creator itself. Each of these shards of

Dressing for God

the big mirror is a soul. And each soul is part of the one imagination of the creator."

"So what you are asking me to *believe*, is that I am a part of this god, is that right?" Eve asked in a very sceptical, soft tone.

"No, what I am asking you to *see* is that each of us is a part of the one whole and that each soul is a particle of the consciousness of the one creator. What I am saying is, that every human being living in a physical body has at the very centre of its being-ness, a unique pixelated essence of the creator and this is what I term as soul."

"And you can prove all of this, can you?"

"Well let me put it like this, I am not out to prove anything to myself anymore. But what I aim to do in the book is to offer an understanding of how life works *from the inside out* and then the reader can take the understanding and apply it to their own life and prove it for themselves. Or not, as the case may be. That's what I'm about and that's why I am looking for an able and willing sounding board research assistant."

Eve pondered on his words for a few moments and then looked him straight in the eye.

"Ok then Adam, I've another question for you."

"By all means, shoot."

"A simple question then, a simple why? Just what's the purpose of it all—can you answer that for me?"

"Why? Why are we here?" He gave a shake of the head and rubbed his hands over his eyes composing himself "Do you have forever to listen to the answer? I jest." He added, holding up his hands. "Here let me get my thoughts together for a second," he paused to look out the window before continuing.

"Would you agree that everything we can imagine has it's opposite?"

Eve mused for a moment before agreeing, "I suppose I can go along with that."

"Right, OK—so before the material universe was created, all that was in existence was the one mind of the creator in a state of... let's call it 'no thing'."

Eve raised her eyebrows, eyes opening wider, looking up at him.

"This mind space is the ultimate in bliss, where unconditional love enjoys a perfect peace of the one creator. It's the home of all intelligence and power. It's where every iota of everything that could be known is already known in perfect stillness." He looked at Eve for comment. None forthcoming, he continued.

"However, in perfect stillness there is zero movement, a total absence of vibration—there is no attraction or repulsion—there is no gravity or ant-gravity—there is no matter or anti-matter—just infinite bliss. The universal mind was not experiencing or feeling anything of what it knew because, when there are no opposites to compare things to, they cannot be felt or experienced."

"I'll have to take your word for that, but carry on. I'm all ears."

"There's a big difference between *knowing* everything there is to know about love, and *experiencing and feeling* love and it also holds true for it's opposite which is hate."

Eve stayed silent watching him talk, obviously fond of his subject.

"I could continue with a list of opposites such as pain and pleasure, forgiveness and anger, with health and sickness, with north and south, I could go on ad infinitum, but I think you are getting the drift."

"Aye, I see where you're coming from, but not sure where you're heading."

"Where I'm heading, is that the creator desired to experience and to feel the extremes of all that *is* and so polarity was created to allow that feeling to manifest. The earth is a part of this universe of polarity and we all live in this world of opposites."

"I still can't say I understand *why*." Eve was resolute in pushing back.

"And I haven't finished yet." He flicked his hands open abruptly. Eve acknowledged his riposte with a chuckle, putting her hand over her mouth "Sorry."

"Nay bother;" he said, "No need to apologise. I'm enjoying your interruptions, now to continue." He was clearly enjoying himself. "So by creating these pixels of Itself, the creator started to experience life *consciously*. Each soul in existence is essentially living their lives for GOD."

"That's a bit of a heady statement, isn't it? I'd need a month to make sense of that, but go on, sorry to interrupt again."

"Just consider that life is all about God experiencing itself through each of us *all the time*—I read somewhere recently that when I smell the perfume of a flower I am smelling it for God, now isn't that a wonderful way of looking at life?"

Dressing for God

"Yes, I like that but even so I..."

Adam raised his hands motioning her to wait. "Please, just one second, let me finish while I have the ball rolling and then I'll take the questions from the floor, ma'am." He gave her a little look of apology before resuming.

"You see each soul is a miniaturised version of the one source, that's what a soul is: a pixel of the creator, who wished to express itself *consciously* through me, through you, through everything in the universe."

Eve watched fascinated as he used his hands to accentuate his words, fingers alive, his energy palpable. He continued, his tone soft, full of feeling.

"And the reason we are here experiencing this life on earth is to *create* and to remember who we really are. We each create our own reality and God experiences life through each of us. I know that seems a bit heady but the reality of it will sink home as you experience seeing the whole picture yourself," he said, "but bear with me until I finish please."

Adam exhaled and laid his hands, palms up on the tablecloth. "And there you have it—that's the *Readers Digest* condensed version. I see life as if the creator is, in some form or another everywhere. Do you remember that song by The Police, 'Every move you make, every thought you take, I'll be watching you'; well for me that's spot on, there's just nowhere to hide. There is no getting away from IT. God exists in some format in everything. It all comes from the Source and everything returns back to the source. Life is the return journey from God to God by God, by way of us, and that's the why of IT."

Eve cleared her throat, and gave a slight shake of her head. "Thank you Adam, I think I have the gist of it... you sound as if you know what you're talking about even if I can't follow everything just now," and gave him a smile to soften her words.

She ran a hand through her hair momentarily and then asked quietly, "So *if* you offered me this research position and if," she paused and moistening her lips with the tip of her tongue added, "IF I accepted it, what exactly would I have to do. The day to day stuff, I mean?"

"That would depend on you really—reading, digesting, discussing, challenging, applying what you learn. It would all rather depend on your appetite and enthusiasm I suppose."

"My appetite? Why, what's my appetite got to do with it?"

"I mean your appetite to learn. It's like if I put a nice meal on the table and you don't eat it to convert it into energy in your bloodstream, then it's just stays a pile of matter. Same with the spiritual material, if you're not really interested in discovering for yourself your truth about the subject matter and you don't have an appetite to work at it, well it'd be meaningless to start wouldn't it?"

"I suppose you have good point there. You can lead a horse to water but you can't make it drink and all that." She stifled a yawn with the back of her hand.

"Of course, and don't forget that the real bonus may just be that both of us may learn more about what makes life tick." He moistened his lips quickly, "Because if I knew all there was to know about the subject then I wouldn't be looking for assistance, now would I?"

"Does anyone know everything, do you think?"

"Oh I'm sure there have been many who have some of it but I believe there's always a different perspective to truth available—I love that quote from Stephen King, 'Fiction is the truth inside the lie'."

Eve repeated the quote, "Now there's something else for me to ponder on, as if I hadn't enough to keep my poor mind occupied."

Adam looked directly into her eyes, "I would like to say this, if you are interested in the job, then I'd be more than happy to have you on board. I like how you've been challenging me and I can tell you're very quick on the uptake so ... well it's up to you. But take your time by all means, don't make a hasty decision." He then looked up as the maitre'd approached their table.

"Mr. King, the car you ordered sir—regrettably there's been a delay due to the weather. The driver just called in and it should be with you very soon. He said it's due to 'an act of God' if you can call this downpour such a thing."

As he receded from earshot Eve laughed, "Did you hear him and his act of God, was he listening to you do you think?"

Adam chuckled, "He may have been, who knows?" And smiled in that enigmatic way that Eve was beginning to find attractive.

"Have you had enough, or are there more questions?"

Dressing for God

"Oh I think I've had enough for one night. My head is reeling. Maybe we can call it a day if that's OK with you?"

They saw the headlights of the white Mercedes 500 as it parked out front and they scurried through the rain tumbling into the back seats. Sirens were wailing from over the river. Adam asked the driver to drop him off at his hotel first and then to drive Eve to Rotherhithe.

"Is it the London Bridge Hotel sir?" the driver spoke over his shoulder as they turned right onto Tower Bridge.

"Yes," confirmed Adam. Up ahead the sirens were whooping away. "Looks like there's a bit bother at your hotel sir." The car slowed to a crawl as the traffic ahead snarled up on the bridge, the single windscreen wiper slapping across the screen, the rain still heavy.

As they neared the turnoff to the hotel, a policeman in yellow luminous waterproofs waved them to a stop, bent his head in the driver's window, glancing into the back at the passengers.

"Evening Constable," said the driver. "Wot we got then?"

"Evening sir, I'm afraid the hotel was hit by lightning earlier. All the guests are evacuated out front. We have four fire brigade units in there." He looked at Adam then said, "Are you staying at the hotel sir?"

"Yes, I am officer."

"Well, if I were you sir, I'd be looking for somewhere out of this rain. There's maybe four hundred guests milling about back there sir. They could be out in the open for hours. Good night sir, madam," he tipped his cap and went to the car behind them.

The driver turned around "What'll it be then sir?"

While Adam was thinking of his options Eve decided, "Look, you can stay in my brother's place. No, really it's OK. You can at least kip out on the sofa. What the heck, driver, take us to King and Queen Wharf please."

Adam looked a bit bemused, "Are you sure?"

"Well it's not as if we are complete strangers, is it? I mean we do know people in common. Those six degrees of separation you were going on about earlier."

They smiled at each other as the driver made an illegal u-turn and drove back over the bridge heading to Rotherhithe and King and Queen Wharf.

Chapter 5
Déjà vu

I'm in the company of women in period costumes. I feel I'm in France and the name Bois de Boulogne seems familiar for some reason. The women are wearing luxuriant dresses, with prominent bodices and plenty of bosom showing and they all have powdered hair styles. Some have fans in their hands which they are using to keep themselves cool. One wall of the room is mirrored and I can see my reflection looking back at me. My dress is pale blue with trimmings of lilac ribbon and I'm wearing a black silk, diamond choker. My hair, strawberry blonde, is piled high on my head, powdered and highlighted with ribbons of the same colour as my dress. I can feel the stiffness of the corset which is pushing my breasts up and out, but I am still restrained compared to the other women. I can just see my shoes peeping out from under my hemline, blue with shiny buckles.

The scene changes suddenly as a commotion breaks out. As if from out of the ceiling these ninja-like, camouflaged figures, heads covered with only their eyes showing, silently swoop down on ropes and in a sickening moment they start a killing spree. The next thing I feel is the shock of being grabbed from behind, my head being yanked back by the hair and the sight of this long, cold blade coming swiftly before my eyes and then slicing through my black choker, blood jetting out in a red fan shape as my body slides crumpled to the floor in a heap.

Strangely I feel no pain. Feeling weak beyond reason I watch the room fade from my vision and I float upwards, aware now of the blood still spilling from my neck, seeing it from above my now lifeless body and the thought, "This is death" runs through my mind, but not "The mind of my body," I hear myself say, because I am not in it any more. I know I am dreaming but it seems so real—so life-like.

Dressing for God

Eve woke with a start. The vision of her death sending a shiver straight through her body as she lay trembling in the dark, the duvet held close and tight, the far wall a backdrop for a wayang shadow show as the clouds wrestled with the moonlight, the shapes tearing at the building across the river as the light flitted in the storm. Never before had she dreamt with such clarity. "Dear God above, what was all that about?"

Slowly running her hands across her bare arms, now all prickly with tiny goose bumps damp with cold sweat, she moved her hands over her body, feeling her throat which felt parched and slightly sore. It had all been so vivid, so life-like, and so real.

Frightened and fearful of what it meant, her breathing became faster. 'Was it a throwback to something she had read or seen or was it something else?' She shivered in the dark, the pillow warm beneath the chill on her face, afraid to move, reliving the experience.

She heard it then. The muffled sounds of someone moving in the corridor outside her bedroom brought her attention back into the room.

Gradually consciousness returned and moving slowly, blinking through a veil of unfamiliar surroundings, she remembered she was in Guy's apartment. She'd had dinner with Adam the night before, the storm, the lightening, and then inviting Adam to stay over because of the fire. Exhaling a deep, deep breath, trying to calm the feelings of confusion, fright, nausea all vying for her attention, but it was the picture of the cold steel blade flashing before her eyes and the spray of blood arcing out, which was so vivid in her recall. The words escaped her lips, "Oh my God, that was awful."

She strained to pinpoint the sounds. Stirring quickly she threw off the duvet, swung her feet over the edge of the bed, switched on the bedside lamp and saw her image in the dressing table mirror.

"I look terrible and feel worse. Oh dear God that wasn't a dream—that was a horrible nightmare." Her hand slowly caressed her throat and spotting her diamond choker lying on the dressing table, she picked it up held it at arm's length. It was smaller than the one in the dream. Remembering the knife, she hugged herself tight, shivers rushing through her body.

Wrapping herself in the oversize white robe she slid her feet into her slippers, then unlocked the bedroom door and peeped into the hallway. Adam was shrugging into his overcoat, the light from the kitchen leaking into the hall corridor. He looked up and saw her.

"Eve," his voice in a concerned whisper. "Hey, I didn't wake you, did I?"

He looked startled, his face pale in the dim light.

"No, I heard you all right. I've just woken up." Her voice was edgy and hoarse—raspy.

She stood in the doorway feeling vulnerable and exposed, confused, visibly quivering.

"I had a really horrible dream. Oh it was frightening, so awful, it woke me up—are you leaving now?" her teeth chattered as she tried to control her bodily reactions.

Adam hesitated, half into his coat trying to see Eve better, not answering her question.

"Are you all right?" He lowered his head closer to look at her, his eyes narrowing examining, searching.

"Are you all right? Do you want a cup of tea, coffee? I've just had one, the kettle won't take a second to boil." His voice was still a whisper.

"You don't have to whisper," she said. "Oh it was hideous. Yes, I'd love a cup of tea please." Another shiver rippled through her as she tightened the robe trying to snuggle into it to escape the chill enveloping her. The thermostat on the kitchen wall showed twenty-three degrees Celcius. "I shouldn't feel this cold."

"Sorry. I forgot I was whispering. I was trying not to wake you," he replied in a normal tone. "I whisper when I creep." He smiled, but concern remained on his face, his eyes attentive.

Busying himself with the kettle, dropping a teabag into a mug, he read the message on it,

> Truth Is Rarely Pure
> And Never Simple
> —*Oscar Wilde*

He poured in the boiling water as Eve took the milk from the fridge.

"Do you want to talk about your dream? Sharing can sometimes help."

Dressing for God

"I suppose you're an expert on dreams as well as everything else," an edge of sarcasm creeping into her voice. Adam stopped stirring the teabag and faced her.

"No Eve, I'm not a dream expert. I'm just being caring, that's all."

"Sorry, I don't mean to be bitchy." She sniffled, tore off some kitchen roll and blew her nose loudly. "Oh God it was creepy."

Adam handed her the mug which she held in both hands sipping gratefully. "Don't you have to get to the airport?"

"It's only six-thirty, the planes not until eleven. I've plenty of time. I'll have a cuppa with you if you want." He looked at her enquiringly. "I called the hotel, they're open for business, and the panic is over. I need to shower and change. I did appreciate the use of the sofa last night. Thanks again, it was good of you." He paused and said with care, "Now do you want to tell me your dream?"

"I don't know if I really want to talk about it, but please, yes, have a cuppa with me."

Adam had his coat off now and stirring his tea, quietly said, "A tip I was given years ago is to keep a journal. I know there were lots of times when there seemed to be neither rhyme or reason to the stuff I was dreaming, but when I began writing them down, I must say I began to make some sense of them afterwards. Not always, but for a lot of the time it did help."

"Thanks Adam, I'm not sure I want to write about it, but yes, I'd like to tell you about it, if that's all right?"

"Sure. Go ahead, take your time."

He placed his mug on the counter top and settled onto a high-back kitchen chair and listened as Eve recounted her dream.

She was visibly upset, holding her hand to her neck and as the story ended he stayed with his head down gazing into his mug, tapping his fingertips gently on the counter. Eve was breathing deeply, massaging the front of her throat.

"I can see why that would upset you, it does sound as if it's something from the past rather than the future, doesn't it? How do *you* read it?" he asked gently.

"What do you mean how do I read it? It's a dream, a nightmare. Maybe it was the oysters or something. I don't know."

"Mmm", he said. "Food, oysters? Well, there is the old wives tale about not eating cheese before going to bed. But no, I don't think the oysters started it, do you?"

"I don't know—what do you mean, it's something from my past?"

Adam took his time before answering. "I noticed a couple of things that could have symbolism for you. But first of all, can I say that I don't believe anyone can fully interpret someone else's dreams for them. They're just so personal and the symbols can only be meaningful to whoever is experiencing the dream. OK?"

Eve nodded comforted by his words.

"My first impression was that it was perhaps a past life recall and a significant part for me was when you realized that you were out-of-body looking at yourself dying. I felt a strong message there. How does that feel—does that ring true for you at all?"

"I suppose so, I don't know. I'm still sort of shocked. What were the other things you noticed?"

"There's the fact that you ended a chapter in your life leaving Scotland and your marriage. That's an end to a big part of your life and now you're at the fringe of a new chapter, whichever way you decide to go. And you did have those questions about life and death yesterday didn't you, the ashes in the river?"

"But why all the violence, getting my throat cut, what could the symbolism be about that?" Eve asked curtly.

"Well," he continued, his tone soft and understanding. "In a past life you could have been a princess or an upper class lady in France and perhaps you died in the French Revolution. You mentioned Bois de Boulogne, that's on the west side of Paris, have you been there?"

"Paris? Yes, I love France. I speak French."

"Have you been to Bois de Boulogne?"

"I don't know, maybe, why?"

"I was wondering if you'd ever experienced a sense of déjà vu there, that's all. You know a deep feeling that you had lived in a place before but have no conscious memory of it?"

"I don't know," she said, running her hands through her hair, conscious of her bed-head and trying to straighten it. "It's all a bit much for me just now. Have you had these déjà vu experiences yourself?"

"Yes, I've had a few in my time—but listen Eve, I know the dream really frightened you but it would help if you could get it down on

Dressing for God

paper. Sometimes doing that triggers an understanding of the dream's real symbolism for you." Adam glanced at his watch. "Time is pushing on I'm afraid, and I need to get moving soon, are you going to be OK?"

Eve rose from her chair, the colour slowly returning to her cheeks, the hot tea and the sharing of her story restoring her confidence.

"Yes. Thanks Adam, I'm fine now, really, thank you. Maybe you can share some of your déjà vu experiences with me some other time?"

Adam turned quickly, halfway into his coat, "Do I take it then that you are interested in the job?" Delight showing in the crinkles around his eyes, grey-blue now, the iciness dissolved with his obvious happiness.

The question hung there for a long moment and was broken by the buzz of the entry-phone intercom in the hall, the limo driver downstairs waiting for Adam.

Eve wanted to take the next step but hesitated to commit. Her head nodding "Yes" to him, while inside she was still unsure and then seeing the funny side, answered, "What the hell Mr. King—Yes I'm in."

"Oh that's brilliant Eve, I'm delighted. You will be most welcome, when can you travel?"

"Today, tomorrow, whenever, just as soon as I check out your references!"

Chapter 6

Noah's Art

Adam watched his breath vaporize in the cold air of the early morning, a steamy, wispy cloud that filtered into nothingness. Another deep breath, then holding it, feeling the chill hit his throat and his chest swelling. The grey woollen shirt straining the buttons to their limit he heard a soft drip-drop sound splash in the icy silence and looking up saw a teardrop shape of water slowly form at the end of the largest icicle hanging from the roof's eave. It stretched slowly downwards glistening in the crisp light of the early morning sun, suspended momentarily, its surface tension fighting the pull of gravity, slipping into the air, hitting the centre of a small pool of water forming on the deck below it. A plop of water erupted from the centre of the vortex marking its entry point, concentric circles rippling out to the edges of the pool.

He tried counting the moving circles… eight or was it nine. 'Who knows?' He sat there for a few minutes, his warm breath now directed at the slowly melting icicles, the light crackling in little bursts of red, orange, blue, green and violet as the sun light streamed through the melting ice canopy above his head. The melting was quickening now and drip by drip, drop by drop, the pools beneath the larger icicles started slowly joining up to form a little rivulet of water in the slushy ice onto the decking in front of him.

Overhead he watched as three birds flew over the garden changing formation, now a vee, now one ahead and two behind, now the one behind moving ahead and on they flew over the fence heading for the open water beyond.

His reverie was interrupted by the sound of the porch door slapping back on its hinges, the loose mosquito frame rattling in its fitting.

Dressing for God

"Got your coffee? Wow, what a beautiful morning."

Adam, sitting on the old timber bench, head tilted back, hands clasped behind his neck, turned slowly and smiled as the smell of the hot brew wafted under his nose. His mouth juices excited by the java aroma elicited an "Mmm, aye it is beautiful."

Taking the proffered mug he sipped the steaming brew, "Thanks, did you sleep well?"

"Yes thanks, brilliantly," Eve stretched her lithe frame, her arms akimbo. The big heather-coloured woolly highlighting the gold and red of her hair. Her grey-blue eyes still dewy from the quick wash in the basin. It was much too cold to shower, unseasonably so, even for early March in Kerry. She took in the breathtaking vista of the Atlantic Ocean glistening in the bay across the frost hardened garden.

A small boat was etching a liquid wake in the grey-blue sea which shimmered like hundreds of flashing silver mirrors, deceiving the eye into seeing dancing gulls as the mirrored light splash flashed and the waves broke and rolled and carried on their separate ways. Feeling she could hear the sea much the same way she had as a little girl playing on the beach holding a conch shell to her ear. "It's magical."

Adam smiled. "I would have called the place Eden, but the locals would have laughed me out of the parish. Just wait until they hear your name." He chuckled.

He moved over on the bench to make room. "Here, sit yourself down."

Eve sat her wool and denim cased body down beside him, swallowed a sip of coffee and turned slightly, facing out to sea but looking at him from the corner of her eye, sizing him up, seeing him on his home turf with new interest. His flinty blue eyes gave a depth to his broad tanned face, his beard mostly grey with flecks of black around his chin area showed the signs of wear and tear of his forty plus years. His mouth was generous; the lips full, sensuous, crinkling in a smile that showed his ivories to advantage. The nose though was slightly hooked, angling just a tad from the vertical towards the left. She thought it looked quite Roman or Jewish, or maybe just broken and badly reset.

"I'm really glad I'm here Mr. King. It really is idyllic, just as you said in your ad."

J.F. Tallon

The Aer Lingus flight from Heathrow to Cork yesterday was memorable only for the trepidation that surrounded her. It was like there were two Eves talking—one saying "Yes I'm starting a new adventure. Great I love it," and the other Eve remembering other disappointments, other memories recalling where she had been deceived and hurt. The other Eve, saying, "It's not too late to turn around and go back. Stick to what you know is safe for you. Tell him you made a mistake—go back to London."

The new adventurous Eve had won the debate and here she was in Sneem, 'The knot in the Ring of Kerry' as Adam had translated Sneem's Gaelic name as they drove through the colourful, quiet, country town, with the drive along the single track boreen to his house 'Namaste', nestled in these lovely wooded gardens overlooking Kenmare Bay.

"Ah, idyllic it is," his breath was visible in the cold air. "I was just marvelling there at the wonder of it all. Do you see the icicle there slowly melting in the sunlight, isn't it beautiful? See the way it's slowly changing form as we look at it. The water from the ocean was evaporated into the sky, formed into a cloud, the wind blew it from over the Atlantic out there," he pointed out to sea, "until it arrives here as rain falling on the roof and then it froze as it dripped over the eaves and now, sure it's reverting back to water again. Isn't it all the same stuff, just in different form?" His gaze was upon her now, waiting for a response.

"Is this the pre-breakfast physics lesson then?"

"Ah sure there's no getting away from nature, 'tis the divine play of life. Tell me, is the cottage going to be OK for you?"

"Oh, it's perfect, absolutely great."

She looked across the garden where the small one bedroom cottage stood. Its ivy coated porch, whitewashed walls and yes, a thatch. "I don't believe the thatch, it looks so new."

"It is," he said. "I had it done last year. The cottage was just a shell, it was in a desolate state, the ivy porch is about the only original bit left."

"It's really beautiful—inspiring." Eve felt excitement at the prospect of spending time in this lovely place.

Adam stood, stretched, rolled his shoulders, rubbed the back of his neck, loosening the muscles, turning his head left and right in small

Dressing for God

circular motions. "I have to go to Dublin tomorrow for some business… I'll probably be back around eight. It means a trip to Kerry Airport but it's probably best if I drive myself. Give you time to settle in. Or you can drive me there and pick me up on my return, it's up to you."

Without any hesitation, hugging herself, "I'll stay if you don't mind—I'm not ready for Irish roads and the sheep just yet." The journey from the airport last night was still fresh in her memory as she recalled the sight of the sheep and mountain goats wandering all over the road in the dark.

Adam laughed to himself remembering her reactions, "Ah sure you'll get used to it." He stood and pointed out into the bay.

"There's our dinner coming in now." Picking up a battered pair of binoculars he focused on the boat now turning in towards the headland, heading for Oyster Bed Pier just visible to their right, a few hundred yards beneath their view.

"C'mon," he said, "let's take a ramble down to the pier." They went through the screen doorway into the kitchen and out into the hall where he removed two heavy parkas hanging in an alcove by the front door. "Here," he said handing a bright blue one to Eve, "this will keep the drizzle out."

Eve shrugged into the oversize jacket as Adam opened the door, gesturing her to precede him out into the conservatory where the sun's warmth was defrosting the windows, leaving little ice crystals dissolving in streaks of light on the glass, as they walked into the garden. The path led into the driveway where Adam's Land Rover, parked in the shadow of the house, was covered in a white haze of frost. A robin, puffed up against the morning chill picked at the frozen grass and flapping in frustration it winged into the branches of the big chestnut tree beside the guest cottage.

Wisps of alto cumulus cloud were streaked across the pale blue sky as Adam led the way down the driveway. Rounding the curve in the road, the vista of the bay opened up as the slope fell away before them, the water shimmering as a light drizzle pinpricked its shining surface. Two boats were moored at a buoy about three-hundred yards offshore. Lonely yachts riding to their moorings, a sentinel seagull keeping watch from a cabin top.

Adam pointed at the small fishing boat approaching the pier, its wake receding as it reduced speed, then turning in a starboard swing it coasted in gently alongside. As Eve watched, a male figure in yellow oilskins snaked a headline through a mooring ring and secured it, then casually picked up a short stern line and made it fast.

The man stood there, hands on his hips, studying them as they walked down the slippery pier wall. Eve saw a ruddy faced man, clean-shaven, six foot she guessed, about Adam's age, but beefier; big shoulders bulging in the wet oilskin, his hair long, black as coal tied in a ponytail. He was shaking his head from side to side, and she saw a smile crease his face, friendly, full of devilment, eyes bright in obvious delight.

Adam called to him. "How's the catch, big fella?"

The man's hands came off his hips and clapped, the sound loud in the stillness of the morning, muting the quiet slapping of the water between the boat and the jetty. The name *D'Ark Rosaleen* was stencilled in gold lettering on the red hull. A laugh escaped him now and he answered.

"It's not half as good as yours Adam. My, oh my," he said eyeing Eve. She felt the humour between them as they stood looking at each other. "Well," he said, "aren't you going to introduce us?"

Adam made a mock bow in Eve's direction. "Eve Archer, nee McQueen, may I introduce you to the biggest rogue in the South of Ireland, my inestimable friend, Mister Noah Mahon."

Eve's mouth fell open and her eyes widened, "You must be joking."

When their bemused looks confirmed that his name *really* was Noah, she tittered, "Oh, I am sorry. I've never heard of a Noah outside of the Bible. And that," she said pointing at the little fishing boat, "*is it really Noah's D'Ark?*"

They were all three standing on the pier now. Noah, with Eve's hand in a handshake that seemed to last longer than politeness ordained. Hands as big as small shovels that wrapped hers in their grip, strong and firm and pulsing with energy, an honest working man's grip. She noted the brown skin, rough and chapped, fingers square and blunt, nails short with the thumbnail showing new growth over an old injury.

Adam seemed to sense her feelings, "In spite of their appearances, those mitts belong to one of Ireland's finest artists...that's *artist* as in

Dressing for God

painting. Have you heard tell of Noah Mahon, RIA—that is Royal Irish Academy?" Eve shook her head, "No. I'm not au fait with Irish art at all."

"Noah, Eve is here all the way from Scotland—she's helping me out—doing a bit of research for me."

"Aye, you did mention you had some help arriving." Noah replied and seeing Adam's raised finger wagging off further banter, he smiled and welcomed her to Sneem. "It's a rare place if you like peace and quiet and sure he has the cottage all fixed up now, good locks on the doors." He lifted his eyebrows and nodded in Adams direction, "But not that you'd need them, sure aren't they all good God fearing people around here?"

"Is that 'God fearing' or God loving, you mean there Noah?" asked Adam.

"Ah sure a bit of both I'd say. Now then, talking of Himself and loaves and fishes, wait till you see this morning's harvest."

He hopped over the bulwark of the boat and hefted a fish-box on to the wall, chock full of gleaming blue-grey scaled fish, glistening with wet iridescence.

"Look'a here, Salmon Bass for dinner, so I think I will just invite myself over to your place later and we can introduce ourselves properly."

The kitchen was bustling when Eve arrived. Adam was standing in the centre of the large kitchen cum dining room chopping herbs at the five foot square food prep area, a glass of chilled white wine to hand, frost beads formed on the glass.

In the background a Beethoven piano concerto was trilling the air, already redolent with the aromas of cooking wafting from the dark green Aga.

"Welcome," Adam said, as Eve poked her head around the door. "My, you're looking great." He admired her navy alpaca sweater and shawl, the grey wool skirt coming as it did to just below the knee and Adam caught Noah appreciating her shapely calves as he raised the wine bottle in Eve's direction.

"And will Eve be tempted with a glasheen of this little tipple? It's a reasonable Chenin Blanc."

"Oh yes please Noah. Thanks. Can I help with anything Adam?"

"Naw, just park your bones there and relax. Tonight I cook, tomorrow you can cook." and in an aside to Noah he said, "I won't be here tomorrow."

Noah chuckled, "Adam fancies himself as a cook. Did he tell you that before you got here?"

"Fortunately no, he didn't. Otherwise I mightn't be here now." She smiled, "What's cooking then?"

"Well in honour of our present company, I thought Angels on Horseback would be appropriate. Are you OK with that? "

"Oh yes, absolutely."

"Good. And for the main course we have Noah's catch of the day—Salmon Bass a la the *Kerryman*. "

Eve watched as Adam placed the chopped herbs and slices of lemon inside each of the three fish, seasoned them with sea salt and pepper, and then wrapped them in sheets of the *Kerryman* newspaper which he then placed under the cold tap thoroughly drenching them.

"Right you are," he said, looking up at Eve who was peering at him wetting the fish parcels, an inquisitive frown on her face.

"This is the oven steamed special; these'll take about 15 minutes in a hot oven and should be, well I'd say, scrumptious is the word." He popped them into the middle oven. "How are you getting on there Noah?"

"Good, good, these little angels will be sprouting wings soon. I've fixed the salads and the tatties are in the pot, sure we're firing on all cylinders."

Eve enjoyed the easy banter of Adam and Noah as they moved effortlessly around the large kitchen area. She watched their movements reflected in the large ornate gilt mirror hanging over the sideboard, the three candles on the table flickering in the slight draught from the open oven door as Adam removed the dish of bacon wrapped oysters and placed them on the table.

"Come on, these are just ready. Noah, can you serve while I get the dressing?"

Adam settled himself in his chair at the circular mahogany dining table, his back to the cooker.

Noah finished serving and held up his freshly charged wine glass to address Eve, "Let me offer a warm welcome to Miss Eve to our

Dressing for God

humble abode. Well," he paused and said in Adam's direction, "to *your* humble abode. Welcome to Sneem and welcome to the kingdom of Kerry. May we all prosper in your enlightenment during your stay here, which can be as long as any piece of string you want."

Adam smiled at his friend's toast and nodding agreement raised his glass in Eve's direction, "Indeed, I second that and endorse it with a new Amen."

"That's Amen as in 'Amen means so be it," Noah explained. "The way we were taught in school."

"Well then, let me propose a toast to …" she paused for a few seconds, glancing at each of them, then raised her glass and said, "a toast to an enlarged …. 'Sobeit union."

Noah burst out laughing, "Amen to that Eve, ruddy marvellous, the lass has the craic Adam."

They intoned the toast together. "To the Sneem so be it union." Their glasses entwined in the centre of the table, Adam's shoulders rocking with contained laughter.

Eve watched Adam tackle the blackened and singed paper-wrapped parcels, the fish skin had fused with the inside sheet of paper and it peeled back cleanly, exposing the pale pink flesh perfectly intact and impeccably oven steamed. She leant over, sniffing the aromas and gave him a double thumbs-up.

Adam watched Eve's reaction as she savoured the fish. "This is really excellent Adam. I think I'll enjoy my stay here with this standard of eating."

"We do our best; it's hard to make a mess when you cook good food simply," adding, "So are you all settled in now?"

"I am thanks. Snug as a bug, but I'm still a bit in the dark about starting work."

"But we have started Eve. We started over dinner in London and I dangled a bit of bait in front of you this morning on the deck. I believe you called it a pre-breakfast physics lesson, did you not?"

"Oops—OK the water and the ice—how spiritual was that?"

"What was that then?" asked Noah. "Is this something private between yiz or can anyone join in?"

Adam described the thunder and lightning bursting directly overhead just as he was telling Eve of the mirror smashing to smithereens. Noah gave a desultory shake of his head and smilingly said, "Sure I've heard it all before."

J.F. Tallon

"*However,* the lightening hitting Adam's hotel, now wasn't that just a wee bit more out of the ordinary than usual, even by Adam's standards?" He had their attention now.

"Tell me then," he swivelled his eyes quickly from one to the other and asked, "were there any big hailstones just before the lightning hit?" There was a definite tonal interest in Noah's question as he gently filleted his fish and placed the fishbone on his side plate.

Eve exchanged an inquisitive look with Adam, "Was there? It's hard to say, it was so ferocious, did you notice hailstones Adam?"

"There well may have been, I can't say. Why do you ask Noah?"

Noah took a sip from his wine glass and continued. "Well you see now, I saw this documentary the other night. This university team were doing an experiment showing how lightning is generated in a storm. Did you know that in these big anvil shaped storm clouds you can get temperatures as low as minus fifty degrees Celsius and what happens is that at around minus thirty degrees Celsius, these tiny ice crystals start forming at the lower end of the clouds and then they rise upwards in the atmosphere, growing bigger and bigger until they become big hailstones. Did you know that?" He asked.

"I didn't, no," replied Adam. "And just where are you taking us with this yarn?"

"Ah 'tis not a yarn at all, not at all." Noah said. "'Tis pure science; these new hailstones you see, they grow bigger and heavier at the upper level of the giant storm cloud, then the law of gravity kicks in and they start falling through the cloud heading down to earth. What goes up—comes down, you understand. Now, as these millions of hailstones are falling, they collide with other millions of little ice crystals rising upwards and that sets up massive friction causing colossal electrical energy to be generated in the storm battery in the sky, which is discharged in a sort of electrical *wham bam thank you ma'am* lightning bolt. So that's why I asked yiz about the hailstones." Noah looked cheekily at them both, turning his head, interrogating, deep brown eyes glinting with merriment.

"There were no hailstones Noah," They said simultaneously.

"Ah but *there was electricity,* I can see that."

"Noah, the atmosphere is chocker block full of energy." Adam steering the conversation away from his probing, "Infinite energy and

Dressing for God

infinite intelligence. Isn't that what the whole mirror reflects anyway?"

"True enough, true enough but ah, I do enjoy my own reflections. I suppose that's the artist in me. Anyway, I haven't finished yet. You'd have liked this bit Adam, because the programme went on to show how the human body is a living electrical powerhouse and it then explained how a single brain's integrated circuits are more complex than all the world's telephone system put together. It was fascinating stuff."

"That's true enough Noah, though I liken the body as an electromagnet rather than as a mere electric circuit."

"Em, I seem to be missing something here," Eve said looking at each in turn.

"Sorry Eve, I think Noah was making a point about the huge ocean of potential energy that we move in and are generally unaware of. Is that correct Mr Mahon?"

"Aye, fair comment Mr King. The programme got me thinking how we take the very air we breathe in for granted. I mean if it was an absolutely flat, calm day with nary a breeze blowing sure you'd never even begin to guess that the air around you held anything but nothingness would you? I mean that got me to thinking what power there is in the atmosphere, from a wee flutter of wind on the side of your cheek to a full blown hurricane. Isn't it all just pure energy in motion and there's not a thing man can do to control it, is there?"

"And then of course," Adam chipped in adding, "and there's all those different vibrating energies of the other consciousness levels permeating everything—not to mention all the junk-thought we have polluting the atmosphere."

"Would you mind telling me just what you are talking about please?" Eve asked, a baffled note in her voice. "What is this other consciousness?"

"Well how about this for starters." Adam retrieved the remote for his Bose music system and switched on the radio. Depressing the search button he tuned in station after station and then with a quizzical expression on his face, switched it off and said, "The atmosphere in this very room is chocker block full with TV and radio signals but we can't see a single one of them. But trust me, the place is crowded with the stuff. If I scan the dial I can pick out every station in range—hundreds of them, short wave, medium wave, long wave,

J.F. Tallon

FM, very high frequency, ultra high frequency—whatever. They're all there and the only thing keeping them separated from each other is frequency. And the same goes for TV programmes, telephone calls, text messages. Sure, they're all over us in the ethers. And yes you're right, I didn't mention consciousness yet, did I? So I guess I'd better return to our wee pixel in the big picture again."

Noah had settled back in his seat, legs stretched out under the table, swirling the wine in his glass, observing Eve.

"Maybe Adam if you give that wee pixel soul a modicum of human perspective, add a bit of skin and bones to it and give it a life, maybe that's a better way to describe what it's all about. I'm always telling you, don't be lecturing, you're not a Bishop. And I thank God for that." Noah's eyes twinkled, delightedly knowing he had touched a nerve.

Coughing and laughing at the same time, Adam wiped a tear from his eye. "And there I was thinking that you were my friend. Ah God, go on then Mr Mahon paint us a picture of what it is you're seeing, oh Glory be," he spluttered and then cleared his throat.

Noah took out a multicoloured ballpoint pen and a small notebook from his jacket and gave Eve a broad wink, "An artist is never without the tools of his trade," he said, rubbing his hands together. He reminded Eve of a magician getting ready to pull a rabbit from a hat.

"Right then, Mr. Writer, now *you can listen to my picture.*" He clicked out the black ink and quickly sketched a pretty recognisable image of Eve, sans clothes, on the side of a page from his book.

"I did say I'd make it interesting, didn't I? Now then Miss Eve, I'll save your modesty," he said, sketching in a green bikini to cover her nakedness.

"I wouldn't want to embarrass you, really." Then on the other side of the paper he drew seven parallel lines numbering them from the top seven through to one. Eve's modest figure sketched on the left side alongside the bottom three lines.

"Now then, this little spark, this soul, you..." he said pointing at Eve," you need to manifest in a human body to experience life as a living being, conscious of yourself. So here you are swimming in this invisible ocean of electromagnetic energy and you're attracting this subtle matter around yourself like a kind of protective sheath."

Dressing for God

With a few deft lines the drawing had come to life, a likeness of Eve in what now looked like a pink wetsuit. Noah continued talking, looking across at Eve, "And so begins the virtual journey through space into time from there to here on this physical place." Noah traced his pen from seven through to one adding, "And then you finally arrive down here on planet Earth in this solar system we know as our universe. Have you got that now?"

He leant over and showed her the sketch.

"I think so—go on." Eve was looking intently interested with a quizzical look on her face.

Noah added some details to the sketch as he continued. "So speaking as an artist, I see soul as a *creative medium* of the Creator—in the same way that I use different types of mediums in my art work, oils, watercolours, acrylics and so on for my painting. I also see that God designed life around each souls' ability to recognise itself in the divine plan and to fulfil the purpose it came here to do."

Noah spotted Eve struggling to follow his drift and asked, "Are you seeing what I'm saying?"

Eve took a breath, her lips pursed, "Sort of, but the question I want to ask is why? Why is it, that if soul is so perfect, why then have we all this strife and terror and economic woe in the world?" Eve felt herself getting wired into the question, wanting some real answers. As she spoke, Eve folded her arms in front of her, elbows on the table looking across at Noah.

"Why is it that if God and soul are so perfect, why then do we have all the…" she hesitated before adding, "why have we got all this crap in the world, why isn't it all milk and honey and happiness that I heard about in Sunday school?"

Noah exhaled and gave a small grunt and asked, "Do you not have any easy questions? And there I was going to give you my opus on consciousness and you want the $64,000 question answered first off."

Noah looked over at Adam, who waved him on. "You started this big fella', so you'd better answer properly or your credibility will be shattered forever."

"All right then, that'll teach me to volunteer." Noah took a drink from his water glass before continuing.

"There's no doubt at all, that when you look around in the world you'll see huge suffering, millions dying from hunger in one place and food surpluses in other places. The news is full of horror stories of murder and suffering and poverty and it seems that the ones to suffer most are the vulnerable and the innocent. Is that what you're asking?"

"Yes, that's it; why does God allow this to happen?" Eve's eyes opened wide looking at Noah questioningly.

"Ah, if only I knew the answer to that..." Noah said quietly with a slight shake of his head. He stared meditatively for a few moments and then spoke.

"What I will say, is that I often questioned myself as to whether or not there really was a divine plan that could encompass such suffering." He paused again looked across the table at Adam, waiting for support. Adam remained quiet, leaning forward, arms crossed in front of him on the table with a bemused look on his face.

Noah continued in a soft tone as he added some more detail to his sketch. "I suppose my viewpoint now, is that life is all about experiencing the results of how we each use our free will.." He directed his words at Eve.

"Our freedom of choice, you mean?" she asked.

"Quite so. Aren't we all uniquely responsible for the effects of our thoughts, words and deeds? And I suppose you could say that the conditions anyone is experiencing in life at any one time is a true reflection of some sort of spiritual accounting process based on how they lived their lives. So the imbalances we're talking about are manifestations of conditions created by man one way or another."

"But why does this creator permit such suffering? I still don't get this," Eve said pushing back.

"But it's not the Creator who causes the suffering on earth Eve." Noah said putting down the pen and notebook. "It's mankind that's creating the mess we live in. The Creator gave man free will and gave him the secret of creating his own experiences. Sure there's no one down here among us that can really offer a judgment as to who deserves what." He stopped to let his words settle with Eve and then continued.

"It's impossible really to see what a divine plan could be when we're limited to our myopic perception of the fairness of life. I mean if I could do a bit of soul travel to another dimension and look down from my seat with the gods and observe the play of life on the earthly

Dressing for God

stage, then I'd have a better understanding of why things appear as they are. But there is just so, so much that is invisible to our viewpoint and I suppose the only thing I do understand, is that the law of cause and effect is the one law that we can never escape from."

He looked at Eve and asked, "So does that help in answering your very tough question then Miss Eve?"

Eve bowed in Noah's direction. "Thanks Noah. Yes it does help a bit. I can see that I still have a lot to understand. Sorry for interrupting your opus."

"Thank you, Miss Eve. It was no bother at all. And yes I'm almost there, just bear with me. All right let's return to Adam's mirror for a wee second," Noah pointed at the top line.

"Here's where it all began. Here in the imagination of God. In the realm of the conscious mind of the Creator, and before you ask the question what is mind Noah? let me add that no one has ever seen what mind is. Any more than you can't put a thought under a microscope or buy a bucket of atoms at a supermarket, but what you can do is this. You can see the effect of the movement of atomic particles in a physics laboratory, or you can switch on the electricity in your home that was generated from a nuclear power station in exactly the same way as we can see the effect of our own thoughts in our own lives."

Noah hesitated for a few moments, picking his words carefully and then continued in a measured tone as he pointed at the sketch.

"So this—I'll call it cosmic consciousness—which is the realm of the mind of God, and I'll show it here as it gave birth to its ideas. Let's say for the sake of argument that's what the big bang was all about. What we have then, is this first cause of everything being itself—bursting into life and everything in the universe thereafter is a series of effects resulting from that desire of the Creator to express its intelligent ideas consciously."

"Noah," said Adam interjecting. "Jeepers, you said I was obtuse. Surely that's way above her head."

"I know it is," Noah said moving his pen above the sketch of Eve. "Look it's all above her head, but I'm coming from the top down. Eve, is this really over your head?"

"No, it's ok. I'm with him so far, let him go on."

Noah, embolden with Eve's support winked at her. "Right then, we're nearly there, so we have this cosmic consciousness and its desire to be totally aware of itself and so infinite divine intelligence is let loose and given life - all these little shards of that big mirror, are expressing themselves in some aspect of a conscious energy life form. OK so far Eve? Are we seeing a bit of the divine in everything imaginable?"

Eve sat in deep thought looking at Noah's drawing. Adam was toying with a teaspoon, making a tiny beam of candle light flicker and dance on the ceiling, seemingly unaware of Noah's question.

"I'll take it then, that no answer, is a yes?"

"Oh sorry Noah, no I'm all ears. Carry on please, you were going on about Life, were you not?" Adam put down the spoon, his attention back in the room.

Noah shook his head in mock exasperation at his friend and said.

"Life is a great subject isn't it? I often have the sense that there is really only the one life and that we are all living in it. I know, I know, that sounds a bit off the wall, but isn't it like we are all breathing this life force, inhaling the air that surrounds us, feeding us life, feeding the plants life, feeding the birds and bees life? Sure isn't the life stuff eternal and infinitely permeating everything perfectly? That's what I mean by saying we live in the one life." Noah finished talking and then drawing in a deep breath, he continued with his little drawing.

"So let me do a reverse. Let's see a diver getting ready for a dive." He started another sketch. "Let's say that Eve, the diver, descends through the ocean in a dive bell. She has a special dive suit, dive hat, watch, knife, all the kit and here's the umbilical cord connecting her to the diving bell and back up to the mother ship on the surface where her dive supervisor and the life support technicians are looking after her. Eve knows her job, she's been briefed and she's confident of getting the job done down in the depths of this earthly ocean."

"She has communications back to the surface and her dive is being video recorded in dive control. Her every movement and detail of the dive, her each and every thought word and action are all recorded here on hard disc memory."

Turning back to the original sketch, Noah pointed to the pink wetsuit, "Eve's soul body is now connected by this very fine silver umbilical cord back to her source. This is Eve's lifeline from the invisible planes to down here on the earthly planes. This ethereal soul-body is now zipped into this once-only suit."

Dressing for God

Noah took Eve's hand in his and squeezed it gently and then moving his hand up over her arm he kneaded it a few times and said, "This is your once-only suit. And it's called a once-only suit because you only get to use it once and then you discard it. Your physical body is just a suit that is recycled after use and the stuff it was composed of, the ninety-percent water and ten-percent matter, well that matter reverts back to where it came from, while your wee soul body is welcomed back to the mother ship in the invisible worlds for a life debrief and review. And you Miss Eve, you will get to sit through your full life review session and you'll get to see just how well you performed in your latest live dive." Noah smiled as he added, "It's the ultimate life lessons learnt session."

Noah's pen fluttered over the lower end of the page, Eves figure was now fully dressed in a black jumper and skirt, the pink wetsuit hidden beneath the new outer skin and bones, a hint of a silver thread rising from her body in the lower planes up to plane number four of the invisible worlds.

Noah slid the drawing over to Eve. "Oh that's great Noah," she exclaimed. "Can I keep it, will you sign it for me? I'll have my own Noah Mahon drawing. I'll have to frame it."

"Here give it back a second and let me show you a bit about consciousness and then I must be getting back home. Thanks," he said, as Eve handed back the sketch.

"I should mention here too, that these planes are not like, you know, going up in an elevator and getting off at the fourth floor—can you take me to the middle astral please?" He looked over at Eve who was grinning back at him.

"No, it's more like climbing a mountain; the atmosphere is rarer and the vibrations faster and finer the higher you go and of course the higher your viewpoint is, then the broader your horizon becomes, if you follow me."

He finished writing on the sketch and placed it on the table facing Eve.

"See here at the bottom, this is what we call the first dimension. Let's say that this is the clay of the earth. Now I'm calling this a single dimension of unconscious energy. I say unconscious because the clay hasn't got consciousness of itself, but it does have different live chemical abilities and affinities. There is stuff going on in it all the time, so when a seed is dropped in the clay, there is this unconscious reaction between the seed and the soil and growth is the effect as life develops." Adam watched Eve's response to Noah's explanations with interest, enjoying her obvious grasp of the subject.

Noah continued, "And that takes us nicely to the second dimension which is the realm of what is called the simple consciousness of the earth's vegetation world." He pointed to the drawing again, adding, "So what goes down also comes up, you understand. It's a sort of anti-gravity in a way. You see depending on the seed's natural design - whether the seed is an acorn or a tulip bulb or a grass seed; it's that seed design which dictates the shape of its growth whether it's the tree, the flower or the blade of grass." He looked over at Adam and gave a conspiratorial wink.

"So we have this simple consciousness for all vegetation growing on earth and you'll notice that this consciousness has only an up and down motion. It's rooted to its own space with just a teeny weenie bit of sideways motion as it tracks the Earth's orbit round the sun, sucking in the power of the light to sustain its growth. It's what I call a prana sucker."

"A what?" Eve asked.

"Prana. It's the life force that all earthly bodies absorb from the atmosphere. It's the energy generated by the Sun and it's what keeps us alive – that's in addition of course, to the nutrients we consume in our food and drink. Prana is also called Chi or the life force."

"I got that, thanks and may the force be with you too." Eve responded.

Noah grinned back at her. "Thank you Obi Wan Kenobi, but we're not at that level of consciousness yet – we're still in the second dimension where there's another level of simple consciousness and that's the animal kingdom. This dimension of consciousness embraces the whole range of the animal kingdom where each species expresses varying degrees of intelligence ranging from the simple amoeba up to the whale. These lads are not rooted to one spot in the soil, but have the power to roam about freely. They live on their natural instincts and exist in the main, by the law of survival of the fittest." He stopped there to see if he still had their attention before continuing.

"So now we arrive into the third dimension where mankind enjoys life and is endowed with self- consciousness. You know that expres-

Dressing for God

sion when two people have different viewpoints? Ah sure we're on different wavelengths. Well that's a true enough analogy for expressing differences of personal consciousness. With the gift of free will in our lives, we are also given the amazing power to think consciously and I might add that besides having his own natural instincts, man has the incredible ability to receive intuition and to be inspired. And we could all do with a bit more inspiration, couldn't we Adam? "

"No truer word ever spoken."

"How is this settling with you Eve?" Noah looked across at Eve who seemed a bit nonplussed. Adam, noting her raised eyebrows, interrupted.

"Noah, I believe Eve is maybe troubled over understanding your 'inspiration'. Can you perhaps elucidate for us in a few simple words?"

Noah acknowledged the question and stopped in mid-flow. "Of course I can. Sure inspiration derives from the Latin word, inspiro, to 'breathe in' and speaking as an artist, sure if I didn't know how to get out of my own way and let the spirit of God give my imagination some texture and colour. Wouldn't it be like trying to make an omelette without having any eggs? It's how the universe talks to me when I ask the question as I sit in front of a blank canvas, what is it I should paint next and how do I want it expressed? Sure I never know from one minute to the next what message the unseen is going to ask me to paint – that's down to me being open to receive and willing to oblige, I guess....letting my Inspiration breathe through me and into life." Adam looked across at Eve and saw her comprehension.

"Thanks Noah – that helps." Noah smiled back and swivelled the sketch in front of Eve on the table, then pointed to it with his pen.

"So it's in this third dimension where man spends his seeming reality. This is the space where all the gazillions of the effects of life on Earth become manifest and are experienced. It's the movie theatre of all life where every soul is an actor or player in some role or another."

"So now we move into the fourth dimension, which is the astral level of consciousness. This is the level of the individual unconscious mind and it's where dreams originate. This leads me nicely into our arrival in the fifth dimension, which is the realm of those wonderful souls who have achieved oneness with all there is."

J.F. Tallon

Noah added a few notes to the sketch before saying, "There's a whole load more up there above the fifth dimension but the atmosphere up there is way too rare for me to even consider climbing from my base camp here in Sneem and try to explain. So that's about it really Miss Eve, and this seems a very good time to be going about my 'father's business', as the man said, and get myself home to bed for my bye-byes."

Noah signed the sketch, presented it to Eve and then rose from the table.

"Are you away home already?"

"Aye, I must go Adam. I want to check the boat on the way home. Did you happen to see the weather forecast tonight?"

"No, I didn't, but by the sound of the wind I'd say it's Sou'westerly and it seems to be freshening, but at least it will be a few degrees warmer. I thought you were taking the boat out of the water for its survey work?"

"Aye, I was meaning to tell you, I'm maybe trading up for something a bit more salubrious. McCarthy Marine have a three year old Cyclone 30 coming in tomorrow, and I'm thinking if the price is right, maybe it's about time to retire my 'D'Ark Rosaleen'. She's served me well, but I could use something a bit bigger with some more cabin space."

"Sounds great, I like the Cyclones. They're good in these kinds of waters. Oh yes, new toys for the boys—I look forward to it."

"Right then," Noah said to them both, but directed his smile at Eve as he pulled on his old olive green wax jacket which had seen better days.

"I'll be off so. Say Adam, if you're away tomorrow I can maybe show Eve a bit of the Ring of Kerry on the drive over to Valentia; would you fancy that?" he asked her. "We can maybe carry on with more *of the revelations of Noah* on the way?"

Eve shrugged, not quite knowing what was expected of her, the issue of research seemingly forgotten since her arrival.

Adam said, "Sounds grand to me Noah. It'll be a good chance for Eve to see a bit of the scenery and sure I can get you started on some pre-reading in the meantime if that's all right. You might as well make hay while the sun shines."

"More like when the cats away, the mice will play," said Noah.

Dressing for God

"Grand Eve, I'll see you around half eleven. I have a few things to get sorted first. I'll bid you both a good night, and thanks for a great evening and sure the food wasn't bad either."

7		Cosmic Consciousness		
6		Supra consciousness		
5	Realm of the One Mind	Unconditional Love	Multi-dimensional Awareness	Causal Plane
4	Ocean of the One Mind	Individual Unconscious Mind of Man	Astral Consciousness	Mental and Astral (Emotional) Bodies
3	Ocean of the One Mind	Self Consciousness – Human Conscious Mind Seeming Reality	Physical Plane incorporating Astral and Mental Planes	Humankind
2	Ocean of the One Mind	Higher Simple Consciousness and Simple Consciousness	Physical Plane	Animals / Mammals / Fish Plants / Trees
1	Ocean of the One Mind	Unconscious Energy – (No self Awareness) Chemical Abilities / Affinities	Lower Physical Plane	Water / Clay of the Earth

Chapter 7

Thoughts Are Things

Snuggled beneath the covers, Eve heard the start-up cough of Adam's Freelander as he set off on an early start to Kerry Airport. The sound of the motor receded down the drive and then there was just the soft sighing and whistling of the wind in the trees as she fell back into a blissful sleep.

The gurgling of the bedroom radiator woke her at 7:30 AM. She burrowed her head into the pillow, pulling the duvet tight around her, thinking of the many changes she had just gone through. Selling the flat, the divorce and then she thought of the future, 'What of my long term plans?' At least this thing in Kerry was turning out better than she dared to expect. They were really nice people, Adam and his friend Noah, even if she did feel a bit *foreign* with all the spiritual stuff, she had to admit that it was different and it had got her thinking.

She reminded herself of the books Adam had asked her to start on. "Please make notes if there's anything unclear so we can discuss it together." She had her own desk in his office with a 20" flat screen for her laptop. He was all very business-like without Noah's presence, more formal towards her, as if he was protecting some vulnerability. 'Not that I am interested in him in that way, anyway,' she thought as she swung her legs out of the bed and headed for the bathroom.

A gentle rain was pattering on the roof, it streaked the windows a wet opaque greyness as Eve, now dressed in black woollen tights and a high neck white Aran knit sweater, her feet in pale pink slippers sat sipping a cup of tea, milk, no sugar; her attention on the sketch Noah had performed over dinner. Turning it over and looking at the diving Eve in the dive gear, she felt wonderment at the coincidence of

Dressing for God

it. She'd never mentioned to either Adam or to Noah her interest in diving. It was her passion ever since getting her PADI certification for open water diving in Australia years ago. 'Another piece of a peculiar jigsaw,' she thought.

"And so to work—first day at the office," she said aloud, walking through to the small sitting room heading for the front door, her gaze fastened on the picture hanging over the mantelpiece.

He was almost life-sized; this saffron robed Buddhist monk, shaven head, sitting lotus fashion on a kind of dais with a pile of old manuscripts and ancient books around him. He looked as if he was beyond the written word somehow. There were gentle wafts of fume-like energy, hints of gold, yellow and red, emanating from a purple aura around his body; his features indistinct in the light except for his eyes. They were a light shade of brown with tiny, silvery irises that mesmerised her momentarily, as she found herself looking into them, unable or unwilling to explain the feelings stirring inside. She felt a sense of presence, a silent sereneness touching her very core and then she noticed the signature in the bottom right. 'Noah Mahon 1999'.

The office door was lying open and there was a note from Adam on her desk.

> *Eve,*
> *Welcome to the office—it's really good to have you on board.*
>
> *I should be back around eight; I forgot to mention that Sheila, the lady who does my cleaning, will be by this morning—take care.*
>
> *Adam*

Eve Blu-Tacked Noah's sketch onto the whiteboard over her desk, sat back in the swivel chair enjoying being alone on her first day. She went through the pile of books Adam had left, trying to decide where to start. "'Pick one that feels right" she thought he'd said. "'Ask yourself which one is for you?" She scanned the various titles, weighing them in her hand and settled for a short list of *The Secret* by Rhonda Byrne and *Notes from the Universe* by Mike Dooley.

Holding *Notes from the Universe* in her hand she closed her eyes and opened the book at random and read:

> *Here's a Little Trick on how to change the scenery in your life radically, fantastically and perhaps, forever (If that's what you really want). Look the other way.*

"This was not what I expected at all." Her thoughts were now running pell-mell, "What do you mean—look the other way—look differently to how I used to look?"

She re-read the words several times trying to imagine even more new scenery in her life. Closing her eyes she started the deep breathing exercise Adam had recommended 'to help to get your energies clear' as he'd put it.

"OK deep breath in for seven seconds. Hold the breath in to the count of seven and then exhale and hold that to the count of seven, another breath for seven; this is not what I'd call hard work at all."

The crunch of tires on the gravel shortly after nine announced Sheila's arrival. Eve was very interested to meet the new arrival and opened the front door to a cheery, middle-aged lady, white haired, with an infectious laugh who was bustling out of a white Fiesta.

"Hi. Hello there, good morning. You must be Sheila."

"Ah Good morning, good morning, good morning…. Isn't it the grand, grand day now with the rain stopped. And you must be who now? Is it the new help from England ye are?"

"Yes, my name is Eve."

Not drawing breath other than to utter a small giggle she carried on, "Well sure now Eve, ye couldn't have come to a nicer spot, and to a better man in the whole world than to Mister Adam. No, no, no, no, no…" she left the words trailing behind her as she blew through the front door of the house leaving Eve laughing quietly in her wake on the front porch.

Eve stood silently sensing the morning air, the sea smells mixed with the peaty smoke of burning turf, enjoying the garden's beauty as she watched two birds busily picking at the grass under a tree and then her trance was broken by the Hoover starting up as Sheila started

Dressing for God

her routine. "OK, back to my reading then, two hours before I get ready for Mr. Noah."

Sitting in the warmth of Noah's Jeep, the smells of turpentine, fish and damp clothing fighting for prominence in the stuffy interior, Eve listened to his running commentary as they turned left from the high-hedged, single track road from Adams house onto the N70 towards Sneem and Waterville, the bulk of the Knockmoyle Mountains throwing a shadow on the road ahead.

The south-westerly wind had cleared the rain and the late morning was bright with just a few clouds in a pale blue sky, the road winding between the hedgerows, mountains climbing away to their right, they passed the entrance to Parknasilla Spa and Hotel complex. Eve noted they had pool facilities and felt delighted that pampering was so close to hand.

Noah was extolling the delights of Sneem as they slowed down and entered a small square with a village green surrounded by brightly painted shops, reds and yellow, green, purple, sandstone, a kaleidoscope of colour, every shop and house a different hue to its neighbour.

"Sneem is called the 'Knot in the Ring of Kerry'—mainly because in the summer with the tourists in their coaches thronging the road, they come to this little bridge," Noah said as they slowed to a stop. A tractor with a trailer load of turf was slowly crossing the single lane bridge over the Sneem River, the driver tipping his cap to them as he passed.

"And you can see for yourself why it's called a knot, 'cause it was *not* built for two way traffic." A yellow, diamond shaped road sign hung askew at the far end of the bridge—ANGER—Eve was about to ask if this was a warning against road rage when she noticed that the D had been crudely scraped off. Noah saying, "Ah sure it's just the local kids demonstrating their spelling skills."

They crossed over into another small square, past more rainbow coloured shops and houses and then headed out the road to Valentia. Noah was relaxed and driving well within the 100 kilometre speed limit, partly because of the winding road and partly due to the age of the Jeep.

The boggy fields behind them now, they drove across a ribbon of road that sliced through a series of long hummocky rocky outcrops that ran like old lava flows from the mountain straight down to the sea. Then they coasted around the shore of the Atlantic and were heading down the curve towards Castlecove and Caherdaniel.

Noah pulled in to a stop on a rising slope above Caherdaniel. Eve's attention was fixed on three sheep, a ram and two ewes, scrambling out of their way. The ram nudged the oldest ewe up onto a dry stone wall and then through a tangled wire fence, where she left a tuft of wool caught in a barb; the ram following over the side onto the rocks below.

"You'll find sheep and goats along the road here all the time, especially at night and in the fog they're a real menace."

"I know," said Eve, "I've seen them."

Noah pointed out the places of interest. The view was panoramic.

"That's Caherdaniel down there. Can you see the roof of the big house nestled in the trees beside the beach? That's Derrynane House and over there to the left, that wide crescent of beach and the surrounding mountain, that's Derrynane Bay. Straight down below us is Derrynane with the jetty in the middle, that's where the dive school is based, 'tis very popular in the summer with the tourists."

Eve, at the mention of dive school turned to face him. "Noah, I didn't want to interrupt you last night when you drew the diver in that sketch of yours, but diving *is* my hobby. I got my PADI cert in Australia—I just love diving. Are there any good dive sites around?"

"Well what do you know. I must be psychic. I know there's a lot of diving out around the Skelligs but other than that, I can't really say but you can always Google Caherdaniel Diving and see what's what."

"Great, I'll do that," she said looking very pleased.

"Alright then, let's get back in the car and maybe we can see the Skelligs on our way into Waterville." He continued his narrative as they drove off, "Ah the Skelligs are famous around here. Skellig Michael and the little Skellig; they stand around eight miles off the coast; the little one has the second biggest colony of gannets in the world and Skellig Michael is famous for the stone beehive huts sitting up there popping the clouds. I think it's about 800 steps up to the monastery and the beehive huts; they're like big stone igloos and were all hand carved by these monks, what 1,300 years ago."

"So where did they come from these monks—I mean 1,300 years ago, wasn't Europe still covered in forests?"

Dressing for God

"I believe they were called Aramaic monks and they made their way here from Egypt. Sure they'd have come though the Med and up the French coast and across here. The way I heard it was they were searching for the most westerly place in the known world and they settled on Skellig Michael. They literally hand carved hundreds of these steps up to the summit. The island was named after the Archangel Michael you understand? It's brilliant out there in summer but in winter sure it's another story altogether."

"What's the small one called again, the one with the gannets?" Eve asked.

"That's the Little Skellig."

"That's funny you know, because I lived in North Berwick, in the Firth of Forth, and I could see the Bass Rock from my window and *it* has the second biggest gannet colony in the world. And that's where I did a lot of my diving, off the Bass Rock."

"Well isn't that a coincidence now, the two second biggest in the world! Ah sure who's doing the counting? Anyways, I'd say the water temperature is a bit warmer here than in the Firth of Forth, what with the Gulf Stream giving us our semi-tropical climate," Noah laughing and switched on the wipers as they drove through a low, grey, wet cloud hanging over the top of the mountain, then as they rounded a bend, Waterville Bay opened up to their left beneath them.

Noah pointed out the megalithic, round stone fort below as he slowed down lowering the window on Eve's side. "See over there," he pointed out to sea at the twin shapes of the Skelligs just visible in the grainy murk on the horizon.

"That's the Skelligs there. You can just see them, the last bit of land before America."

Eve strained to separate the shapes on the horizon through the drizzle, "They're almost like pyramids aren't they?"

"Aye they are that; sure maybe that's what attracted the Egyptians to them. It was George Bernard Shaw himself after a visit there, who said something about them having 'the magic that takes you far out of this time and out of this world.'"

Noah popped a stick of chewing gum into his mouth, Eve declining his offer of some with a shake of her head, a half smile on her face.

"Well do you suppose that the magic that takes you out of the world is a good enough point to continue with your Noah's revelations then—but can you talk and chew gum at the same time?"

"Hey, whoa there—I can talk and drive at the same time but as for chewing gum, sure I generally end up chewing my own cheek!"

Eve, facing away from the window, gave Noah her full attention, her uplifted eyebrows preceding her question. "Can I ask a personal question please Noah? About yourself and Adam I mean, when did you meet, how do you know each other so well, it's just, well you seem so close..." her words drifting, "Is it ok to ask?"

"Aye, of course 'tis," he replied, meeting her eyes momentarily and breathing deeply.

"Sure Adam and I go back a good while now; we knew each other as kids growing up in Dublin. My dad, he was a vet," he said, smiling to himself, "which explains his sense of humour in naming me Noah."

"That's not so bad is it?" interjected Eve "It's not like in the song *A boy named Sue* is it, I mean Noah it's well, it's a Biblical name."

"Aye it is that. Anyways, dad passed on when I was nine and mother returned to Kerry, to Sneem where she grew up and I didn't see young Adam again for oh, the best part of twenty five years I guess."

They traversed Waterville, passing the whitewashed walls of the Butler Arms Hotel, its windows and doors picked out in black paint, Noah nodding his head in its direction.

"The Butlers there used to own the Skelligs once but they sold them for a few hundred pounds to the lighthouse people when they wanted to build on it. I bet they wished they still owned them now. Did you notice the statue of Charlie Chaplin back there on the seafront? Sure this was his favourite holiday spot in Ireland. He loved the Butler Arms. He used to do salmon fishing on the lakes behind us. Anyway I'm digressing again, so back to your question about Adam and meself."

"I like your digressions," Eve said. "They're full of colour and they help me understand the place much better, but yes back to you and Adam."

"Did he mention to you why my boat is called the *D'Ark Rosaleen*?"

"No," Eve shook her head. "He never mentioned it."

"Well," another of his deep exhaled breaths. "Well I was married to Rosaleen..."

Dressing for God

Noah took his time before continuing.

"Rosaleen was the love of my life." He gave Eve a sideways glance catching her eye. "You'd have loved her, everyone did. She had that effervescence, that caring touch, always seeing the best in everyone, and she was beautiful to look at, tall, slim, raven black hair, sea green eyes…" his words trailed into a sacred silence. Eve became conscious of her shallow breathing, intensely aware of Noah's sharing.

He looked over at her as he said with a sigh, "And then, and then she was no more. We were married just three years, a short illness and…" he clicked his fingers, "and she was no longer with us."

"Oh I am so sorry Noah. I shouldn't have asked you to …"

"Nah Eve, its fine. I'm well reconciled now; anyway that's why my *D'Ark Rosaleen* is special to me. I named it for her when we bought it together, and many a happy hour we had fishing in it when she was here."

They drove in silence for several minutes before Eve asked gently.

"But now you're trading your Rosaleen in for a new boat, why?"

"Ah it's only the shell of the boat that will be changing, I won't be letting go of her name. No, her Spirit is in the name. And the new boat will be my *D'Ark Rosaleen II*."

"And the old boat, the old *D'Ark Rosaleen*, what about her?"

"Well she's due for her major survey soon and God willing she'll pass without too much bother and McCarthy's over there can sell her on. But her spirit stays with me in my memories forever."

He gave a shake of his head as if to clear away the memory. "So that was when Mr. King and I met up again. It's what, all of seven years now. He was back from some project in Australia or somewhere and he read about Rosaleen's passing in the press. She was a well known actress and Adam knew there was only one Noah Mahon in the universe so he flew down from Dublin to spend time with me. God knows I needed it. I was distraught for months. I tried to drown my sorrows in the bottled spirits, even looked at joining her on the other side at one time and Adam it was who was there for me, and eventually he made me look at myself in that mirror of his. Some reflection it was too…. that's about it really."

Eve was still digesting his story as they passed the 'Welcome to Portmagee' signpost and Noah pulled in to the car park at the edge of town.

J.F. Tallon

"We can have a bite of lunch here and then head over to the yard." Noah pointed across the water to the boat-yard, myriad masts and hulls etched against the shoreline, "The Bridge Bar does a really good fish chowder."

Eve rubbing her hands together to get her circulation going in the brisk March air replied, "Sounds great Noah, what a lovely place." The gulls overhead were squawking and crying as they made their way along the quay enjoying the multi-coloured façade of the splendidly painted shop fronts, the yellow of the B&B, the green post office, a deep russet hue on The Bridge Bar and the Moorings, and then white, turquoise, yellow, blue, sandstone, the colours of the houses went on and on to end of the road.

Opposite was a large slipway that fronted the L shaped jetty. An old blue skiff that had seen better days lay upside down awaiting a good scrub and scrape; there were bundles of old green filament fishnets piled in a corner and red pellet marker buoys, old rope pennants, rusty boat cradles on double axel wheels, the very essence of a working fish harbour. Eve felt her heart churning, the memories of North Berwick flooding through her.

"Can we...," she tilted her head towards the jetty, "take a wee ramble? It reminds me of home."

"Do you mind if I just head on inside?" answered Noah, "I need to pump ship, check the plumbing, if you know what I mean. Sure take your time and meet me inside. Can I order anything for you or would you prefer to see the menu?"

"No the chowder sounds fine Noah, and maybe a coffee to finish? Thanks."

Eve wandered along the jetty, past the creels stacked in a five-high tier, just as she remembered them from home, exchanged hellos with an old, wizened faced man in a small wooden boat, fag end in the corner of his mouth, filling his outboard fuel tank from a red can, bilge water slopping around his dirty white Wellies. She fancied the red and black RIB moored at the inner steps, its 120 horse power Johnson outboard tilted out of the water, life jackets strewn across the seats. It stirred memories of other days heading into the Forth for a day's diving. Three inshore fishing boats were moored at the offside end of the wall, just starting to strain at their lines as the wash from a passing launch surged in the short chop of the tide.

Two gulls were having an almighty row over a piece of bread roll, shredding the air with their racket, fleecing each other with snapping beaks, feathers flying, the sounds and the smells, the feelings all surfacing in a rush of emotion. Eve leant against a lamp-post, she closed her eyes and saw the memory clip replay in her mind, "It wasn't that long ago and yet.." And then she felt a surge of relief as the scene receded, emotions calmed, feeling grateful for where she was right now, remembered the quote from the book this morning—'Look the other way'.

"Yes," she thought, "*look forward and don't look back.*"

"You recommended well, the lunch was excellent, thanks." Wiping her mouth with her napkin, Eve rose to join Noah, who fixing the collar of his coat, was eager to get going. "Let's go see this boat then, shall we?"

Five minutes later the Jeep turned right off the Shore Road in through the gates of McCarthy Marine Services and parked up.

"Noah, you go ahead and do your stuff I'll just stay here out of your way—maybe read a bit. I brought one of Adam's reading course books with me." Eve took *The Secret* out of her small carry bag.

"Are you sure? You're very welcome to come along."

"No. you go on and when you've done the business, sure I can have a look at it with you then. I'd only be in the way."

Eve settled in her seat and started rereading Chapter Two again; her new notebook balanced on her knees, trying to write her notes neatly.

> *The law of attraction: Like attracts like.*
> *Thoughts are things!!*
> *I attract things to me as I think.*
> *As I feel so I attract.*
> *Feelings are feedback.*
> *Feeling of Love is the highest vibration.*

She closed her eyes, wondering, "How thoughts could possibly be things? Things are *things, they're physical,* you can touch them," she wrestled with the concept in her mind. "I can't see it," and thinking those thoughts, she dozed.

The thump of the books hitting the floor woke her as she felt herself snap back into her body with a jolt. Looking around she saw Noah approaching the Jeep with a tall, well built man, in his thirties with fair hair, a determined look about him, dressed in a navy fleece jacket, dark blue cargo pants and tan safety boots. They stopped in front of the car talking amicably and then they shook hands. The man waved at Eve and then headed back into the office building.

Looking very pleased with himself, Noah opened the door with a big loud, "Yess—yess, I've done it; that was Pat McCarthy, we shook hands on it, the deals done." A big cheesy grin was eating its way across his ruddy face. "Do you want to see her? C'mon, c'mon, c'mon."

Eve bundled herself out of the front seat and quickly joined Noah who hurried her to the boat parking area. He stood in front of this boat with a duck-egg blue hull and a red bottom, twin propellers with a large white deck cabin bristled with radar and whip antennas. Noah with a showman flourish, hands sweeping down and upwards said proudly, "Eve I would like you to meet the soon to be—my new *D'Ark Rosaleen II*."

"But she is so big!" Eve exclaimed, her eyes taking in the craft.

"She's a thirty foot Cyclone Patrol," Noah was saying, as he rattled on about tonnage, displacement and range. "Speed thirty knots, sleeps four, toilet, shower, galley."

Eve read the name Serenity painted on the stern, port of registry, Tralee.

Noah was so excited, running his stubby hands over the hull, caressing her. Eve felt so happy for him and his new love. "What about *D'Ark Rosaleen* then, is he taking it from you?"

"Oh yes, he has to get all the survey stuff finished on this one, fix up the interior the way I want it and do the change of name and registry. He says it'll be ready for me in about ten days, I just have to bring in Rosaleen and a bankers draft and we're away. I can't wait to tell Adam."

The return journey was filled with Noah's talk about his new boat. He told her of the fishing trips he was planning, of the brilliant little harbours in West Cork where he could find his solitude and great

Dressing for God

scenery to paint. His excitement was palpably touching her and she began to realize how true it was, that 'like attracts like'.

Driving into Caherdaniel, Noah turned and asked, "D'ya fancy a celebration drink? The Blind Piper will be open, will you join me?"

"How could I refuse an offer like that? It's a bit early for champers though isn't it?"

"We'll settle for a pint of Guinness then."

They were seated around the small, open turf fire. They had the place to themselves except for a middle aged man reading a newspaper sitting on a high stool at the bar, a pint of ale and a whiskey chaser in front of him. Noah was sipping on his 'pint of black,' as Eve nursing a half of Guinness, read the lunch menu on a blackboard over the fireplace, her thoughts on supper at home tonight.

"I see you were reading *The Secret* back there. How are you getting on with it?"

"Ah good, I'm enjoying it, but a lot of it is just common sense though, isn't it? I mean positive thinking and all that. It's the way they stress that 'thoughts are things' that I'm really struggling with. Like a hammer is a thing and a boat is a thing, but I fail to see how a thought can be a thing. You said yourself last night you can't put a thought under a microscope to see it, so how can it be a thing?"

Noah took a long pull at his pint, put the glass back on the table, and used his thumb and fore finger to wipe his mouth, his tongue licking his lips savouring the black creamy potion.

"Ok then, I can see where you're at. Well for me a thing is something that is real. It has substance, it's an inanimate object. In fact, I suppose you could say it has its own existence in time and space."

"Exactly."

"Right so. Let's say that I have an idea and I'm going to give it some thought and maybe you can join me here. My idea is, I want a new boat." Noah took his pen and notebook from his pocket, opened it and wrote the word boat and then made a simple drawing of a boat.

"Now this is only a thought of a boat, I can't really walk up to it and touch it, can I?"

"No, but you can touch the picture of the boat."

"Very good, you now understand that I gave the idea of the thought of a boat a physical presence by picturing it as a rough sketch. This is the start of my design blueprint for the boat to appear in my life. I can elaborate on the blueprint by writing about it and describing it in as much detail as I can. In fact I am in essence writing a specification for my requirement. I'm going to try to be clear on what kind of boat I am looking for. So I want a boat for fishing, about 30 foot and it's for four people and so on."

"Yes, I can see that."

"So I define my requirements. I select these thoughts around my requirements. I write them down and visualise them. My thoughts are forming around the idea of what it is I'm looking for and how I am going to use it. I am feeling what it's like to have it. I am breathing it. I love it so much. It's mine. It's MY secret. I'm passionate about it. I'm dreaming about it all the time; I'm in LOVE with it. Now do you get the idea? I'm sending it the energy for it to grow and develop. I'm working from the very centre of the *feeling*. It surrounds me completely."

"You are seriously into this aren't you?"

"Absolutely, there's no question about it. What I am *not going to do* is to start destroying my idea by saying to myself, ah Noah that's a crap idea, that boat is too big, ah I can't afford that boat, sure you don't deserve that boat and all those kind of influences. And I'm not letting anyone else do my thinking for me. I don't need anyone telling me that my idea of having this boat would be bad for me, because if I listened to any of those negative energies it would divert my own energies from staying focused and could simply destroy my idea and it would never appear in my experience except as an unrealized dream."

"So a totally positive diet is a necessity," Eve stated. "What you're saying is that each thought I choose around an idea is a building block?"

"Yes, it's a building block using thought as a hammer to help build my boat or a thought as a hammer to destroy my boat. Build or destroy—that's the process. *So thoughts are real things.* There now, you asked about tangible things earlier hammers and boats you said."

"Touché, Mr. Mahon, you are a clever clog aren't you?"

"Ok then, let's get you back into the ocean there in your dive gear and look at all the zillions of different types and shapes of creatures in the sea. Every single one is uniquely different to the other. Now imagine that as *each* fish *moves* in the water it effects a tiny movement in the ocean that has an impact everywhere in the ocean."

Dressing for God

"See the stingray rising off the ocean floor where it has been hiding flatout not moving a fibre of its skin and now it senses food and rises up in the water, it's body moving majestically and the water moves in response to its movements. As small as that movement might seem, as a part relative to the whole, it's all part of the one connected body of water in the ocean; so the whole is impacted by each moment of any of its parts."

"You seem to enjoy getting me in the water."

"Yeah well, you can come out of it now and dry off, because I'm taking away the water in the story."

"You are? Why?"

"Because when we take away the water we can see each and every person in the world thinking on dry land and as each thought goes out into the atmosphere so the whole world's atmosphere is impacted. And that's the very atmosphere that equates to the one consciousness we talked about last night."

Noah was pleased to see that Eve was following his train of thought as she nodded affirmatively.

Noah continued, "That consciousness is the one mind where everything is created by thought. As we each think a thought, we send a wave of energy into the ocean of mind and it moves in response to the force of the thought. So the thought is the motive energy and the ocean of the mind is in relative terms a static mass of energy—creative intelligent energy—that responds in a plastic way to form what the shape of the idea is in the invisible worlds and then it manifests tangibly in the physical world."

"I think I'm beginning to see that now," Eve interrupted him. "So instead of the water of the ocean surrounding me and reacting in response to a movement—what you're saying is, that it's the invisible atmosphere that surrounds us that responds and reacts to the dynamic movement caused by a thought. Thanks Noah, that'll keep me occupied for a while."

"Sure, I'm delighted to share the little understanding I have, and wasn't it Adam himself who got me going in this direction in the first place? He has a grand way of looking at life. Tell me did he ever tell you his ghost story experience?

"No," she said hesitantly. "He hasn't mentioned it. A ghost story! Is it very scary?"

"No, not any more but maybe you should tell him we were talking and say I told you to ask him and I'm sure he'll share with you. It'll make a good bedtime story. Now then shall we be on our way?"

"Can we stop in Sneem on the way through please? There are a few groceries I'd like to get. I might just surprise Adam and have supper ready for him when he gets in tonight."

Noah pulled in to the driveway of 'Namaste,' the outside security lights switching on as he drew up at the front door.

"So there you are Miss Eve, home safe and sound. And now I must be off. Have you all your bits and pieces then?"

Eve gathered up her shopping and carry bag. "Yes Noah, I'm all together now thanks." She gave him a wide smile. "I really enjoyed today, it was great. See you soon, safe home, Bye."

Chapter 8

'Move The Car'

Eve sat at the dining table, the casserole cooking gently on the Aga cooker, feeling her mouth juices drool as the aromas of the Coq au Vin filled the kitchen, a glass of Burgundy in front of her, willing Adam to hurry up and get home. She was starving and furthermore it was lonely here in this big house. The Bose, tuned to Lyric FM, was wafting Paccabell into the air stirring fond memories.

She'd finished her journaling for the day, *The Secret* lay closed on the table and Eve again picked up *Notes from the Universe* closed her eyes, opened it at random and read.

> *Using your physical senses to assess your options is kind of like driving while looking in the rear view mirror.*
> *Not too swift, unless you want to go backward.*
> *Mostly, the physical senses show what has been and not what will be. For direction, look within, to your feelings, your heart, and most important, your dreams.*
> *Though I must admit, you do look smashing in mirrors.*

She sat there mouth hanging open, reading and re-reading the words, understanding the meaning of gob-smacked. "'You do look smashing in mirrors'. Adam and his smashed mirror and this morning look the other way and now this and all of it picked out at random. Is there a message in there for me, or am I just being foolish?"

The sound of Adams car outside, broke her train of thought. Straightening up she ran her fingers through her hair, did a quick pursing of the lips in the mirror and was tying an apron over the Ben Sherman blue tunic blouse when Adam entered the room.

J.F. Tallon

"Eve, how are you? Oh my goodness that smells wonderful and how nice it is to have a welcome like this," he quickly threw his coat over a chair and gave Eve a peck on the cheek, pleasantly surprising her.

Eve, the laughter lines around her mouth stretched into a full smile answered, "Welcome home Mr. King. Gosh that was a long day you had, you must be bushed. I heard you take off in the dark and now here you are returning home in the dark. I do hope you've got an appetite. Have you had dinner?" Eve was busying herself at the cooker.

"No, I came straight from the airport, I'm famished. Boy that looks good," he said taking a peek into the casserole dish as Eve gave it a gentle stir, proud of her cooking initiative.

"Coq au Vin and parsley creamed tatties."

"Wonderful, well done, it smells great. Let me get out of this suit and I'll be right down."

There was nothing left of the casserole on the table. A mound of chicken bones on his side plate evidence of the two full servings he'd enjoyed.

"That was marvellous, and I thinking to myself on the drive home that you'd be sitting by the fire in your little house and I'd be eating some tinned soup and a cheese sandwich on my own."

Adam, hair still damp from one of the quickest shower he'd ever taken, wearing a pale blue rugby top with broad navy stripes, navy Dockers, his bare feet in a pair of soft tan moccasins was leaning back in his seat, his look one of unabashed admiration. Eve sat hands folded under her chin, her elbows on the table surveying the empty plates, not stirring herself to clear the table.

A thought occurred to Adam that he'd forgotten to ask about her day and he was just about to broach the subject when she asked.

"So how did your day go then? Finished the business in Dublin?"

"Eve, I had a fine day. Yep I finished that part of it. Now I've just one more trip to London and I can wrap it all up and start on the writing full time. But I do apologise. I really am sorry but I was so famished and the meal was so terrific I never asked you how you got on with Noah today. Did *you* have a good day?"

Eve thinking, 'Well that's a bit better then,' replied, "Actually Adam, I had a brilliant day. I loved the drive to Valentia and Noah

Dressing for God

is such a sweetie and just you wait 'til you see his new boat. It's huge, duck-egg blue, sleeps four and he says it'll be ready for him in ten days. His new *D'Ark Rosaleen II*."

Adam perked up visibly, "He's bought it! Ah that's great. He's been talking about getting something bigger for ages. He must have done a good deal then, Noah doesn't like to part with his coin too easily. Ready in ten days you say?"

"Aye, he's chuffed to bits with it, really excited. I was delighted for him." Eve paused, "We had a good chat together on the way and he did...," she hesitated before adding, "he did tell me about his dear wife Rosaleen passing on and how you were there for him." Eve was conscious that Adam may have had some scars around the memories.

Adam took a deep breath as the thoughts replayed in his mind. "Yeah Noah is a tough old soldier. He was besotted with Rosaleen. Sure I had lost contact with him since we were kids together and then when I read of Rosaleen's death in the papers and saw Noah's name as the widower. Sure the penny dropped that there could only be one Noah Mahon in Ireland. So I flew down to offer my support in his hour of need and then I stayed on here afterwards."

Adam picked up his glass of red, took a sip, looking pensive as he said softly.

"I'd never been to Kerry before. I'd travelled most of the world but this place was something else. I loved it, the scenery, the air, the people and of course finding Noah again. So I stayed. And truth to tell," a silence, as he fixed his gaze somewhere in the middle of the table, his face controlled, mood sombre, he continued in a low voice which Eve strained to hear. "Sure Noah was just as supportive to me as I was for him at the time. The only difference was that I didn't know that I was in need of support at all."

Adam standing now, cleared the dishes from the table and emptied the dross into the garbage. Eve rinsed the plates and stacked them in the dishwasher wondered if this was a good time to ask about the ghost story, but decided against it.

"Well then shall I get a fire going in the sitting room and maybe I can fill in some of the gaps in my life for you, or maybe you'd prefer an early night?" Adam asked, pushing the start button on the dishwasher.

"No. I'd love that Adam. Actually I'm a night owl kind of person—just as long as you don't want me at the desk for seven o'clock or some other ghastly hour in the morning."

"Not at all, sure haven't we all the hours that God gave us? Right so, let's go inside then—the fires all set, it just needs a match."

The sitting room was warm and snug. Eve curled up on the two-seater settee in front of the fire. Adam crouched on one knee watching the flames catch, adding lumps of coal and sods of turf strategically on the kindling and then satisfied that it was well under way turned and caught her mischievous glance.

"Were you a boy scout?" she asked.

Adam stood there looking pleased at the fire, grinning back a reply. "But of course, some things you never forget."

They sat in silence for a while watching the flames rise and then subside to a low red-orange glow as the coal and turf combined, the rich peaty smell adding a flavour to the glass of wine which Eve nursed carefully. Adam, sitting back comfortably in his cream, leather recliner, moccasin feet up on a foot stool, a glass of Jameson Irish Whiskey in his hand, looked over at Eve.

"Well isn't this the life? Tell me before I start my story, how did you get on with the books today, did you manage to make a start at all?"

"I did indeed, and I had a good chat with Noah about how 'things are thoughts', as well."

"Ah ha. Good one. Was it *The Secret* then that you started?"

"Yes. It's very good, I'm working through it. But I am enjoying the *Notes From The Universe* though, that one seems to be speaking to me."

"I love it when that happens. Which I suppose is as good an opening to this story of mine as any."

"Noah did sort of strongly suggest that I prompt you to tell a ghost story but I didn't want you to feel I was prying."

"Is that so? Well I suppose that *was* a major turning point in my life, so I guess maybe his prompt was correct."

Adam was looking at the fire through his tumbler of whiskey. "Ah where to begin, at all, at all?" He lay back in his chair, looking up at the ceiling as he waited for his thoughts to settle, then sat up and took a sip of his drink.

Dressing for God

"OK then. Before I get to what Noah calls my ghost story, let me recall an event that happened to me a few years before that. D'ya remember last night, we spoke about intuition?"

"Did we?"

"Noah did, when he was saying the difference between the consciousness of the animal and man, the animal has instinct and..."

Eve interrupted, "And the man has intuition and inspiration. See I was listening."

Adam wet his finger and gave her a mark in the air, "Top class, well done. I'm impressed."

"So let me get back to my story then. It was wintertime and I was home in Wexford, on leave from the St. Patrick, a car ferry which ran between Rosslare and Le Havre. My neighbour Jimmy, asked me to do him a favour and pick him up from his work in Johnstown Castle and drive him to collect his car from the garage where it was being serviced." Eve settled back on the settee and tucked her feet beneath her as Adam began his story.

"So there I was being the good Samaritan on this cold February morning. I drive up the long, oak lined driveway leading up to the castle and being about thirty minutes early, I decide to park in the drive and do my crossword rather than be conspicuous and park outside the front door. Being naturally shy you understand."

"Yeah, Right." said Eve.

"I remember I was sitting there in the car—it was a red Morris Maestro—and it had a voice box gizmo that gave you prompts in a woman's voice. She'd tell you stuff like, 'Fasten your seatbelt', or as you'd leave the car she'd say, 'Your keys are in the ignition'—I found her really, really annoying."

"So there I was parked halfway down this big driveway, struggling with my crossword when I heard this voice say *'Move the car'*. Now it wasn't the nagging woman in the voice box that was talking to me. Not at all, at all. In fact it wasn't the *sound of a voice* as such that I heard, but it was the pressure of the message that was so clear that without questioning it for a second, I immediately dropped the paper, started the car and reversed about fifty yards back up the drive."

Adam had a faraway look on his face as he continued.

"It was only then after I had switched off the engine and picked up my crossword again that I asked myself, *'Just what the hell was all that about?'* In answer to my question, I watched dumbfounded as this giant Oak tree slowly, slowly, toppled from the vertical and in a tearing, ripping, crunch, it slammed across the road *exactly where I'd been parked just seconds earlier."* Adam saw Eve sit bolt upright.

"Wow—that's just incredible." She said with an amazed expression in her voice.

"Yeah it certainly was, and it was the start of my learning to trust completely in this inner voice. I can still see the hole where the roots of that tree were—it was so enormous, well you could have parked two double-deck buses in it easily."

"That's amazing, I mean if you hadn't moved?"

"I'd have been brown bread, *dead*. Back across to the other side again."

Eve felt a chill run down her spine thinking about it. "That's awesome. I've never had anything quite like that happen to me. I've had some little prompts, you know a kind of gut feeling, the sense of danger, but never anything like that."

"Do you want a refresh on your wine there, or would you fancy a taste of a proper whiskey, a dram of Irish to salve your Scots soul?"

"If that story there was just a taster before the real ghost story, then yes please, I'll have one, but just a real small one, thanks."

Glasses charged, Adam added another lump of turf to the fire, gave it a poke to stir some life in it and resumed his narrative.

"So indeed my life moved on from Wexford and I left the seagoing career behind me. Ploughing waves I called it. I got this job with an American offshore construction company and moved out to Singapore with my family. This is where the story really begins." Eve watched him carefully as he composed himself taking his time recalling the memory.

"We were renting this rather nice bungalow off Bukit Timah Road. It was a two bed house with a nice big garden, the usual kitchen and lounge. It had a veranda with maid's quarters—a tiny bed and bathroom, and a small cooking area in the back. Our Amah was a lovely lady named Elsie, my wife's right hand since we moved to Singapore. I guess we were there about seven years at this time. Elsie lived in her own kampong nearby and rarely stayed over with us." Adam had a faraway look in his eyes, gazing into the fire as he told his story.

Dressing for God

"Some months after we'd moved into this bungalow, my wife had a very frightening experience in the spare bedroom as she was doing some tidying up. She felt this cold, eerie presence totally surround her. She'd actually felt it touch her physically. She had long black hair which was down to her waist—well, such was her fright—that her hair actually straightened up and hit the ceiling and just missed getting tangled in the ceiling fan. She was, as you can imagine, scared witless. So she called me and I got home, but whatever it was had disappeared and well what could I do about it in any case?" Adam stood with his hands behind his back to the fire as he continued.

"A few weeks after this, my wife and our children came down with different illnesses and they all ended up in hospital. Elsie was staying over helping out and next thing I knew, I am woken up in the small hours of the morning. She was in a terrible state, standing there in my bedroom doorway, in a terrified voice saying, 'Master, master, terrible evil, terrible. Oh master I so scared." She was petrified out of her wits. I got up and put on all the lights, walked around the house trying to sense any spirits or whatever entity it was, but I felt nothing. I tried to reason with her but she'd had enough and just high-tailed it back to her family and never returned. Now I had to tell the wife that she'd had done a runner and now we're without any home help. That didn't go down well at all, at all."

"So a few days later the family was back home again and the wife and I visited the Singaporean family who owned the house. Very kind people indeed—so we told them our story. They listened with inscrutable kindness and suggested that they seek help from the monks in their local Buddhist Temple. They were absolutely sure there was someone there who could deal with this strange happening. It sounded good to us, so we said, 'Yes please, can you arrange it as soon as possible."

Adam was moving his shoulders in that rolling motion Eve was familiar with now, getting his circulation moving, head moving sideways, little crunching sounds from his neck as he flexed, rolled and stretched.

"It was a few days after this—I remember it was Sunday lunchtime. I was having a midday cold beer, just wearing a pair of shorts on the veranda, hanging loose in my hammock, reading a book when I got this feeling to get properly dressed. I was about to receive a visitor- another one of those little intuitions. So I put on a pair of slacks and a shirt and I had no sooner returned to the porch when I saw this saffron robed Monk walking down our neighbours drive looking in my direction."

"Maung was a Burmese Buddhist Monk. We got a telephone call from our neighbours just as he was walking down the pathway, telling us that their temple had nominated him to clear any entities that might be present in the house."

"Maung was a beautiful soul. He had the most amazing eyes you ever saw in any man or woman alive. I can still remember shaking hands with him after he did a Namaste welcome and I being the westerner returned the salute as best I could. Did you know Namaste means, *the God in me salutes the God in you*—hence the name of the house here?"

"And," Eve asked, "that painting of the monk by Noah in the house. Is that Maung?"

"Yes, that's Noah's interpretation of my description of him, pretty good it is too."

Eve nodded for him to continue, remembering the eyes in the painting, how they seemed to be always looking straight at her no matter where she stood in the room.

"So Maung has this instrument; it looked like a hand compass or something and he walked around the house and gardens and eventually he sat down with us. Said sorry but he couldn't detect any spirits or entities around and then, looked me straight in the eye, he added, 'But if there were any then *you*', meaning me, 'would know them and deal with them."

"I can still see my chest swell out with this recognition of my spiritual understanding—what a prat I was. So off he went, back to our neighbours and next thing I saw was their car going down the drive as they delivered him back to the temple. It wasn't the last I saw of him by any means, but back to the story in hand."

"The wife and I had enough of this interference. If the monk couldn't clear the house of this spirit then we would have to move out. We gave notice and started packing. The family were returning to Dublin for a holiday. I would go with them but I had to immediately head straight back to Singapore for my work. So we arrived in Dublin on a Friday and next day, Saturday, I'm in Heathrow getting

Dressing for God

ready for my Singapore Airways flight back east." Adam sat back in his chair and resumed.

"I was in WH Smiths in Terminal four buying a few books for the flight and for some reason was shocked to see a book stand displaying a book titled, *The Ghost of Flight 401*. I thought it was such bad taste to tout a book like that in an airport book shop. Truth to tell, it made me nervous for some reason. So I paid for a bunch of books and magazines for the flight and headed off on the mile trudge to my gate."

"You didn't buy the book then?"

"No not then. But the voice just wouldn't stop. It was incessant, 'Go back and get that book'. So eventually I stopped, sat down and took stock and against what I thought was my better judgement, I returned to the shop and bought the book. As soon as I was seated on the plane and had my first glass of bubbles, I opened it up and started reading. I read it from cover to cover non-stop. And yes, it had a message for me."

Adam rose from his chair and retrieved a copy from the bookshelf. "Here it is," he said and looking at the cover read out the caption: '*The Real Life Supernatural Incident that Grounded a Jumbo Jet*'. Let me tell you about it...."

"Flight 401 was an Eastern Airlines flight that took off from New York for Miami but unfortunately crashed in the Florida Everglades with a huge loss of life. December 1972, it was just before the New Year. A subsequent NTSB investigation laid the blame for the crash on pilot error." Adam handed Eve the book as he went on.

"Eastern Airlines recovered the wrecked fuselage from the swamp and brought it back to their base. It's quite usual in such cases to cannibalise the wreck and strip it of whatever bits of kit that were undamaged and could be used on other aircrafts as replacement parts, such as radio gear, galley equipment and the like. And that's what Eastern did with 401."

"This guy, John G. Fuller, the author of the book, was a scientist. He'd written several books on deeply hard science factual issues. He began to hear rumours of strange occurrences happening on different Eastern flights and then he had a conversation with a flight crew member who had a personal experience of seeing the head of one of the deceased pilots appear in a galley oven. This was an oven that had been salvaged from flight 401." Eve's face had a scared look on it as Adam continued with his story.

"Now John Fuller was a self confessed utter sceptic on anything that smacked of the psychic but he became intrigued with the stories of strange appearances of ghosts that he was hearing about on his travels. So he did some follow up work and eventually after a lot of sleuthing he made contact with one of the deceased pilot's wife. It seems that she'd been having dream experiences about her husband's death and she told this John Fuller all about it."

"Evidently the cause of the crash was not 'pilot error' at all. The real cause was an intrinsic design fault in the planes auto pilot system that disengaged with the slightest of touches. This happened on Flight 401's approach to Miami and went unnoticed as the flight deck crew tried to fix a faulty bulb in the instrument panel. This is what led to the aircraft losing altitude and crashing into the Everglades. The deceased pilots on the other side of the veil, so to speak, were now fatally aware of this design fault and just wouldn't rest until the truth was established and another disaster averted."

Eve had a perplexed look on her face said, "That's incredible—but how did they get the message across?"

"The pilots were manifesting on whichever aircraft a part of the old flight 401 had been installed in. At one stage the chief pilot of 401, Captain Loft, was seen in full uniform sitting in the first class section beside Frank Borman, the astronaut who was a vice president at Eastern Airlines at the time. Borman later went on to become CEO of Eastern. You'd have thought that having one of your deceased captains sitting beside you in first class was maybe a pretty strong message to send to the Eastern board wouldn't you? But oh no, not at all, Eastern's policy was, Eastern's policy was, 'Do Not Scare the Travelling Public' – that was the management strategy. So the airline tried to put a total blackout on the reports but there were too many of them happening and eventually news of the ghost appearances began leaking out everywhere."

Adam pointed at the book in her hand. "The book details how communication with the deceased was carried out, including the manner of the silent inner conversations with the deceased pilots, which for me was really pertinent, although obviously I had no idea why at the time. And yes, a subsequent CAA investigation proved the flight crew's message was correct and the initial crash investigation

Dressing for God

findings were reversed and technical fault was properly adjudged to be the cause and not 'pilot error'."

Adam took a sip of his whiskey and asked, "So how's that for an interesting introduction to the ghost story?"

"I can see now why synchronicity is a key thing with you," Eve replied.

"Indeed yes." He poured another dram of whiskey into his glass before continuing.

"Well now, that's the background for starters. So let me head into the main course. I got home around five on the Sunday. I had the movers arriving the following morning to collect all our furniture and bits and pieces for storage until our new condo in Orange Grove Road was ready."

"I remember pouring myself a Canadian Club and dry ginger and I was sitting at this small rattan bar I had in the living room, trying to decide what music to play on my stereo when this feeling crept all over me… my skin was a rash of goose-bumps. My hair was bristling. I could feel the charge of electricity in the air. It was there again. My first reaction was one of utter fear and then I remembered how the communication went in the book I'd just finished. So I carried on silently, feeling a bit of confidence return, but only a little bit. A very little bit…"

"*I said hello and welcome. There was no reply.*"

"*I repeated, 'Hello, I know you're here. I can feel you—I can help you—it's OK your friends are here also.'. I could sense these souls calling him to let go and join them 'Look their hands are stretching out waiting to welcome you. Please go with them—it's time to move on—your time here is done.*"

"*And somehow I knew who it was. He was an Indian gardener who used to live in the kampong across the road and who had worked for the house owner looking after both gardens. He had expired in the garden and he didn't want to leave. He liked it here. It was his place of peace. I told him 'Your friends are here to help you, look at them. They're reaching out for you'. I kept the communication going but it was all one way. I kept talking silently to him as I had read about in the book.*"

"'*They want you to join them. Reach out and let go. There's nothing to fear.' But he would not go. I carried on talking with him for some time telling him that he was in his Astral body, that his physical body no longer* existed, that the reason he could walk through walls was because he was actually, physically dead... he needed to let go, to trust and reach out, his friends were there, just let go please."

"He wouldn't leave; he was more scared than me. He told me he just couldn't do it...he was so afraid to let go ....and then I said it."

Eve asked in a whisper, "You said what?"

Adam sniffed; his face pale in the dimmed light, "I said that I would go with him if he was afraid."

Eve could feel the electric charge as he recalled it. Her skin was crawling now, goose- pimples all over her as she shared this recall.

"So I went with him. He was so afraid and I said 'OK. OK you guys over there, guys get ready, here we come' and next thing I know was the reunion had taken place. He was with his friend and I was in the middle of, of this whirlwind of time and space, aware of what seemed like all knowledge, aware of everything that was an unanswered question in my understanding, the answer was there simultaneously to every question I wanted answering.... they came catapulting so fast that I was on my knees, then I was lying on the floor my arms wrapped around myself, the incessant questions and answers streaming through me for what seemed like an eternity and then I was back. Sobbing uncontrollably with the thought running through me of how fine the line is between sanity and insanity. This was not an experience I would recommend to anyone. It was literally and metaphorically out of this world."

Eve visibly confused, brow furrowed, tension showing in the way she straightened up, moved her legs from under, placed her feet firmly on the floor.

"Well, then..." she searched for words, "Why you... why did you get yourself into this situation, could you not just have... I don't know, just left the house and not gone back?"

"Aye, maybe I could and maybe I should have, but I didn't, did I? I didn't really have a chance to sit down and rationalise it. All I had was this feeling of confidence that I was..... I don't know how to describe it other than I was being asked to do something to help a lost soul cross over. The bit of going with him wasn't in the script or I doubt that I'd have had the courage."

Adam stopped mid-thought, "Courage? It was more naivety than courage, when I think about it now. In any case, I paid the price eventually."

Dressing for God

"How, in what way?" Eve asked, her voice hushed.

"Oh when I came back, I was so psychic, it was unreal. My energies were all over the place. I would be in an elevator and unbeknownst to me, it would stop mid floor and stay that way, until I began to realise I had somehow stopped it and then I'd sort of consciously start it up again. Or I was in a car with a friend, it was a 7 Series beemer—he had been a test driver for BMW and as we were driving along the engine started coughing and spluttering and I had to own up that it was probably me doing it. Those sorts of things were happening all the time."

"Ruddy heck, so what did you do?"

"I was back in Dublin then. The marriage was strained beyond survival and I was literally too scared to do anything. Eventually the wife had enough and I can't blame her for that and I found myself alone, adrift, back home staying with my dear mother and having to take stock of myself trying to pick myself up again."

Eve nodded, wanting more.

"So that's when I started studying spirituality more or less full time, to see if I could get a real grasp on how life works from the inside out and that I suppose is why we are here now talking about it. I did learn later, much later, that if a soul dies and is really afraid, like desperately panic stricken, that it can get stuck in what is termed the quantum realm, a sort of half-way house between the physical and astral planes, and that's where I think our gardener was stuck."

Adam, standing now, put his back to the fire, "Anyhow it took a few years and I eventually got myself back in the mainstream of life, working in the offshore scene again, and then when I read about Noah's wife Rosaleen passing on, I flew over to Kerry to see him and that was it. I stayed."

Adam placed the fireguard over the fire, his signal she knew, that the storytelling was at an end, for tonight, in any case. "Now what say we call it a night?" Adam gave a long yawn as he stretched and checked the time. "Jeepers, it's nearly midnight."

"Thanks for sharing that Adam, it really is an amazing story. I can see why you're motivated to get this book written."

"Thanks Eve, there's a long way to go with the writing, but at least I've made a start. C'mon, I'll walk you over to your house—lock the car on the way."

Chapter 9

EFT

The bird song started her on the journey from deep slumber to half wakefulness. It seemed to come from directly overhead. The distinctive whistled pitch and trilling of a black bird welcoming the day and then the repetitive twitching, whistling, symphonic melody as a song thrush answered and from somewhere in the distance another trill, 'Was that a robin?' she asked herself as it added its staccato chirp, chirp, chirp to the morning song. The music lent a joyous edge to her slumber and then with a harsh raucous cawing and rustling of feathers scurrying on the roof, a pair of magpies scattered the sound asunder bringing Eve to full wakefulness.

The clock blinked 7:20, the weak March sunlight filtering in through a gap in the curtains. Eve lay there listening, waiting in hope for the bird song to resume and wondering what the day had in store.

A peek through the window made her mind up and ten minutes later, clad in a pink hooded jersey top, grey bottoms with a pink leg stripe to complement her silver and pink Nike Air trainers, Eve did some warm up stretches in the garden. A solitary bird scratching in the grass keeping her company. The sky was a hazy greyish blue, the temperature five or six degrees above freezing.

Starting easily, Eve felt her body find its rhythm as she kept her pace intentionally slow. It had been over a week since her last run, so she figured twice up and down the single track road, about four miles, would be enough. Staying focused in her body, mind in neutral, she worked up a good sweat in the crisp air. Her breath evaporating as she breathed easily, letting her thoughts return to Adam and his ice and air analogy and then, 'What about his story of last night?'

Dressing for God

Finishing the run with another stretching session, Eve leant in against the front wall feeling her tendons pull and tighten and then relax, repeating the exercise, left and right, centre stretch, rotate and again relax. "I'm stretching more than my imagination in this place, and that's for sure—but so far so good."

Showered and dressed for work in a navy wool sweater, white button-down shirt, blue denim jeans with her feet in soft brown suede pumps, her appetite sharp and ready for breakfast, Eve quietly opened the door to the big house, as she was beginning to call it, headed for the kitchen for some low fat yogurt and orange juice. The smell of fresh coffee brewing told her that Adam was already up and about and then she heard his voice talking with someone in the office next door.

"Funny there's no car outside, whoever it was must have walked here. Maybe it's a neighbour." She busied herself getting her breakfast and waited for whoever was with Adam to finish their business and leave.

The background conversation ended and Adam, in a red Munster rugby top and faded Levis, emerged looking very relaxed and pleased.

"Eve, good morning," his voice cheery, full of the joys of spring. "Did you sleep well? Isn't it a lovely morning outside? I saw you coming back from your run, was it good?"

"Morning Adam and yes to all of that. I slept like a log and the run was great. God knows I need the exercise with all the rich food and wine."

Eve peered behind him to see who was with him in the office. Adam turned following her gaze and asked, turning his head, "What is it?"

"Haven't you got company in there with you? I heard you talking with someone… someone talking with you, I mean."

Laughing, shaking his head.

"No, there's nobody there, physically I mean." He saw the perplexed look on her face.

"No it's not an entity from the other side. Come in, let me show you."

Adam, moved a chair for Eve to sit and share his computer screen, logged on to a website, entered his password, selected a YouTube video from the menu, and sat back quietly as a soft West Coast American voice spoke.

"And now it's time for Tap O Morning' with Brad Yates."

A yawn, as a coffee mug with the title appeared on the screen and a bleary eyed Brad Yates in a slept-in navy T-shirt, stretched his body awake.

"Morning.... So tap of the morning to you," another yawn. "And let's do a little tapping to start the day off right. A little positive phrasing to start, just follow along and tap where I tap ... sometimes negative emotions will arise and you're not ready for them...." Adam hit the pause key, turned in his chair facing Eve.

"What you heard in the kitchen was Brad and me doing this exercise together; EFT, ever heard of it?"

Eve made a slow sideways shake of her head, "No, what is it?"

"Emotional Freedom Techniques, it's really good. I've been using it for a couple of months and I can truly say it's helped me shift some emotional stuff I didn't even know I was carrying."

"What kind of stuff?"

"Stuff I don't need. It's a really simple tool to help clear blockages in the body. I use it the same way as I take a shower to stay, ya' know, clean and fresh. And I do this tapping whenever I feel a need to flush out any negative feelings and emotions that are blocking my drains. Guess what happens when the drains are blocked, what overflows?"

"Crap?"

"Exactly, except in this case its emotional crap."

"So what's going on then, how does it work?"

"Well I can show you now; you can follow along if you want—is that ok?"

"Yeah that's fine, go ahead, run it."

Eve sat forward on the chair, her eyes intent on Brad as the clip continued. Brad warned first time users to be careful of negative emotions surfacing if they're not ready for them, and then he set out his intentions to have a great day—to use the law of attraction—to release any negative memories or feelings that could screw up having a great day and then he finished by saying, "I deeply and completely, love, forgive and accept myself and anyone else involved in my life."

Adam followed Brad—tapping on the corner of the eye, on the side of the eye, under the nose, under the mouth, collarbone, under

Dressing for God

the arm and then crown of the head, repeating the phrases after him, then he finished with a request to have all these energies release at a cellular level. Adam took a deep breath, held it for a few moments and released it, smiled questioningly, "So what do you think?"

"I don't know. I've watched it, but I don't understand it."

"Well that's as good a place to start as any! Let me get a coffee and I'll see if I can show you what's going on."

The phone ringing in the office interrupted him, Adam picked it up on the fourth ring. "Ah, its yourself, grand thanks, yeah got in before eight—had a brilliant supper waiting for me."

Eve thinking, "Noah."

"Eh, Coq au Vin and parsley mash, you'd have loved it."

Adam began to laugh.

"Hey great news on the boat, can I ask how much?"

"You're joking. That'll take a lump out of your pension fund then."

"I'll bet you are—me too for that matter."

"What are we up to? I just introduced Eve to EFT—well the Tap O Morning bit."

"Oh, excellent. Tomorrow, what time? When are you off?"

"Fair enough, I'll ask her." Another belly laugh.

"I will I will, take care then, bye, bye, bye."

Adam returning the phone to the charger, rubbed his face, fingers smoothing the moustache, and then pulled gently on the tuft of hair under his lower lip, a faraway look in his eyes.

"I take it that was Noah." said Eve.

"Aye. He's off to Cork this afternoon, picking up someone from the airport, wants us to join him for dinner tomorrow and said to tell you that he has a surprise for you."

"A surprise! What kind of surprise?"

"Well, if I told you that, it wouldn't be a surprise would it?"

Seeing the look on her face he added, "No, he didn't say. I take it you have no objection to the invite then?"

"No. That's great. I'll look forward to it and I'll get to see his place. So can you tell me more about this EFT?"

Adam finished off his coffee, rinsed his mug in the sink and looking out the window over the decking said, "It's as the man says, it does what it says on the tin. EFT brings to the surface any hidden feelings and emotions that are causing me grief in my life."

J.F. Tallon

He picked up a yellow scouring sponge from the sink-tidy, ran it under the tap, letting it fully absorb the water. "Can you hand me that elastic band there please?"

He pointed in the direction of the dresser. Eve handed it over and he twisted it around the sponge near the top, and then held the sponge up by the head.

"Now let's say this sponge is a human body with a small head on top of a big body."

"Yes, I can see that."

Adam held up the sponge which was slowly dripping water into the sink, gave it a squeeze and then soaked it again under the tap.

"The body is just like the sponge that's absorbed all this water. We're exactly the same, we absorb consciously and unconsciously all the impressions we're constantly immersed in. All of our unseen reactions to stimulus are programmed into our own unconscious minds. The unconscious mind is what makes you tick, it's transmitting all of the time on auto without you having to think about it."

"OK, I certainly never heard that before, and so where does this EFT come in then?"

Adam dropped the sponge into the sink and headed back to the office. "Let me find my journal entry for an experience I had very soon after I started tapping."

Adam rummaging on a lower shelf, picked out a black covered A4 size notebook, leafed through it, "Here we are," and he looked up at Eve. "This is precisely as I wrote it."

"This is dated seventh of December, 2008."

"*Well my EFT sessions seem to have opened up ages of suppressed feelings—I was a wee baby in a blue baby cot in the corridor of Jervis Street Hospital in Dublin, feeling totally abandoned and screaming my little lungs off as my mother had to leave to go home and the children's ward wasn't ready. I had this feeling of being abandoned—it was a devastating feeling of loss and it had obviously been lodged deep in my consciousness—my earliest memory of this lifetime. It seems like the feeling of abandonment set the tone for the rest of the life experiences I was attracting to myself....*"

"I was just fourteen months old when that happened, but that feeling of being abandoned was stuck inside me, hidden away below decks in my unconscious. It was shortly after I started tapping with

Dressing for God

EFT that I became very, very upset with emotions churning inside me when these feelings surfaced. I'd no idea what was causing them. I just felt the eruption of deep, deep impressions bubbling up and overflowing and I was feeling so swamped by them that I emailed Brad and asked for help to get rid of whatever was causing this effect. He forwarded a suggested tapping exercise and that worked immediately and over the course of a few weeks the feelings evaporated completely."

"Now I don't have that little child within me feeling abandoned any more. It really was incredibly liberating, like finding a missing part of myself that I didn't even know I was missing."

"You got that from tapping?"

"Yes, EFT uses key acupressure points—have you seen one of those models acupuncturists use to map out the meridian lines throughout the body?" Adam asked.

Eve nodded, "Yes I have."

"Well if there's a blockage in any of the energy paths in the body you'll get an imbalance of energy flow and this results in a build up of negative feelings or emotions being experienced in the body. It's a chicken and egg thing, negative beliefs can cause disruptions in the energy flow or physical trauma can set up an imbalance. Either way, tapping is a process of releasing the negative energy pattern, clearing it out and replacing it with a counter belief and positive energy flow. It's like weeding an inner garden of self consciousness."

"And can anyone do it?"

"Yeah of course they can. But like anything it's best to understand the potential side effects you might open up. Here, I'll send you a link to Brad's website it's www.bradyates.net now, I don't want *to tell you* to try EFT, but it's an essential part of what I'm writing about, so maybe take a look at it and see for yourself."

"Thanks Adam, I will. I know acupuncture. I've had it a few times in Scotland. It works. No problem, I'll give it a go. You talked about your writing there—it's just that you don't seem to be doing an awful lot of it, what with all your travel and such."

"Oh, you're right there Eve. I'm really looking forward to finishing this project with Lloyds. I've one more trip to London at the end of next week and then I'll get stuck in full time. Would you like to see where I am with it so far?"

"Oh yes please."

Adam checked the time. "It's close to ten now. I have a bit of shopping to do and I was thinking," he paused, standing, hands behind his head, "I have a surprise for you too. Why don't you join me and we can catch up with the writing after lunch?"

"Oh I love surprises—what is it? No forget I said that, I'll wait and see."

"How many laps of the boreen did you do this morning?" Adam asked, as they were waiting to turn left onto the A70 into Sneem.

"Just the four, up and down twice; I didn't want to overdo it and I didn't fancy running on the main road with the traffic flying past. They don't half give it wellie, don't they?"

"Ah, you can't be too safe here. Tell me Eve," Adam waited for a white van to pass before pulling out, "are you happy enough here just now, I mean is there anything you need to help you settle in?"

Eve chose her words carefully, "Well it is just a bit isolated and," she hesitated, "no, it's really fine and no I'm grand, thanks."

"The reason I ask is, I was thinking of getting you a set of wheels. Nothing salubrious mind you, just a wee runabout—something that will get you out and about and give you a bit of freedom."

"Oh Adam, that would be brilliant, thank you. That would *really* make a difference. Is that the surprise?" Her eyes widening as Adam indicated to make a right turn into the garage.

MURPHY MOTORS SALES AND SERVICE.
CAR HIRE, COACH SERVICE.

The sign in large, blue letters was blazoned across the front of an old two-storied whitewashed building, Ivy spreading like a rash across its façade, black window sills, a battered petrol pump stood outside at an odd angle to the vertical. There were two vehicles parked by the office door, a small red Seat van looking the worst for wear and a dirty grey Volvo estate, a farmer sitting under its open tailgate patting the head of a black and white sheep dog. A wide side gate also painted white led into a back yard, the top of a cream coloured coach visible over the top. Adam pulled up and parked beside the van exchanging silent hellos with the farmer with the ubiquitous hand flick that Kerry folk used in passing.

Dressing for God

"Can you wait here a mo'? There's something I want to check out," he said pulling on his blue parka. He disappeared into the office leaving her contemplating quietly.

'Sneem—Adam and Noah'—agreeing with herself, that 'Life wasn't so bad after all and maybe this job, if I can call it that, was if not demanding, it was at least refreshing.' She fiddled with her Blackberry thinking how little she used it here.

"It's different, that's for sure," the words spoken under her breath as Adam reappeared accompanied by an elderly man, dressed in navy dungarees over an old pink sweater, a broad greasy leather belt corseting his ample midriff. He unlocked the padlocked side gate and propped it open with old Guinness beer keg.

Adam followed him through into the yard. Eve sat and waited expectantly and a few moments later a vivid green VW Beetle with Adam at the wheel zipped out trailing vapours from the tailpipe and pulled up alongside the Land Rover.

Eve stood beside the Beetle, pulling her jacket close, arms folded in front of her, lost for words as she took in the unusual puce greenness of the car.

Adam was saying, "Now isn't she lovely, what do think? Sure nothing a good wash and a polish won't put right. Isn't that right Tim?" addressing the old man who'd joined them, his wispy grey hair rain streaked across his wide forehead, brown eyes humorously watching Eve's reaction.

"Ah 'tis a grand motor that and a lovely shade of green to go with your lovely red hair, a match made in heaven, I'd say meself. Look Adam I'll leave you to it. Have a look-see and let me know if you're interested and I'll have it serviced and valeted like new. Good day to you Ma'am." He tipped his hand to Eve, turned and headed indoors.

Eve sat in the driver's seat, hands on the wheel, fixing the rear view mirror, winding the window up and down. "Tell him it's not red, its strawberry blonde!" She gave Adam a cheeky grin, "Well it has all its bits, steering wheel, pedals and actually it feels not bad but, I'm not sure how to put this… but it's so green!"

"Well you are in Kerry so maybe this is the greening of Ms. McQueen. Away you go there and have a drive and see what you think." Ten minutes later, Eve parked beside Adam, nodding her head, looking really happy. "Adam she's really grand. She drives perfectly and I guess I can get used to the green. Thank you." Squeezing his arm, she gave him a peck on the cheek.

"Great—I'll have Tim get her titivated and delivered to the house. Right, I'm ready for a spot of lunch, let's hit the road."

Eve stood by the window in the lounge looking out over the patio, her eyes moving down to a small grass topped stone jetty below her where a red cabin cruiser was moored, bobbing quietly in the shallows. A short distance off, a white cigar shaped speedboat lay tethered to a mooring buoy, and about fifty yards beyond that, a long dark wedge of rock stretched out into the bay forming a perfect breakwater from the prevailing winds. An attendant was coiling a rope at the top of the steps leading down to the cruiser; the steps glistening slippery wet from the recent drizzle.

Her eyes scanned beyond the reef to a small island marked with a long swathe of grass sweeping to a peak and then the seascape stretched across the bay. The sea and sky were melding inseparably in a haze of grey-blue, purple sheen of serene light.

Adam was seated by a small crackling log fire, chatting with the barman who had brought the lunch menu to the table. Eve turned and walked slowly across the room, enjoying the richness of the moment; amazed at this place being literally next door to Adam's house. They were in the Doolittle Bar in Parknasilla Hotel and Eve was feeling very enthused at the prospect of living in Sneem for a few months, the spa and the large swimming pool, well this was better than she could have imagined.

Lying back in the tan leather chair, hands clasped behind his neck Adam stretched his legs out, crossed his feet, a tuft of chest hair peeping from under his button-down tartan shirt, his mouth crinkled in that half smile he favoured, "Not bad for a local hostelry, is it?" he asked.

"Oh this is really nice. I think I'll stay. It's my kind of place. I must check out membership in the spa before we go, if that's OK with you."

"Not a problem." He pushed the menu across the table to Eve, "Is you hungry?"

"Oh just a toastie for me I think and sparkling water please. Oh Adam what a great day this is turning out to be. A new car—well a green car—wheels anyway! And then finding this place with the spa

Dressing for God

and the pool, you asked if I'm happy to stay? It's a BIG yes *and* a big thank you."

Eve's enthusiasm lit up Adams face, "Nice to see you so happy."

"Well then I guess it's about time I filled you in on this book project of mine," Adam said, wiping his mouth with a napkin. "Let's sit by the window there with our coffee where we won't be interrupted," and then added, as he rose from the seat, "With the progress I've made on the writing up to now, this shouldn't take too long."

Eve sat watching him as he settled back, looking deeply into his coffee cup as if it contained all the secrets of the universe, his hands folded on his lap. Eventually he spoke.

"My writing—well it hasn't really been going too well to tell the truth. You know about writers block?"

"Of course, I do, it's not unusual is it?"

"I guess not, well I've a severe dose of just that and in essence that's why you're here. You see, I'd reached a point where Captain John in his little boat, *My Trust* just couldn't get clearance to enter Port Abundance and pick up his rewards. There's something elemental stopping him from reaching his goal and I can't for the life of me figure out what it is. I've tried literally everything to clear the block but he's still stuck in the quarantine anchorage waiting to get the all clear."

"And Captain John is your alter ego and when he has a block, it's really your block, is that it?"

"That's it precisely. Well for starters Captain John had a lot of trouble with his self steering. Whenever he left the cockpit to do something on deck or left to cook a meal or take a nap, the autopilot had a mind of its own and he'd end up near as dammit back where he started. But EFT sorted some of that and I got the steering gear on the mend, but there's still something else holding him back from gaining clearance and I'm hoping when I get into the writing in a few days time we'll be able to find out exactly what it is and get it sorted."

"And where are you exactly in the writing now?"

"*My Trust* is anchored outside Port Abundance waiting for it's clearance inwards so Captain John can have his 'life lessons learnt' session with Finity Muze."

"Well then Captain John, you'd better hurry up and finish off your other wee project and hurry back here so we can make a start on finding out where the block is, won't you? And in the meantime can I read what you have written so far please?"

"By all means, yes, see if you pick up any clues on where I should start looking."

Chapter 10

Upside Down

Later, back in her cottage, curled up in front of the fire Eve opened up the draft of Adams book and started reading.

My Trust—The Voyage Home

I am Sailing
In a boat named
Trust
On an Inner Sea
Of Being
Knowing that My Pilot
Has my Eye
To bring me Home
Aye
Bring me
Home

Motor Yacht *My Trust* Logbook Entry Wed. Feb. 4, 2009.
0554 Following received from Port Abundance radio control on VHF channel forty eight as follows: proceed to small vessel quarantine anchorage and await port health– no pilot available—follow previous port entry instructions…

Eve read to the last page, closed the folder and placed it on her bedside table, switched off the light and lay there quietly, drawing sleep inwards, calmness all around her, thinking thoughts of sailing across the silent seas.

J.F. Tallon

The morning air was moist, a low bank of cloud shrouding the tops of the trees, a crowd of crows strung out in a row on the telephone lines at the side of the road, looking as if they were grounded by avian air traffic control. 'Much too foggy to fly big birds, you'll have to wait for the visibility to clear.' Eve smiled as she lengthened her stride in the middle of the rhododendron lined single track road, concentrated on her breathing, getting into her rhythm, wondering just how birds communicate with each other.

Heading back to the house on her last lap of the morning, she mentally planned her day—a long hot shower, shampoo and maybe dress in the pink gingham shirt and black cotton trousers; get another wash in the machine, a bit of housework and then it's over to Noah's for late afternoon. 'Didn't Adam say Noah was planning a barbecue? A barbecue in March? I must be missing something.'

She started her stretches, feeling her fitness return slowly—thinking of the first coffee of the day, listened to the crows cawing away in the background. The air scented with fresh, green moistness, she breathed in deeply—holding it—releasing it 'God it feels good here.' Happy and smiling she headed indoors looking forward to whatever lay ahead.

The washing machine was on its rinse cycle in the kitchen. Eve sat at the table considering what Guy had just told her on the phone. His friend Tomas owned a four star boutique hotel in Brighton and would, he was sure, make her a lucrative offer to take over as general manager, probably with profit sharing. Would she please think about it?

'Bless you Guy, you always have my best interests at heart, but I don't want to face that kind of life right now. I couldn't just walk out on Adam and anyway I'm beginning to like it here. Though I won't get rich at what he's paying me will I? Still it was sweet of Guy to look after me like that—he was always the perfect big brother.'

A knock on the door interrupted her thoughts. Adam stood on the doorstep looking dapper in a navy blue Nautica fleece, chinos, tan loafers, his hair ruffled in need of a trim. The day was dry and bright with sunlight streaming through the trees behind him.

"Good morning, good morning." Adam's greeting lilting in the fresh air.

Dressing for God

"And how is every little thing in the universe today? Isn't it lovely? Did you sleep well?" Eve smiled at the way he seemed to become more Irish every day. Four questions wrapped in the one greeting.

She laughed as she considered which question to answer first, decided that if you can't beat them, join them. "Ah it's just grand, grand, grand and did you sleep well yourself?" Eve tried her hand at the local accent.

"Like the proverbial. Look, I'm heading into town, just wondered if you wanted to pick up the car. It should be ready by now and I fixed the insurance for you yesterday," his eyes questioning, waiting for her answer.

"Sure. I'd love to, thanks. I'll just grab my bag and be right with you."

Adam headed for the car as she fetched her jacket and bag, thinking to herself, "'Now where would I rather be, here or in Brighton?" She pulled the door shut behind her with a confident show of decision making and looked at Adam waiting patiently in his car. "No doubts. Here. Right here, right now and no question about it," she said quietly under her breath.

It was four o'clock and Eve was sitting at the wheel of Felicity the Beetle getting ready to leave for Noah's supper. She had chosen the name Felicity because Felicity Green was a childhood friend and Felicity, she knew, meant 'good fortune', so Felicity it was. And she loved her, even if her green skin was just on the wrong side of puce and it didn't really go well with her strawberry blond hair, but the little 1.3 litre engine performed well and Eve was excited to have a bit more independence at her fingertips. Adam was strapping himself into the passenger seat cradling two bottles of wine like new born babes.

"Well if you don't mind being the designated driver, I don't mind being the designated passenger," he said. "So let's get your anchor up and away we go."

They drove out the road towards Kenmare and after a few miles took a sharp right along a rutted drive, a crumbling dry stone wall on one side and a high gorse hedge on the other before they emerged into a clearing where Noah's house and garden stood overlooking a vast reach of Kenmare Bay.

A red sailboat was parked beside a locked garage, an old boat cradle, minus a wheel lay cockeyed beside it. The house was stone clad in warm, pinkish purple stone, two stories, L shaped around a large Valentia slate patio with a small fountain gurgling at one end. A separate single story building with large windows, easels and canvases visible inside, sat to the right of the patio. Adam pointed to where Noah's Jeep was parked.

"You can moor Felicity over there beside the studio."

Eve stepped out of the car enthralled with the view, yet another panorama of mountain, sea and sky.

"Wow you guys sure know how to pick your houses," she enthused.

Adam nodded, "Yep, it's not too shabby is it?" in a typical understatement, "C'mon let's see if there's anyone home."

As they rounded the corner of the house they heard Bobby Mc Ferrin's vibrato voice from an old 80s hit wafting out the doors onto the patio:

"….In your life expect some trouble, but when you worry you make it double, don't worry, be happy……"

Adam picked up on the tune, bottle in either hand, swaying to the rhythm, ushered Eve in through the open doors. "Whatever it is…." Noah was draped in a big, white apron over a red woollen shirt, faded jeans, open-toed leather sandals, long filleting knife gleaming in his right hand, joined in "Don't bring everybody down like this," their enthusiasm much greater than their harmony, "Don't worry, it will soon pass, whatever it is—Don't worry, be happy."

Noah and Adam laughing hard exchanged a bear hug. Eve stood back shaking her head in amusement and then this woman, tall, trim, raven black hair swishing around her shoulders, rushed into the kitchen from the hallway, positively jumped into Adams arms and kissed him on both cheeks.

"Mmm. Oh my, it is good to see you Adam. Here let me look at you," she partly disengaged from their hug then held a flushed but pleased Adam at arm's length.

"Hannah oh goodness me, you look great—you haven't changed a bit." he said in a rush and then turning towards Eve, catching his breath, tapped on his chest with his fist still holding a bottle of wine.

"Excuse me. Can I introduce Eve…. Eve this is Hannah, or should I say, Dr. Hannah Dubois?"

Dressing for God

"Oh how nice." Hannah greeted Eve with cheek to cheek air kisses. "Leave the doctor bit out of it please, I'm just plain Hannah," she held Eve by the elbow and beamed a welcome smile at her. "I am so pleased to meet you Eve, I have heard all about you from Noah."

She took Eve's hand in hers, held it up in the air, winked at her conspiratorially saying, "Aren't they the right pair of eligible bachelors then?"

Hiding her surprise, Eve returned the welcome smile wondering who this doctor was. She was beautiful, same height, maybe early thirties, big brown eyes, deep set under a broad forehead, shoulder length jet black hair, the face angular, almost chiselled deep dimples at the sides of a generous mouth set in a mischievous grin. She wore a v-neck cream satin shirt, white satin pants, gold and white sandals. Eve's eyes locked on the diamond choker she wore around her very elegant throat.

She found herself agreeing with Hannah's question saying, "Indeed," thinking 'Who is she? Was this Noah's surprise?'

"Em, Eve," Adam said, a little wince crossing his face, "I should have mentioned that the good doctor here is, eh, Noah's little sister."

Her hands joined in front of her mouth, Eve let out an involuntary gasp and looked from Hannah back to Noah searching for a family resemblance. Yes, she could just about see it in the shape of the face.

"Noah takes after our dad and I take after mom. Now aren't I the lucky one then? Just imagine if it was the other way round and I had to go through life looking like him."

Eve defended Noah. "Ah no he's lovely, you're both lovely," she looked across at Adam, "Oh you got me, you rotter. Why didn't you tell me Noah's sister was here?"

"I asked him to keep it as a surprise," said Noah. "Now then Miss Eve, you've arrived at my humble abode, so make yourself at home and maybe Hannah you could show Eve around while Adam and I start fixing dinner?"

"Come on Eve, let's leave them to it." Hannah took Eve by the elbow steering her into the hall, "I'll give you the Cook's tour."

Adam was standing at the wide kitchen window looking out over the patio down to the shoreline and saw the girls deep in conversation emerge from Noah's studio, Hannah locking the door behind her. Noah pointed his glass in their direction.

"Well they seem to be getting on like a house on fire."

"I never doubted it for a minute. Tell me how long is Hannah staying?"

"Ah she's away back to Paris on Monday evening, it's just a flying visit."

They remained there for a few moments looking over the water. The sky was a clear blue with just a few wisps of high alto stratus to the south west. Noah pointed them out to Adam.

"Isn't that just like a Japanese brush painting?"

"God yeah it is and what a great canvas too. I hear the weather is set to stay warm for a few days with that high pressure system staying over us. I can see your egg is smoking away there." His eyes strayed to the Big Green Egg smoker sitting in its nest in the corner of the patio. "So what's the menu for the day then chef?"

"Some home smoked wild salmon and a lump of rib. C'mon I'd better check the fire. Let's go look-see." Noah removed a large platter of salmon from the fridge and headed out to meet the girls on the patio.

Eve watched curiously as Noah opened the lid of his Big Green Egg and placed four thin slabs of cedar wood on the grill and then ceremoniously topped them with the sides of wild salmon, blew them a kiss as he closed the lid then he set the vents and checked the time on his watch.

"Forty minutes to the finest hot smoked salmon you will ever taste," Noah said emphatically, as he gave the ceramic Green Egg a warm pat.

"She's the same colour as my Felicity," laughed Eve, explaining to Noah the name of her recently acquired wheels. "Aye," said Noah, "well I hope Felicity doesn't smoke as much as this fella." As the cedar smoke and rum aroma spiralled out of the Egg's top vent.

They were seated around the dining table in the conservatory off the kitchen watching the sun set in the west, the sea reflecting the deep red and gold weft of the few clouds on the horizon, warps of soft yellow, orange and turquoise a palette of cosmic colour in the purple sky; the scene changing tone and texture with every passing moment.

The salmon course had worked its magic getting approval especially from Eve who considered herself a bit of a smoked salmon con-

Dressing for God

noisseur. "I'm not used to speaking in superlatives but I have to say Mr. Noah, that's up there with the best smoked salmon I ever tasted."

Noah accepted the praise noncommittally. "Just you wait 'til you taste the beef and then you can try superlatives, I say modestly," he added with a wink, as he left the table to check on his rib of beef, slow cooking in the egg.

"'Twill will be a while yet," he announced as he returned to the table, handing Adam a bottle of Beaune Reserve and a corkscrew. "If you would do the honours there my good man and let that breathe." Then he handed Eve a long cardboard tube, "And now Miss Eve, here's a wee present all for yourself."

Eve pried off the top and extracted a poster, the title, *Hidden Depths* printed on the bottom. She stood up from the table unrolling the poster. It was an underwater photo of the most amazing iceberg she had ever seen. The little ice cap bit sticking out above the waterline was dwarfed by a huge ice mountain extending beneath the surface. "It's just amazing—how did they ever photograph that?" she asked astonished with the picture.

"It's like an upside down Matterhorn, look at all those caverns, they're like cavities in the decayed root of some enormous molar." Hannah said.

"This is so beautiful, oh thank you Noah." Eve spread the poster out on the table where they could all see it.

"I think I know where this is leading," said Hannah. "Is this more of your mind stuff Noah?"

"Yeah, it's great isn't it? I thought of it when Eve told me she loved diving and we'd been talking about consciousness and I'd seen this on art.com. Here, let's stick it on the door and we can all look at it."

Noah fetched a packet of Blu-Tack and started to hang it on the conservatory door. "Noah, why don't you try hanging it upside down?" said Hannah, "Really. Turn it around and see what I mean."

Noah, glanced over his shoulder at Hannah, his brow furrowed, questioning, but turned the poster as she asked and stuck it on the door.

Noah stood back and gazed at it for a while. "She's gone and made a tarte-tatin out of my apple pie, but I'll grant you this much Hannah, it does show just how relatively powerful the unconscious is in the whole scheme of things."

"I do like that," said Adam. "It changes the perspective when you see it that way up and you can see how any changes in the shape of the unconscious effects the ocean it breathes in and vice versa."

Eve interjected, "Can I ask a question please?"

"Of course you can," said Hannah, sitting down and taking a sip of her white wine.

"So, that big unconscious bit beneath the surface which we can't see, is it our subconscious or unconscious mind? I'm never sure on that."

"Good question," Hannah replied. "I can understand your confusion. Some people call it the subconscious mind and I suppose it is, in so far as it's the space it occupies in the one subconscious mind. The way I learned it is, there is just one subconscious mind where we all live and breathe. That's the ocean of energy that it's floating in there. Every one of us, each person has an individual conscious mind, the bit sticking above the water controlled by the brain. And an unconscious mind is the big bit below the surface, swimming in the big subconscious mind. So conscious mind is about ten-percent of our mind that we use logically and the other ninety-percent is the unconscious part we use through our programming one way or another."

"I hate to throw a depth charge into our conversation," said Noah, placing a four rib roast of beef on the table, "but this critter is ready for carving, so you can all start having group consciousness salivation, in anticipation of the eating."

Later resting in his chair, hands on his tummy, Noah looked around the table at the clean plates. "Well now Miss Eve," he said. "I'm ready for your superlatives, platitudes and gratitudes. Actually you don't have to say anything, the smile on your face speaks for itself."

"Noah, as the speechless writer said, words fail me!. That was a truly magnificent feast. You should open a restaurant."

"Well I'm pleased that my little sister was here to explain the iceberg picture for you. I take it there are no further elaborations required then?"

"Well I do have just one please," piped up Eve again. "Your tarte-tatin for dessert… Upside down or downside up, I don't know, but where does soul come into all of this?"

"Hands up who wants to answer this one?" Noah looked around the table.

Dressing for God

"Adam put your hand up there, you're volunteered."

"Alright so," Adam laughed quietly, stroked his beard for a few moments before he continued. "I'll stay with your upside down apple pie analogy then. OK so we agree that what goes up, must come down according to the law of gravity?"

"There'll be no arguments about that," Noah said.

"Well I'm not saying that we live in an upside down world, but I do say that we live in an *inside out universe*. Our outside world is wholly determined by our inner attitudes and desires. So in answer to your question Eve, soul would be at the very centre of that big iceberg of self-consciousness, surrounded by all the mental and emotional stuff it has accumulated during the experiences it had during its many lifetimes on Earth. Now Eve does that answer you?"

Eve held her hands up in surrender. "Yes enough is enough—I'm afraid to ask any more questions."

"No, no!" cried Hannah. "Questions are great. It's good to challenge these two."

"All right then a silly question, can we take a break? Is there any chance of a cuppa tea?"

"Can you make that tea for two, guys?" Hannah asked as Noah and Adam cleared away the dinner plates leaving the girls talking.

"So tell me Eve, are you enjoying this work you're doing with Adam?"

"I am actually. It's like, I don't quite know how to put it. It's like I've been wearing a watch to tell me the time and now I get to open up the back of it and get a glimpse of its workings. It's very different from running a restaurant. Now I have to learn to think quite differently and I'm trying to understand how life works for the first time, if you'll pardon the pun." She shared a smile with Hannah.

Hannah, her hands clasped together under her chin said, "Oh life is all about facing our own challenges but for me what's really exciting is learning how to use the energy of life constructively." She opened her hands out wide and added, "But you are right. Life does have its clockwork elements but it's really the fluid part of it that's, to use the poster analogy there, that's absorbing."

"You mean absorbing, like in a sponge?"

"Well yes, like a sponge." Hannah moistened her lips quickly with the tip of her tongue and continued. "Have you ever seen those Russian dolls, you know the ones, when you open one up, there's another smaller doll inside it and a smaller one inside that and so on?"

"Indeed I have."

"Well that's really how our bodies operate in this ocean of fluid energy. It's like we have several overlapping force fields of energy surrounding us; invisible layers of sheaths or skins that are our interface between the energy of this ocean and our bodies."

"A bit like a wetsuit?" Eve asked, thinking she might be back in dive mode anytime soon.

"Yes, precisely, these subtle bodies are made of varying vibration rates and fineness. I like to view them as my Wonder Woman suits!" Hannah reached over and squeezed Eve's hand as they enjoyed her joke.

"And just how many of them are there?" asked Eve.

"Here let me draw a quick sketch. I must be getting like Noah, I have to draw everything. I'm going to show you four of them."

"So here I am at the centre and the first body surrounding me is what we call the etheric body. This is the connection between the physical skin and bones, the meat parcel of your physical body with the unseen life force. This interface is the distributor of the life-force throughout the physical body system. And it feeds seven different energy nodes like a seven point plug delivering different vibration rates of energy throughout the wonderful human body. You have heard of chakras, haven't you?"

"Sure, yes."

"They're here," Hannah moved her right hand just above the crown of her head, then in front of her forehead, throat, heart, solar plexus, sacral and base. "Our chakras are just the charge points for our energy distribution. They strip out the different energy frequency rates automatically and send them around the body to the various demand centres to keep us in vibrant good health." Hannah looked to see that Eve was keeping up with her explanation and continued.

"And then moving outwards we have the other bodies of different consciousness. We have the emotional body and then the mental body and outside that we have the causal body, before we reach our true essence of the soul in the spiritual body."

"So are they all working like that, you know like the Russian dolls, one inside the other?"

Dressing for God

"You're a quick learner Eve, I'll grant you that. No actually, they don't work like that, because this life energy field is an ocean of everything invisible to our conscious perception and it only responds to a vibration of consciousness that corresponds with it exactly." Hannah saw that Eve had difficulty here.

"You see Eve, each of the different bodies have differing degrees of fineness from the very fine of zero matter at the spiritual body level, down through the various planes of consciousness until we, at our physical level, can only see the dense bodies of our selves. Each level interpenetrates with the level below it but they are all present as one energy source all the time."

Hannah continued talking as she passed Eve the sketch.

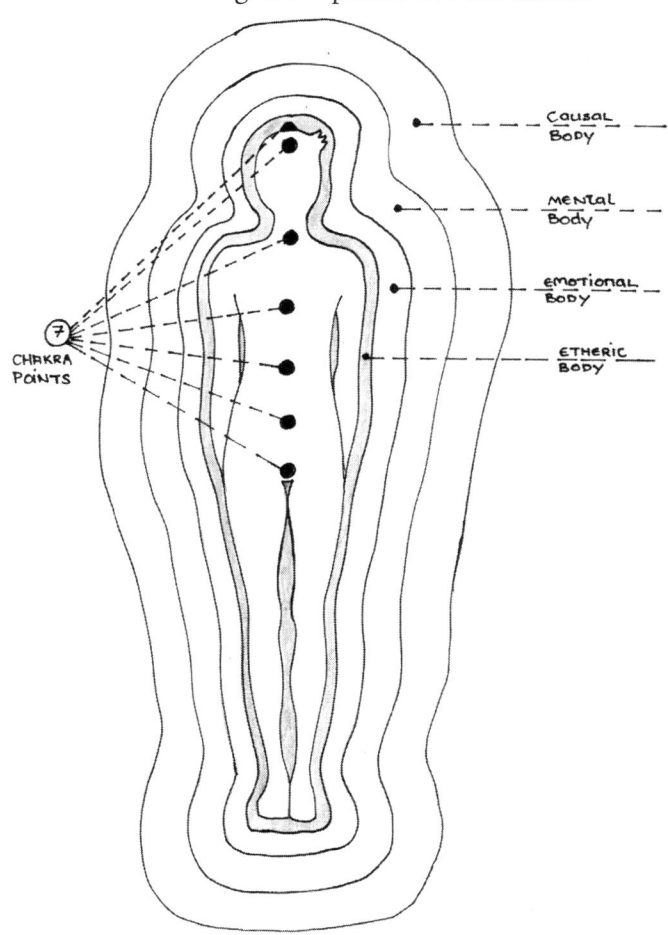

"At the next level up from the physical is the emotional body level on what we call the astral plane. The astral plane contains, believe it or not, an exact mirror image of your life here on this physical plane."

"How scary is that?" Eve said with a little grimace on her face.

Eve and Hannah were giggling together as Adam placed a cheeseboard centre table, Gubbeen, creamy ripe Brie and a Camembert oozing at the edges. "Did the Brie and Camembert come from duty free Hannah?" Adam asked.

Hannah nodded, "Yes and there's a bottle of very fine Pinot de Charentis as well Adam." She rose from the table, "I'll fetch it, I know where it is."

Noah placed a plate of biscuits and cheese crackers along with the tea and coffee on the table as Hannah returned holding her laptop which she placed on the table and the bottle which she handed to Adam.

"You seem to be the sommelier this evening Adam, you're not driving are you?"

"No not tonight. I have my trusty designated driver Ms. McQueen in her Felicity tonight. So yes, I'll certainly enjoy a drop of this very fine Pineau, thank you very much indeed. It reminds me of happy days of youth spent grape picking in the Cognac region."

"Talking of designated drivers," Noah spoke up, "Hannah, I must tell you a story that was in the news last week. It'll remind you of your Irishness. Picture if you will, a busy public house in the Midlands near closing time on a busy Saturday night. The car park was jammed with cars and a lone garda car was quietly parked, hidden in the dark behind some bushes. The two men, the sergeant and young garda, are sitting there watching and waiting. Five minutes before closing time, this fella' staggers out of the pub, looks around the car park for his car, fumbles for his keys, finds them, gets into the car, starts the engine, the headlights go on, off, on, then the windscreen wipers go on, off and then very slowly he drives out of the car park onto the road. Instantly the garda car pounces, headlights on, blue light flashing, pulls up in front of the 'yer man, forcing it to a stop and the garda approaches the car."

"The usual question, 'Have you been drinking sir?"

"Yes garda—three pints of coke."

"Would you mind stepping out of the car sir and blowing into this?"

Dressing for God

"Meanwhile as the garda attend to the breathalysing, the car park has emptied slowly and after a few more blows into the bag, the Garda asks 'What's all this about?' and 'yer man pipes up 'Shure garda, wasn't I the designated decoy for the night? Goodnight now', says 'yer man and he started the car and drove away."

"I can well believe that," said Hannah, "It sounds like an 'Irish solution to an Irish problem', as they say."

"Indeed so," said Adam. "And pray tell, what have you two been up to while we were doing the washing up?"

"Washing up is right," replied Hannah. "Having another tipple I'd bet. Well, we were having a conversation on subtle body anatomy—women in Wonder Woman suits as opposed to men in tights."

"Yes, we'd reached the astral plane but returned just in time for the cheese," added Eve beginning to click in to Hannah's humour.

"It sounds like they're ganging up on us," replied Noah.

"Actually Noah, talking of sounds," said Hannah, "You know of Stefan's passion for sound and language. Well he emailed me last week to check out this lady Mrs. Watt- Hughes. She invented this contraption in1885 called an Eidophone—have either of you ever heard of it?"

Hannah looking round at the shaking heads. "OK, let me boot up my lap top and I'll Google it up for us. Here we go, now have a look at this from way back then." Hannah swivelled the laptop so they could all see the screen.

"Right so—the Eidophone is a pipe and a bowl with a thin membrane across the top which has a very thin layer of fine sand or pollen on it. Mrs. Watt-Hughes sang into the pipe and with each note she sang, she produced vibrations in the sand and these amazing shapes took form on the membrane. Have a look at them."

"So what you are saying is that sound is actually a carrier of a specific shape. Just like the daisy form there has a corresponding set of harmonic vibrations in synchronicity with say, its seed form?" asked Noah.

"That's what it looks like doesn't it?"

"That's brilliant," said Adam. "So out there in this mind stuff, in this plasticine of the Creator, is the thought form of everything in intelligence and all it takes for it to take shape, is to call it into being? Well OK, a lot more than just call it, but like that daisy pattern that happened when she sang a note, what you're saying is that a different shape forms as a result of different notes. Is that it?"

"That's it and when you consider that she discovered this in 1885..." Hannah said with admiration in her voice.

"I wonder how far we have progressed since then." Eve asked.

"Oh we have moved on quite a bit since. I remember reading about the work of a Japanese scientist, Dr. Emoto I believe, who experimented with playing different types of music to water samples. He'd play classical and jazz or heavy metal to different water samples and then after they'd absorbed the sounds he'd photograph frozen water crystals from the samples. And guess what? Each crystal sample had a totally different configuration from the other. Each one retained the vibration of the sound it had been subjected to."

"That is fascinating," Eve said. "So the water retained the imprint of the sound wave?"

"Yes and if I remember correctly, he then moved on and experimented with subjecting water to different emotions. He labelled the sample jars with positive and negative stuff like 'I love you' or 'I really hate

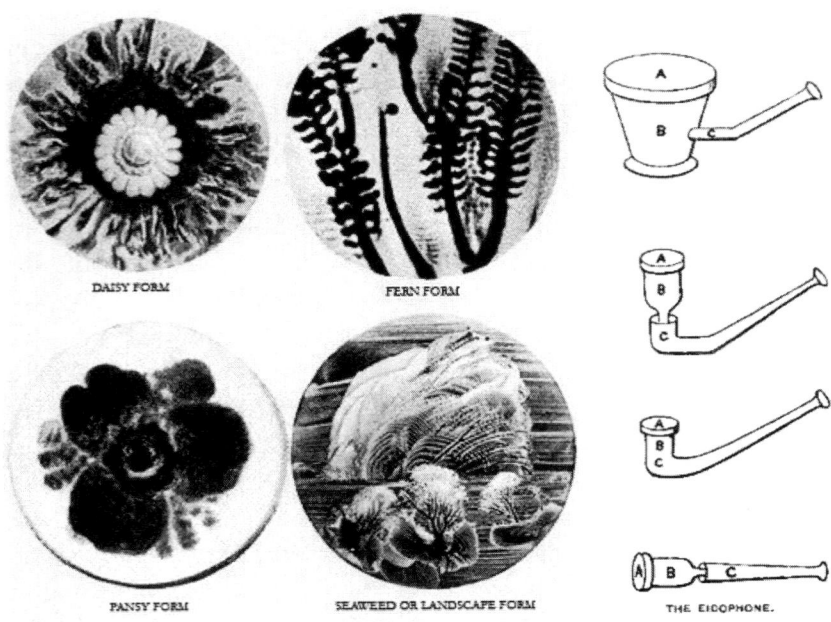

you' and the samples that were positively influenced had beautifully formed crystals and the ones with the negative influences were horribly ugly. I saw some of his photos, they're really impressive. But what stuck in my mind was the fact that water retained these conscious emotions and we are composed of what, ninety-percent water?"

"That explains a lot about the workings of EFT then, doesn't it? I mean trapped emotions at a cellular level—I've always wondered why they remained stuck?" Adam said.

"We've always known that sound is caused by vibrations—well what is sound, but the music of vibrations in any case, and so sound is the resonance of energy."

Hannah wet her finger and started to run it along the rim of her wine glass, creating a humming note that as she increased the tempo of the friction, it produced a higher and higher pitch.

"Aw crikey, don't break my glass please," asked Noah, seeing his Reidel glass vibrating away and worrying more about the potential wine loss than the broken glass if truth were known.

"We know that all matter, from the atom to the molecule, from the pebble to the mountain, from the armadillo to the human being—wherever matter exists, it's always vibrating. The only difference is that every particle of matter has a different rate of vibration. A stone has slow vibration, wind is fast vibration and very high vibration registers as sound and we have all the various layers and spectrums in between," Adam explained to Eve.

"So where does this equate with light?" Eve asked.

"Which comes first, light or sound? I'd say light, but really in some ways they'd be parallel aspects of the one power source," offered Adam. "Would you agree with me Noah?"

"Yeah, for sure, take colour for instance. We have the seven colours of the spectrum and music has a seven note diatonic scale. So in the beginning was the word and out of the void of nothing emerged sound and light. They're inseparable really, just different aspects of the one energy. And did you know that you can actually see sound waves by illuminating them?"

"You mean like in the expression 'I can see what you're saying'?" asked Adam.

"There he goes again," said Hannah. "Our resident Sneem philosopher. Well sound is the consequence of motion isn't it? And isn't vibration motion? So the first cause of a vibration would result in the first sound wouldn't it?"

"Absolutely and you know if you transmit two sounds of the same pitch and frequency opposite each other, they will cancel each other out and create silence... which is a quality we could all possibly do with now," added Adam, smiling at Eve.

"OK guys." Hannah said, "But don't forget that if you could actually *hear* the very high frequencies that the primary colours—the red, yellow and blue light waves are vibrating at—you'd actually hear a major chord and listen to this," Hannah noted as she accentuated her words with her hands. "You can tell I'm married to a sound aware Frenchman. If you could see the sound of notes in a major chord relative to the scale used by light, then you would be able to see chords in primary colours also. Primary colours are major chords."

"You must get Stefan over here soon Hannah," Adam said. "I really enjoy listening to him and his theories—you'd like him Eve."

"Just as soon as we can make it we will Adam and now," Hannah stood up closing her laptop. "Lady and gents, why don't we make this the carry-out for the evening otherwise Eve here, will be getting an overdose of the spiritual and will be up all night looking for some celestial Pepto-Bismol."

Adam stifled a yawn with the back of his hand and stood up ready to go.

"That's probably a very good idea Hannah. I could do with an early night. I still have my report to finish and get it off to London before Monday afternoon. C'mon then Eve. Let's give these good folks some space and head back to the ranch."

Noah and Hannah walked Eve and Adam to the car, the sky bright with an almost full moon, threads of cloud scudding across the night sky reflected in the waters below. Eve and Hannah exchanged hugs.

"I'm really delighted to have met you Eve," said Hannah. "I do hope we can meet up again before I go back."

"Mmm, that goes for me too. I feel I've known you for ages, maybe we could meet up for a walk or a jog tomorrow—do you run, you look pretty fit?"

"Oh I'd love that. Look give me a call in the morning and we'll see what we can arrange, maybe do the dunes at Caherdaniel?"

Dressing for God

Watching Felicity's lights recede down the lane, Hannah looked at Noah, "Do you think there might be something brewing there then?"

"She's a fine lass there's no doubt. Who knows? Sure you'd probably have a better clue about it than I would, being a woman and all that."

Chapter 11

'It Sticks Where It's Stuck'

"Just park there where it says *Coaches Only*," Hannah told Eve as they drew up outside the front gate of Derrynane House.

"But it says *Coaches Only*," Eve questioning the advice.

"Sure there are no coaches here at this time of year and the car park is closed. You're in Ireland—when it says "don't walk on the grass" you don't—you run on it. C'mon you'll like it here."

Hannah in a blue beret, white Adidas track suit and silver Puma track shoes, led the way down the track to the dunes. Eve following a pace behind, enjoying the warmth of the Sunday morning, thinking how much she liked this chic chick from Paris. The pathway opened up and Hannah loped to her left following a set of arrows marking the trail, past a broad altar stone, slowing, pointed it out to Eve, "In the penal times, when priests were banned from saying Mass by the English, they used this stone for secret outdoor mass." And then she turned and headed uphill, picking up the pace gently. Eve followed in her wake, both comfortable in their own space and then they rounded the blind side of the dunes and the breadth of Derrynane Bay opened up for them.

"Wow," said Eve, "Just look at that, it's magnificent." She stopped to take it all in. The curve of golden sand flanked by towering grass topped dunes swept to their right as far as the eye could see before it arced seawards, the land rising to a knoll where the ruins of an ancient abbey stood in jagged relief on the skyline.

"That's the local graveyard there," Hannah said, pointing to the ruins. "It's only accessible between tides." They continued their run along the top of the dunes. Hannah leading Eve on a circuit that

Dressing for God

ended outside Derrynane House. Hannah explaining that the estate was now state property and was managed by the OPW, the Office of Public Works—like the national Trust in the UK only not as well funded.

They did their stretches leaning on a visitor's bench beside the private chapel where Eve had a chance to see the triumphant chariot that Daniel O' Connell was gifted on his release from jail in Dublin.

"Do you know anything about Daniel?" Hannah asked.

"No. I was afraid to ask," Eve replied shyly with a little grin. "I take it he was a famous politician?"

"Indeed he was all of that. He was born up the road in Cahersiveen and his uncle took him in and brought him up. He went to university in France during the French Revolution and the terrible butchery that he saw there gave him a lifelong horror of violence. He was the first Catholic MP in the House of Commons and I suppose he's best known for leading the campaign for Catholic emancipation in Ireland. He tried to get a separate Irish parliament and that really got up the noses of the British establishment, hence the name Daniel the Liberator."

Eve looked duly impressed being so close to an Irish icon, as Hannah continued.

"This was the Uncle's house. Sure it was a haven for smugglers in those days, French brandy and wines and the like. Here let me show you the gardens, they're my favourites—I always try to come here when I visit."

They were seated at the top of a small hill section of the garden wildly cultivated as Hannah put it. A tree long since fallen formed a natural arch, orchids and flowering micro plants trailing from its withered trunk.

Hannah asked, "Last night wasn't too much for you then?"

Eve looked puzzled, "No. Why?"

"Oh, we can go on a bit about our spiritual stuff, especially now Adam seems serious about writing. Mind you Noah is just as likeminded. They're a right pair."

"No, it was fine. I'm enjoying it—it's different—it wasn't anything I gave much thought to before. In fact I never really thought much about thoughts." A bird calling overhead interrupted her. They looked at each other and shared a smile.

"How did you get into this stuff anyway?" She asked Hannah.

"Ah my mother was big on that kind of thing and my dad was way ahead of his time. He used acupuncture and homeopathy on his patients—his animal patients that is."

"Adam was saying that you're a doctor of homeopathy?"

"Yes I did a diploma course in France after qualifying in medicine in Trinity. That's when I met Stefan and now I have a practise in Paris. Homeopathy is very popular in France you know. We're probably the biggest users in all of Europe."

"What does Stefan do, is he a doctor also?"

"Yes, but not in medicine. His degree is in Earth science. He specializes in animal communications." She paused and looked off into space for a few seconds. "He's finishing off a study in the Antarctic on Emperor Penguins."

Hannah let out a soft sigh and turned to Eve with a smile. "He's due back home next Thursday. I can't wait to see him. He's been away ten weeks now."

"I'll bet you're missing him. What's he doing, talking with the penguins?"

Hannah laughed quietly. "Yes, he's part of a French team researching how penguins communicate with their young. Did you know that every penguin Mother gives its baby chick its own special penguin name that it answers to and that done, she leaves the chick with its dad and heads out to sea to fatten up on fish. Then, when she returns weeks later and calls its name, 'Hello Jean Pierre Penguin where are you, dinners ready', the little chick recognises its Mother by its name sound and Mother and chick are reunited again."

"Wow, really? Is that what you'll be doing at the airport when he returns then," asked Eve "standing outside arrivals, calling out your name so he'll remember you?"

Hannah broke into a belly laugh, "What a great idea. I think I'll do just that and maybe get myself a penguin mask too!" They giggled at the idea.

"Listen to that," Eve said, her ear raised upwards.

The oak, chestnut and beech trees with early spring-growth budding on their tips were coming alive with song; the birds started a cross garden symphony discussing the visitors in the garden below them.

Dressing for God

"Can you tell which bird is which?" Eve asked

"I know some but not all of them. Stefan does though. He can whistle back to them and really get them going." Hannah had a dreamy look in her eyes talking about Stefan—she got to her feet, rubbing her hands together.

"C'mon then, let's keep the circulation going. Do you fancy a coffee or something? The Blind Piper should be open."

"Yeah sounds great; I had a drink with Noah there last week, it's nice."

The bar had just opened and they grabbed a table in the corner beside the fire and ordered coffees.

"That was a great run," Hannah said. "It was kind of you to ask me to join you."

"Not at all," Eve replied. "I thoroughly enjoyed it too. I feel like I've known you for ages, instead of just meeting you last night."

Hannah reached across and gave Eve's hand a gentle squeeze. "I know, I feel the same way too. Isn't it funny how you can feel an instant rapport with someone you've just met?" adding, "Or indeed, how you can take an instant dislike to someone?"

"Yes, it really is. I felt that with Adam when I met him," laughing. "No, not distrusting him, but feeling very comfortable in his presence."

"Oh Adam is terrific," Hannah said. "He's like a big brother to me." She leant her head close to Eve, "Is there, maybe something brewing between you two, did I detect a little spark of romance there—just between us girls?" Her eyes wide with enquiry.

Eve gave a small laugh, "No, really. Adam is nice, I know, but no we are very much in professional mode and I'm not ready for anything like that just yet." She said looking Hannah in the eye.

"Well you did say '*just yet*,'" Hannah replied, patting her hand conspiratorially. "I do understand, honestly I do."

"Thanks. I appreciate it. The truth is, I'm still healing from my breakup. The pain memory seems to want to stick around. I'm letting go all the time and trying to stay removed from feeling hurt, but it's taking time. Anyway," Eve let out a deep breath, "I'm happy to be unattached and actually Adam doesn't seem to be, well you know forward, if you know what I mean. He's very much the gentleman."

"That he is. Noah did mention to me that your marriage had broken up recently. Are you coping OK? I hope you don't mind my asking, it's just that talking about it can sometimes help, so if you want to talk, well I'm happy to listen. I'm not a shrink, but I can listen."

Eve took a sip of water. "Thanks Hannah, I appreciate it. I'm OK about the break up now. I'm not angry with my ex or indeed with myself anymore. I've managed to get that out of my system. In a way being here has helped me see how much we'd grown apart from each other."

"Did you work together, your ex and you?"

Eve nodded in reply. "Yeah, we owned a restaurant together. It was brilliant in the beginning. I was front of house and he was the aspiring Michelin chef. We built up a good business; had a regular clientele. But gradually life became a drudge of work, work and more work. I remember thinking when we started the business together how ideal it was, being with your loved one all the time, really sharing everything."

"Yes," Hannah said. "We do need our own space, don't we?"

"Exactly so—it was a recipe for disaster and eventually the strain just got too much and we had to face the reality that we had grown away from each other instead of growing closer. I love reading and he only read recipe books. I remember reading *The Celestine Prophecy* once and I suggested that he read it. He threw it back at me." Eve gave a wry smile, adding "No the book didn't hit me—poor James, he missed a lot in life," she said with a laugh.

Hannah raised her head silently asking if there was more.

Eve, catching her look, continued. "Well I love change and doing the same stuff every day, I found wearing. I love travel and he didn't; he loves Scotland. I'm into diving—I love exploring underwater but James was only interested in cooking the fish that came out of the water. Gradually we stopped conversing about anything other than the business. We became strangers to each other and then he had an affair...." Her eyes strayed to her left hand ring finger.

She caught Hannah's expression of empathy. "It was understandable I suppose, but I didn't really see it coming. I couldn't see the wood from the trees and all that. Anyway—it's over now and I'm sort of in that place where I can look back and not add any more energy

Dressing for God

to the drama, *and* I'm learning to forgive and am starting to quite like myself again."

Eve covered her mouth with her hand as she let a small yawn escape. "Excuse me, but yes you are right Hannah, talking about it does help, especially with another woman, and I appreciate your asking. Adam was saying that if I use the EFT tapping to bring the feelings of hurt to the surface, I can release the trapped energy and the feelings won't recur, so I've been doing that."

"Yes the tapping certainly helps," added Hannah.

"Well I've just started really and I did feel some sort of energy shift in my," she patted her belly, "here and when I do it I also find myself yawning. Adam calls it a physical energy release. It does seem to be working. Why, I'm not really sure yet."

Hannah said, "Well you know the feeling in the belly will be the energy moving in your solar plexus which is the key area for the emotional body. You remember your wonder Woman etheric body suit from last night? Well that's where the emotional body links in to the physical body via the ethereal body and the solar plexus is the link for the emotions into the unconscious. So if you're feeling energy shift there, it's a very good sign that you've started clearing the negatives out."

"Thanks Hannah, I have to say I'm beginning to feel lighter in myself, so something is shifting."

"That's good, as they say when you start tapping, 'shift happens'. It's great when we can begin to see the root cause of our pain and you're dead right that the best place to start your healing is by starting to love yourself for who you really are. Because if you can't love yourself for whom you are, then you can't really begin to love anyone else. And now," she paused, looking up as the waitress placed their coffees on the table. "There I was asking you if you wanted to unburden yourself and it's been me doing all the chat. I'm sorry about that," a little giggle escaped, "But I can get carried away on this subject."

"Tell me," asked Hannah, as they were leaving the bar, "did Adam discuss bio-rhythms with you at all?"

Eve shaking her head, "No, should he have?"

Hannah had a warm smile on her face and said, "Well if he hasn't yet, you can be sure he will. It's one of his pet subjects. He has a story to tell about it that's quite something. I think you'd enjoy it."

Eve rejoined, "When I was in here having a drink with Noah, he told me to ask Adam about his ghost story, which I did and yes that was out of the ordinary. Now you are telling me to ask him about another of his experiences. I suppose you know about his ghost story?"

"Indeed I do. Yes he shared it with Noah and me when he was here after Rosaleen's passing. I suppose it's why he's interested in how life works for this book of his, which I'm pleased he's finally getting around to getting off his chest. God knows he's been on about finishing it for as long as I can remember."

They were passing Carroll's Cove when Eve said, "I've been thinking what you said about those chick penguins remembering their names. That's really quite fascinating, I mean a human child wouldn't recognise its own name until it was maybe three or four at the earliest, would it?"

"I suppose you're right at that. I must ask Stefan if penguins survival instincts are keener than a child's, but that will be after I get him home, you understand. I may have some other things on my mind to go over with him first. You're right, ten weeks is a long time...." which prompted them both to laugh at the shared intimacy.

"Tell me Eve, are you using your married name or your maiden name now?"

"Funny you should ask that because I've been using my maiden name again and enjoying it."

"Why's that do you think," asked Hannah.

"I don't really know, but I feel more my old self as Eve McQueen. It's like wearing an old pair of jeans; it's a tag I'm comfortable with. I suppose names are important in how we feel about ourselves."

Hannah agreed. "Very much so, they're important and very personal. Again our names represent the vibration we resonate to. Did you feel different when you changed your name when you married James?"

"Well, yes I did, but my name wasn't the only big change I was going through in getting married. You know living with someone new, in a different environment, in a different everything really?"

"Sure, getting married transforms a bit of everything. Yet names are really important to how you feel within yourself. Consider how you'd feel, if say, you were recruited as a spy, and you had to live with

Dressing for God

a completely different name. So imagine you're not Eve McQueen or Eve Archer but your new name was, I don't know, let's say it's Marley Lamour."

"Marley Lamour?"

"Yes. How does that feel? Now imagine that you had to completely immerse yourself in this Marley persona and you'd only answer to that name and nothing else, what changes do you think you'd undergo?"

"Marley Lamour…." Eve was quiet, driving slowly concentrating and then started speaking in a soft American accent, "It feels like I'm some sort of Hollywood vamp—I'm Marley Lamour—sounds like a can-can girl in a Wild West saloon. Anyway that's what it feels like. Or I can just picture her in another movie: Marley and the Harley." Eve reverted back to her normal voice.

"Yes, I see what you mean about feeling your name. I think I'll stick with McQueen for the time being. Do you think that's why some women keep their maiden names when they marry? Because they don't resonate with the new name vibration and the strange sounds they need to resonate with?"

"Without a doubt, yes. Do you know Stefan can hear someone's name and give a summary character reading of their strengths and the challenges they face in life and he does it purely from how they spell their names. He says it's all about character resonances and challenges and values, I can't really follow what he does, but it seems to be very accurate. He calls it numeronics."

"Really? Oh I hope I can meet him someday, he sounds fascinating."

"That's like something he'd agree with."

Eve looked questioning at her.

Hannah replied, "What you just said, 'sounds fascinating', it's his field of specialization, sounds and communications. Well you never know, you might just still be here when we visit again, Ms. McQueen."

Eve parked Felicity in Noah's drive and they stayed looking out the windshield at the clouds beginning to mask the horizon in a dark almost black, sheet of rain.

"It looks like we got the best of the weather for our run."

"Aye, we sure did." Eve turned in her seat facing Hannah. "Can I ask you something personal before we part? It's just something that triggered in me when we met yesterday and I was too shy to bring it up until now."

"Of course Eve, what is it?"

"Well, you remember that diamond choker you were wearing yesterday? I don't want to sound silly but I was wearing one just like that when Adam and I had dinner in London and afterwards, that night, I had this nightmare. It was really awful. Can I tell you about it?"

"But of course," Hannah replied. Eve recalled the details of the dream, the ninja like figures dropping down from the ceiling and the bloodletting. Then the blade slicing her throat and having the feeling of watching the scene remotely and the pain in her throat when she woke up.

Hannah was silent for a long few moments after Eve had finished.

"Was this the first time you had a dream like this?"

"Yes it was. Of course I have dreams like anyone else, but they are just sort of bits of things and I forget them as soon as I wake up. Adam has me keeping a journal now and I try to write them down as soon as I wake up but there is no real pattern to them that I can make out. But that one was so scary and then I saw your choker and I was wondered if there was any, well any connection between you wearing a similar choker and the nightmare? Well I'm sure you know of Adam's sense of synchronicities and I was wondering."

"Yes I know Adam's sense of synchronicities. Look, the rain is getting closer. Why don't you come in and see if we can find some sense in what happened. Have you got to be back at Adam's at any particular time?"

"No, my times my own today, he's finishing off his report for Lloyds anyway."

They were seated facing each other across the circular, oak kitchen table waiting for the peppermint tea to brew. Eve with Hannah's choker in her hand admiring the diamond's lustre, watching it sparkle as the light caught its movement. "Was there anything that happened earlier that day that could have triggered the dream?" Hannah asked.

"Not that I can recall. We'd dinner in a French restaurant and there was a French navy ship moored at the bridge, but no there wasn't anything out of the ordinary." Eve placed the diamond back on the table, her hand involuntarily going to her throat, rubbing it gently.

Dressing for God

"I mean I'm pretty sure it was based in France and the period seems, I dunno, I suppose it could have been the eighteenth century, but if it was around the French revolution shouldn't that have been a guillotine thing rather than a knife?"

Hannah picked up the choker and fastened it on her neck. "It does sound as if it could have been around that time. I mean wearing a red or black choker became a bit of a sympathy symbol in England during the Revolution and even now you'll see them worn by women in Paris especially around Bastille Day. And as for the guillotine, I think it was actually developed *during* the revolution after the killing spree had already started."

"Really, I didn't know that. It was just the coincidence of seeing you wearing a choker that seemed a bit strange to me. I don't suppose you ever had dreams like that, did you?"

"No, I can't say I have, though I must admit when I moved to France full time, I did feel very much as if I had lived there before. I couldn't quite explain it other that there was a strange familiarity about it, particularly in some of the older quarters of the city. I put it down to previous lifetimes. I mean who knows where we've lived before this time around?"

There was a flurry of draught as the door opened and Noah entered shaking his head, casting wet drops from his hair. "Bloody rain again," he said, smiling warmly at Eve and Hannah. "Hello Girls. I saw the car parked there, how was the run, did you manage to stay dry?"

"The run was grand, yes thanks. We managed to stay dry between the showers and how's the painting going? We saw you in the studio as we came in."

"Ah the creativity's dried up. I'm just pushing paint today; my inspiration seems to be on holiday. So I thought I'd cheer myself up and see how yiz are doing?" He pulled out a chair at the table and sat down.

"We're fine thanks, grand—we're just having a wee girlie chat," Hannah replied.

Noah peered at Hannah wearing the diamond choker. "Tell me you weren't out running in your jewellery! Would you not be just a *mite* overdressed for Kerry? Adidas and diamonds, glory be to God."

They both joined in laughing, Hannah wondering how to reply, not wanting to divulge Eve's confidence. Eve saved the situation" Of course we wear our jewellery when we're running—we're raising the tone of the place," which brought a mock grimace from Noah.

Eve added. "Nah, I was just admiring Hannah's choker. I actually have one something like it."

Hannah sat eyebrows arched, a bemused smile crinkling her mouth, wondering where Eve was going with the story as she continued, "No. Truth to tell Noah, I was telling Hannah how my choker was the death of me."

Noah blinked rapidly, then shaking his head, asked "The death of you, what do you mean?"

Hannah relaxed in her chair as Eve recounted her dream experience.

"I suppose you could well be right, about being the death of you I mean," he said. "No one can interpret the meaning better than the one who's doing the dreaming. But that's just my own humble viewpoint and I'm a big dreamer myself. Sure my life is nothing but a waking dream. What was it your man, Lau Tzu said—ah yes—it was this, 'Last night, he said, I dreamt I was butterfly and when I woke up this morning I wondered… am I a butterfly dreaming that I am a man, or was I a man dreaming I was a butterfly?'. Now which is true do you think?"

"Do butterflies really dream?" asked Eve.

"Do you know, I never really paused to ask," Noah replied. "What's a dream anyway? Just images we indulge in unconsciously when we're asleep and I suppose consciously when we're awake too."

"There's also lucid dreaming and nightmares," added Hannah, "and as Eve *was aware* that she was 'dreaming in the dream' that could well have been a lucid memory flashback delivered to her for some reason."

"You mean like 'old karma' from a previous incarnation?" He asked.

"I suppose it could be; why don't we ask the lady herself what she thinks?"

Hannah turned to Eve, "Well do *you* think your dream was caused by karma from a past life?"

"I can't really say. Isn't karma about doing good and bad? Are you saying that maybe it was about something bad I inherited?"

Dressing for God

"No, no, no, not at all," Hannah said. "No karma's not about good and bad. Karma is just like gravity. It's how life affects you according to how you think and act. It's just cause and effect in action. It's neither good nor bad—it's just the result of the choices you make."

"Oh, I'd always assumed that it was like brownie points you accumulated. You know, if I did good deeds and gave money to charity, or if I helped someone in need, and you're saying it's not like that?"

Hannah turned to Noah, "Do you want to come in on this one?"

"Ah sure I'll try my best." Noah ran his fingers through his hair as he ruminated for a few moments.

"Let me say first off, that what we are talking about is what I call the law. There is no avoiding it in life. It's every single thing I experience from every thought, word and deed that is reflected back to me for my personal experience. You could say that when I tell the universe what I want, then that's what I get to experience."

"So then," Eve paused collecting her thoughts, "If for instance, like in my dream I was killed for whatever reason—where would the old karma, as you called it, where would that apply to me right now?"

"A good question Eve deserves a good answer, but I don't really have access to the lords of karma library to see where you'd be right now in the chain."

"What chain?" Eve asked eyebrows arched, inquiring.

"The chain of cause and effect; it's made up of the links between you and whoever you've been involved with in past and present lives. The links are ties of emotional energy between you and whoever, until such time as there is mutual release from them."

"But can this linkage be wiped out—like erased from us completely?"

"Yes it can be cleaned. Karma is an energy pattern. It's a tension that you carry in your consciousness. connecting you with anyone that you still have stuff to sort out and it'll continue until the soul accepts responsibility for his or her actions and asks for forgiveness."

"But that could take forever," Eve blurted out.

Noah gave a deep laugh before answering. *"But we do have all the time in the world Eve*—we live in a three dimensional universe of time and space, energy has no timetable: it sticks where it's stuck."

Hannah's shoulders shook as she stifled a laugh. "Oh Noah, where do you get them from—*'sticks where it's stuck'*? Karma will never be the same for me again."

"But it's true isn't it? We just need to be aware that it's not just enough to ask for forgiveness—it's a two way stretch—it may be that the one you are asking forgiveness from, may not want to forgive you in this lifetime. It might be many lifetimes before he or she is balanced enough to forgive and forget. The feelings are so deep and painful that they get *stuck*, like I just said."

"So what would happen then I cannot get forgiveness even if I'm repentant?"

"You can always ask your higher self to petition the Creator for forgiveness to help break the chain. It's impossible to know where we really stand though, who really knows what we were responsible for in previous lives?"

"It sounds a bit like driving in the dark without any headlights—how can you possibly know who you are karmatically connected with?"

"You don't, simple as that. So treat everyone the same. We're all fish in the one ocean, so we're all probably karmatically connected at some level somewhere. So treat everyone as your own reflection; love yourself and love whoever is in your face. Be compassionate. That's as good a place to start as any." Noah leaned back in the chair looking sanguine as he stirred his tea.

"It's not easy is it, this life thing?" Eve asked. "Now I really have to start thinking about how I think about 'what I think about'... is that Irish enough for you?"

Rising from her seat Eve smiled at Noah, leant over and gave him a peck on the cheek.

"Thanks for that Noah, Hannah. You've given me a lot to think about. I'd best be off and head home and rest assured, I will drive—compassionately.

Chapter 12

Divine Breath

It was late Monday afternoon before Adam had emailed his report to London. He emerged from the office into the kitchen where Eve was preparing vegetables for supper, a satisfied look on his face, rubbing his tummy through his navy blue cotton shirt, his hair dishevelled and still in need of a trim. "Well that's that then, my reports finished and gone. I think I'll treat myself to a drink, do you fancy joining me?" he asked Eve.

"Oh well done," she replied. "Yes, I'll have a glass of white please. I thought you'd never finish, the place has been as quiet as a church with you in there tapping away at the keyboard. It's just as well I enjoy my own company."

"Sorry about that, I'll make sure I'm noisy for the rest of the evening. What's cooking?"

"I was just making a vegetable soup and there's some chicken left over from yesterday."

They were dawdling over the remains of the bottle of Semillon Blanc, Eve guessed Adam was deciding if he'd open another bottle when he apologised again for being immersed in his report and ignoring her.

"It's not a problem," she assured him. "Honest. I've had so much stuff to try to assimilate and so many ideas to get straight in my thinking; I have been very, very occupied. I was saying to Noah and Hannah yesterday that I had no idea that life was so complex. I thought it was all about being nice to people and keeping my word and only saying nice things and now I find I have to really think about what it is I want to think about. Will the karma dumpster fly overhead and drop its load on my head?"

"Ah you've been down karma alley with Noah then. Interesting was it?"

"Well it really started with Hannah and her diamond choker." Eve told Adam the feelings she had seeing Hannah with the choker in Noah's house and the subsequent conversation about dreams and karma.

"That's great Eve," Adam said. "You know I haven't forgotten that question you asked me on our first dinner with Noah. You know the one about why life seems so full of crap and why it isn't full of milk and honey. Do you remember?"

"I do yes, but I think after listening to Noah I'm beginning to see why. It's all a matter of how you see life *and the beliefs that you are living* that dictate whether it's the milk and honey diet or the scraps and bones diet that is delivered to your doorstep. Is that the answer?"

"Yes, and then we'll give everyone a tattoo on their foreheads saying: 'There is no such thing as a bad experience—I'm doing this for God' that'd be a great reminder of the law of cause and effect now, wouldn't it?"

"Well you can have the body art," Eve replied. "I'll stick to remembering it in real time, thank you very much."

"Listen, I'm away tomorrow, have you any easy questions you want to ask now or will they keep until I get back from London?"

"Do you know Adam, there's been just so much to get aligned with in my thinking that I am looking forward to having the space to get my questions organised for your return; so no more questions," she paused. "Though Hannah did say to ask for another of your stories."

Adam looked at her, sitting there a coy smirk on her face. "Go on" he said. "Which story is it this time?"

"Bio-rhythms, she said you had another of your experiences to share."

"Ah that story," he said. "I suppose so."

"Are we back swimming in Noah's ocean of energy again?"

"We are, yes in a sense." Adam poured the last of the wine into his glass, Eve covering her glass with her hand, declining more.

"Let me digress into talking about colour for a moment if you don't mind." He swivelled around in the chair, his legs stretched out as he continued.

Dressing for God

"Let me take you back to the seventeenth century, where a young Isaac Newton one fine summer day was in his study, the sunlight streaming through his window and he accidentally refracted pure white light through a prism and saw how it split into the colours of the rainbow. He then placed another prism upside down in the path of these colours and lo and behold, didn't all the colours coalesce back into seamless pure white light again. So Isaac concluded for the first time ever in the history of man, that light is colour."

Eve lowered her head looking at him through raised eyebrows, getting used now to his tangential approach to storytelling.

"You're wondering where this is going. I can see from the look in your eyes, well you did ask—so hang in there—a bit of colour should help in getting to the gist of bio-rhythms, whenever I manage to arrive there."

"One of the great illusions in life *is* that there is such a thing as a state of stillness. Would you agree that we can look at a scene and perceive perfect rest, calm and stillness and see a state of no movement?"

He raised his hand and peered at it, turning it over and holding it up to the light.

"I can look at my hand and it looks perfectly still in this light, yet if I put it under a microscope, I'll see the intense energy action of its vibrations. Because everything of matter is in some state of movement, it's just that we are deluded into seeing stillness."

"Sure, yes, *I can see* that."

"Yet we know without any shadow of doubt, that the whole physical world is an electromagnetic field. Everything in the universe is flowing *with, through and by* electromagnetic waves, or as it is also known as energy, chi, prana, The holy spirit or as the Hawaiians call it the divine breath. I bet you didn't know that the word Hawaii means just that, "divine breath" did you? So there, more trivia for your next quiz night."

"I somehow knew this wouldn't be a straight forward story. Go on, I'm all ears."

"Well, as you know these electromagnetic waves flow in different frequencies and different colours arise when certain wavelengths are separated from the spectrum. Notice what I said—when they are separated from the spectrum. It's the absorption of the wavelengths of an object that decides which colour it displays to our eyes. How a stone vibrates in the sunlight is how it absorbs the light's energies at that frequency and the rhythm of the frequency is the key to its colour."

"And the colour of the stone is what?"

"The colour we see depends on what wavelengths the stone absorbed and what it rejected OK? Let me give you another example. Let's say we take a red rose. What we are seeing is the rose's resistance to the wavelength of the colour red. It will have absorbed all the colours yellow and blue and what we perceive as a red rose is in fact a rose that has rejected red. A daffodil absorbs blue and red wavelengths and rejects yellow so it's a yellow daffodil that we see…"

"Life will never look the same again, you know that?"

"Well good, I'm glad you're taking it in." Adam was clearly enjoying the banter.

"The key here is that as everything is vibrating so rapidly that we cannot see it happening, and what we are left with is the surface rejection of the energy that wasn't absorbed. So while everything in the physical world resists the energy of light, it is also penetrated by the light. This leads me perfectly into bio-rhythms; so if you want to kick start your laptop there and log on to www.bio-chart.com, I'll show you a really valuable life tool and then I'll tell you my story."

"OK now, before you enter in your date of birth, let me quickly explain what you are looking at. We are going to speak of the three bodies: the physical body, the emotional body, and then outside that, your mental body; they all interpenetrate and surround your physical etheric. We'll stick to these three for the moment. These are different density energy fields that make up your total being and as they have different densities they vibrate at different rates and have different frequencies. Just like the stone, the daffodil or the rose, they bodies absorb life sustaining energies which they accumulate, just like an invisible battery, for the first half of a cycle and then they discharge that energy during the second period of a cycle."

"Yes, I have that."

"Now at birth, as soon as the cord is cut and the baby starts breathing, the individual life cycles commence. The body start absorbing this chi or prana at different wave lengths and frequencies. The physical body has a twenty three day cycle, the emotional body has a twenty eight day cycle and the intelligence or mental body has a thirty three day cycle. It's a sine curve, a wave form, meaning it's

Dressing for God

above the line in charging mode for the first half of any cycle and in discharge mode below the line for the second half."

Adam made a wave action with his hand.

"Our bio-rhythms demonstrate visibly why you can feel energetic on some days and be knackered on others and more especially it shows the days when you are accident prone. That's when the batteries cross over from charge to discharge and vice versa. It's as if there's a shift in our awareness and statistically it is proven without doubt, that most accidents occur on double critical and triple critical days. It also explains why top performing athletes—the Tiger Woods of the world suddenly become nervous over a critical putt and have off-days when nothing goes to plan."

"The trick in using these bio-rhythms is to be aware of where your energies are and take note when you are having a critical day. It doesn't mean you should stay in bed or be afraid to go out on these days, but they are times when you should exercise better awareness and realize that you are not at your very best. So on to my story then."

"I was living in Dublin at the time of this story; in recovery mode from my journey to the astral with the lost soul and I was very much into studying the law of vibrations. I'd been using bio-rhythms for several years and I had this little hand held calculator, a Casio Biolater it was called, and I was showing an acquaintance of mine, let's call him Simon, how to interpret the bio-rhythm results. He was really interested and asked me lots of questions and gave me different dates of births and different bio dates."

"After a while he asked if I would meet with him and his brother in a pub, in the city the following day for a spot of lunch. I forget his brother's name now, but let's call him Roger. So I arrive at the appointed hour and join Roger and Simon for a pint and a sandwich. I gave Roger an overview on bio-rhythms and then he gave me his d.o.b and a date he wanted to check out from his past, a few years previous. I plug in the data and it comes up as a double critical with physical and emotional bodies combined with low intelligence."

Adam stood and retrieved another bottle of wine from the fridge. "Thirsty work, talking," he said, as he pulled the cork, topped up his glass and settled back in his chair.

"Right so, let me continue. I could see from the reaction on Roger's face, that I had struck a nerve with him, he was open-mouthed-stunned. I asked what happened that day and he told me he was run over by a car as he crossed the road and ended up in St. Vincent's Hospital with compound fractures of his left leg."

Eve was visibly taken aback and turned her head looking sharply at Adam.

"Roger just couldn't wait to give me a second time which was about ten months after the first date. I plugged it in and darned if it wasn't a triple critical day. I remember it well because there was a long pause in our conversation as Roger and Simon exchanged serious looks between them and Simon said to the brother, "I knew you'd be impressed with this bio stuff. "

"I'll never forget what happened next. I asked Roger what occurred that day. He reached over, took my hand and then tapped it on his thigh. It gave a hollow metal sound. It was a prosthetic. He had been released from hospital that very morning, walked across the road to his brother's car and was knocked down in the middle of the road. He was whisked into surgery where his leg was unfortunately amputated."

"Dear God above, that's awful." Eve's voice hushed.

"Trust me Eve—that is a true story. I gave Roger my little Biolater as a memento. Casio unfortunately have stopped making them but there are plenty of bio-rhythm programmes on the web. It can be worth your while to get familiar with them. So there you have it Eve, another little insight into the understanding of life's subtle energies."

"I'll definitely use this, thanks Adam."

"Nay bother, as you canny Scots like to say." Adam stood and started clearing the table.

"Listen as I'm away in the morning, can I suggest that you review all of this life stuff that we've been talking over and make a start on all the questions you feel need answering. I think that'll be a good way to tackle the book structure when I get back. Are you up for that?"

Eve smiled at his question.

"Actually Adam, I have started a list, believe it or not. I'm getting myself into Finity Muze mode. I've been writing every evening and yes, I can be ready for Friday with my list. Are you flying out from Kerry?"

"No, I'm on Aer Lingus from Cork to Heathrow. Tell me, are you picking up the boat with Noah on Thursday?"

Dressing for God

"I am indeed. I'm really looking forward to it, it should be fun."

"Aye, that it should. I'm just sorry I'm not going to be there as well. Have you got a wetsuit with you?"

"I have yes, my shortie one, why?"

"Ah, it's just that Noah's boat can be a bit damp at this time of the year so you might just want to wear it under your jeans for a bit of insulation."

"Oh good idea. I'll do that, thanks."

"Right then, I must away and pack and get to bed. You have my contact numbers and you can always get me on my mobile if you need me."

Chapter 13

Critical Day!

Eve was standing in the driveway as Noah's Jeep streaming wisps of exhaust, pulled to a stop alongside Felicity. Noah's face was brimming with excitement, laughter lines crinkling his face, eyes twinkling as he hopped out waving his arms.

"I get my new boat today—oh it feels so GOOD." His voice sang the words.

"My, you are excited aren't you?" Eve greeted him.

"I can't wait," he said. "Are you all ready?"

Noah pulled a small, canvas bag out of the Jeep and slammed the door shut.

"Aye all ready Cap'n. I have the sarnies and the coffee here," Eve held up her laptop backpack. "All ready for the off."

Noah gave her a quick peck on the cheek.

"Will you be warm enough in that get-up?" Looking at Eve dressed in blue denim jeans and navy wool sweater, trainers, a waterproof jacket in her hand, "It could get a bit wet when we get around the corner and into the ocean."

"Ah appearances are deceptive," Eve replied. "You can't see what I have on underneath this lot—and," she added, seeing the look on his face, "to save you the bother of imagining, I'm wearing my wetsuit, so I'm well insulated thank you very much."

"Fine girl ye are. C'mon lets head out."

"Ah Rosaleen," he said standing on the pier, looking fondly at his twenty three foot timber hulled boat "Do ya' think she knows I'm trading her in?" he asked.

"I doubt that," Eve replied. "Do boats have feelings?"

Dressing for God

"I dunno—maybe yes, maybe not, but she sure has many memories for me; ah well," he said with an audible sigh. "Sure everything passes."

He threw his bag aboard, stepped over the rail and held out his hand to steady Eve's jump aboard.

"You know what?" he said, "I can understand that Viking thing—that ceremony where they set fire to the long ship when the chieftain dies. You know the funeral pyre bit—it seems fitting really—to let the memories evaporate with the passing."

He paused, looking around the deck, rubbing his hand across the timber of the half cabin roof, a far-away look in his eye.

"Aye," said Eve, "they do that every year in Lerwick for Hogmanay. They set fire to a specially made Viking galley and then have a rave up and a ceilidh, 'Up Helly Aa' they call it."

He nodded his understanding, a sense of reminiscence shared between them.

"OK so," he said and exhaling noisily he started the engine, pushing the bow off clear of the jetty, he swung her head out into the river.

"Let's get to what did you call it? To "Helly Aa" away from here. Say goodbye to Sneem, my *D'Ark Rosaleen*."

"What's the forecast like?" asked Eve, as they cleared the Sneem River heading down Kenmare Bay into the Atlantic. Rosaleen was churning a dirty, white wake, her motion easy, just a small pitching motion making around eight knots on the ebbing tide.

"Ah, I checked it last night on the web and it looks set fair for today. This old high from the Azores is still with us giving us the bit of heat. There was a low coming down from Iceland but we should be OK for good weather there and back."

"Do you not have VHF?" Eve asked, looking around the small cockpit.

"I do of course, I've a handheld. It's in the bag there. Can you get it out for me please and set it on channel 16 like a good colleen?"

Eve took out the ICOM handset and switched it on, set it to channel sixteen, fiddled with the volume, then handed it to Noah. "Do you have another battery with you Noah because, I think this is, em, flat as a pancake."

"Ah sweet God, didn't I set the charged battery on the hall table to pick up on my way out and then the phone rang in the kitchen and shit—excuse my language but I must have left it there."

He took his hand off the wheel and patted his grey fleece jacket, and then the back pockets of his dungarees, picked up his yellow oil-skin jacket from the back of his seat and patted it down, then looked at Eve with a drooping hangdog expression.

"And I've left my bloody mobile in the Jeep haven't I? Ah dear God—what a cock-up!"

"I have my phone with me, if it helps," said Eve.

"Ah thank God for that. Is it charged?" he asked, a relieved humour in his tone.

"Of course it is." She rummaged in her backpack, finding it.

"Have you got service?"

"Yes its fine, do you need it now?"

"Ah not just now, but I told McCarthy's I'd give them a bell to let them know when I was about two hours off, so I'll call them from The Skelligs. I take it you still want to go there first?"

"Oh lord yes, definitely."

They had rounded Sherky Island about half a mile to starboard, and were heading now for Skellig Michael, a long, low, south westerly swell hitting Rosaleen on the port quarter, the sea calm in light airs. Eve, her elbows braced on the cockpit counter, focused the Nikon binoculars on the pyramid shaped island on the horizon.

"How far off are we now?" She asked.

"Oh about eight miles—we should be there elevenish."

Eve checked her dive watch, just 10:10 AM.

"Can you make out the twin peaks of Skellig Michael yet?" Noah asked.

"I can yes, just...why?"

"Ah just a snippet of history for you; I think it was in February 1944, an American navy plane was flying an anti-submarine mission around here. It was what they called a PB4Y. Anyway it was a thick foggy night and they picked up a radar echo of what they *thought* was a U-boat on the surface and then they did a run to drop depth charges on it but instead of a U-boat, they hit the south peak on the island and crashed into the ocean. All eleven perished—God bless them."

"Oh how awful."

"Aye, that it was. One of the lighthouse keepers saw the flash as it exploded in the sea and he climbed up the following morning and

Dressing for God

sure enough there was a scraping of white paint where it made contact with the side of the peak before it went crashing into the sea."

Noah pointed to the far shoreline. "Do you see Mount Brandon over there to your right, the big mountain on the Dingle Peninsula?" Eve studied the mountainous range as Noah continued his narrative.

"Well that mountain collected crashed aircraft like you wouldn't believe during the war. Again it was caused by flying in thick fog and sure they only had very basic instruments in those days and of course the lighthouses were all blacked out for security. It was 1948 I think before they started up in service again."

Overhead she watched three gannets trailing skeins of seaweed in their beaks, heading for their nest making back on Little Skellig. The air over Little Skellig was peppered with birds rising in wave after wave, like chaff blowing in the wind. Eve's memories went flowing back to The Firth of Forth and the Bass Rock when Noah's voice brought her up with a start.

"I'll head over to the lighthouse end of Skellig Michael first and maybe we can try our hand for a few mackerel, though it's still early in the season. And you can get a close-up of the gannets on Little Skellig on the way in to Portmagee, how does that sound to you?"

"Thanks Noah, that sounds terrific, it really is awesome."

Noah reduced speed as he approached Skellig Michael, pointing out Blind Man's Cove where the local boats disembark the tourists in the open season. Eve trained the glasses on the landing place, as Noah sailed slowly along the east edge of the island he pointed out the walkway carved into the cliff as it trailed past and around Cross Cove, a deep defile into the cliff where two seals lay asleep on a rock ledge, the sea slapping at them gently.

"Noah, I'm looking at the steps up to the monastery." Eve had the glasses trained on the centre of the island. "How in the name of God did those monks manage that, what thirteen hundred years ago? I must go up there when its open, I'd love to see it close-up. Have you been up to the top?"

"I have indeed. 'Tis magnificent—it really has something spiritually elemental about it. Ah it wasn't the going up that bothered me. No 'twas the coming down—there's nary a hand rail, nothing to hold on to—and the vertigo had me coming down the steps on me arse, if you'll pardon the expression."

"They're the OPW huts over there." Noah pointed out the grey huts at the side of the pathway leading up to the lighthouse. "They're for the workers doing maintenance work on the island in the summer months. Nobody lives there in the off season at all."

"Can you just imagine the difficulty of building a lighthouse on this place?" Noah said, as they rounded the southerly tip of the island and stood off under the cliffs into Seal Cove. He pointed up at the light, "How far up do you think that light is?"

"I haven't a clue, it looks very high."

"It's all of one hundred and seventy-five feet up in the air and would you believe that a wave knocked out the light in a December storm some fifty years ago. Now you wouldn't want to be at sea when that happened, would you now?"

"You're right there." Eve answered, trying to imagine how a wave could reach that high.

"Are you ready for a bit of fishing?" He asked, heading a short way off the south end, he cut the engine and let Rosaleen come bow up into the tide, drifting gently.

Noah pointed to a second lighthouse nestled on a cliff top, "Do you see that disused lighthouse there? That fella' was shut down in 1854 and now there's not a soul living on the island at all, since the main lighthouse was automated in 1984."

"Japers, look at the way the current is taking us inshore," he said, starting up the engine he took Rosaleen well clear of the rocks fringing the island.

"There's a true story I must tell you about drifting on to the rocks here. Did you ever hear of a famous fellow countryman of yours called John Paul Jones?"

"No, I can't say I have, why?"

"Ah, he was something else was John Paul. He was born in the Solway Firth, went to sea as a lad and at the time I'm telling you about, he was a Captain in the American navy. Some say he is the father of it but we know here in Ireland, that it was an Irishman, John Barry, who has that honour. Just like St Brandon discovered America centuries before that Columbus fella. Anyways, this John Paul was seconded by the American Congress to France—to King Louis' French navy in the war against England. The French gave him a frigate called the 'Bonhomme Richard' and he set out on a fighting voyage around

Dressing for God

Ireland and Britain, capturing merchant ships and pillaging and all that sort of stuff, if you follow me?"

"I'm really getting the tourist guidebook spiel here, aren't I?" Eve quipped.

"Less of your lip there girl, sure aren't I just making it interesting for you." Noah said, affecting a look of being offended.

"Ah Noah, you know I'm only having you on, sorry. I am really interested—go on please."

"Ah I suppose I can forgive you." He brought Rosaleen about and headed into the slight swell and continued his story. "In 1778 it was- that was what, eleven years before your French Revolution? So you may well have bumped into John Paul in Paris in your earlier life. Sorry, sorry I don't mean to make light of your French experience."

Eve shook her head in mock exasperation, her eyes twinkling merrily.

"So our John Paul arrived here on this very place, exactly where we are right now, give or take a few boat lengths, in the month of April and wasn't he becalmed with a strong current setting him straight onto the Skelligs. There wasn't a breath of wind to fill the sails so he launched his longboat with his coxswain and six sailors, attached a hawser to the boat and had them tow the frigate clear of the rocks and the island. That would be a common enough practise. Anyway, what he didn't know was that the boat crew were all pressed men from…" Noah pointed into the shore, "from over there in Valentia Island and didn't they just cut the towing hawser when the frigate was clear of the rocks and then rowed like the clappers into Portmagee and were never seen again. That's a true story—honest to God," he said, crossing himself in emphasis.

He switched off the engine and let Rosaleen drift and they resumed their fishing.

It was early in the season but the mackerel were running and in no time they had a good dozen in the fish box. Eve broke out the coffee and sandwiches and they sat there watching the gulls scavenge as they enjoyed an early lunch.

"We'll just finish these and maybe head over to Little Skelligs," Noah said, sniffing the air and looking at the sky which now had a goodly cover of cloud. "It looks like that low pressure system I told you about is heading our way."

J.F. Tallon

He got Rosaleen under way and headed towards Little Skellig. Eve busied herself stowing the flask and mugs into her backpack then placed it on the deck.

"Eve can you take the wheel here for a minute please, and I'll clear the deck gear away, it's time we started back. Just keep her on that heading there and sure give her some more wellie if you want."

Eve perched her behind on the stool, feet on the deck, eased the throttle forward gently and then squeezed it on to full ahead—felt Rosaleen lift and churn into the waves, enjoying the surge, she glanced back to where Noah was bent over securing the fish boxes, his body swaying with the boats motion, the last burst of speed causing him to straighten up suddenly. He glanced at Eve, a look on his face, about to say something when everything erupted in turmoil.

Eve felt a massive crunching collision as Rosaleen was upended slamming into the sea, the boat slewing sharply to starboard, bow down, cold seawater sloshing all over the place. Eve was flung in a heap landing in a corner of the cabin. The hull had splintered open, directly below the steering wheel where she'd been sitting seconds earlier; the water gushing in was over her waist as she pushed herself to her hands and knees—trying to get to her feet—the sea rising rapidly in the small cabin—the sound of the single screw, a screaming whirring in the air, as the stern lifted clear of the water, the deck at a crazy angle. "Bloody hell we're sinking," her nerves were tingling, adrenaline surging through her body. "Jesus—what the hell is happening?"

On her knees now, she pulled herself upright against the sucking water, her shoulder hurting like gyp, looking aft for Noah. "Oh Mother of God, where is he? What the hell happened? What did we hit?" Rosaleen was sinking in a slow sliding movement on almost sixty degree angle now.

"Where's Noah—oh dear God," the words escaping her as she looked around, the boat turning on its side, sliding under the waves, big bubbles of air erupting around her, the taste of diesel in her mouth. She kicked off from the roof holding onto the life-ring, took two deep breaths, filled her lungs and kicked off, dove down following Rosaleen's air bubbles searching for Noah.

Rosaleen was slowly slipping downwards along the side of a submerged container; an empty forty footer—Hapag Lloyd she saw the name—its thick insulated door, a scalpel lying below the surface. It

Dressing for God

had knifed Rosaleen's wooden skin open and she lay now tethering on top of this box, as air and fuel blubbered slowly to the surface. Eve swam down along Rosaleen's deck, saw Noah desperately trying to free himself, blood streaming from a head wound. She pulled herself in beside him, got a grip on the bulwark—Noah's foot was caught in a tangle of rope—bubbles of air escaping from his mouth, his movements frantic. Eve pulled herself beneath him, grasped his leg and levering with all her might wrenched his foot clear of his boot and heaved him upwards towards the light. They surfaced together, Eve breathing desperately at the limit of her lungs, Noah was retching and puking seawater. Eve turned him on his back, mentally kicking herself for not wearing a life vest. She lay there floating, panting with exertion, looking up at the sky thinking 'Bloody hell—what do I do now?'

She looked at Noah's head wound; it was ugly. He must have taken a blow on the rail as he was pitched overboard. A piece of white bone lay exposed beneath a flap of skin, high on his forehead. The blood flow was seeping into his eyes. Eve saw the life-ring fifteen yards away; she left Noah floating on his back, recovered the life-ring, swam back and flopped it over his head and then forced his right arm and shoulder into the ring.

"Noah, dear God, speak to me." Noah strained to speak, his mouth working but no sounds, just more retching as he spat out gobbets of seawater. His head wound looked awful; she felt a futility sweep over her. They were over half mile from Cross Cove and all she could think was to make for it, get into the shelter where they'd seen the seals earlier.

Continuously checking her bearings, Eve slowly swam towards the cove alternating between pulling the ring with a side stroke and pushing him ahead of her. The swell was helping her progress, slowly lifting them in little surges as she stayed focused on her stroke. The tide was on the flood now and she could see it was carrying them past Cross Cove towards the east end of the island. Eve redoubled her efforts, Noah a passenger—still breathing, but he was in and out of consciousness an occasional "Ah Jesus," escaping his lips. Eve wishing she had a set of fins, kept kicking with all her might.

She could feel the wash back from the swell on the rocks as they neared the shore, Eve calling on all the spirits in the Universe to help her get Noah safe—then stopped for a breather, treading water, readying for the final effort—only another sixty yards or so to go and the rocks at the corner of Blindman's cove were twenty yards to her right. 'If I keep on heading straight in, the tide will hopefully get us in the lee of the rocks and into some shelter. I'll figure what to do when I get there—but first I've got to get there.' She kept kicking and stroking with her free arm.

The push of the tide lessened as they slowly edged around the rock face into Blindman's Cove. Eve gave it her all; her eyes half closed with tiredness and sea spray, she came up against the sheer rock face with a bump. The swell was heaving them up and down a good five or six feet—looking to her right—'over there, pushed off and struck out, panting, another kick, towing Noah behind her now. Another ten strokes and there were the steps, greasy-wet, seaweed strewn, "Oh God, I don't have the energy to go another yard."

Eve managed to sit on the greasy bottom step and holding onto the red tubular hand rail, hauled herself up step by step out of the swell zone, dragging Noah with her. Tying the life-ring to the rail with a tail of an old rope, she leaned over the edge of the steps and was violently ill, vomiting her guts up. Shock set in, hitting her in waves of nausea; her shoulder ached where she had fallen on it. "I've done it—I got here. Now, how do I get him up the steps?" Exhaustion overcame her—fatigue and cold and fear. Her eyes closed for a moment, "Have to rest for a minute…oh dear God above—help me please." Her head hung low on her chest, both hands numb with the cold, totally done in. Faintness overcame her.

A slight shake on her shoulder, again, firmer this time, then the voice, "Here, let me help you. "

Eve raised her head and looked up. A man stood on the steps above her, bent forward, "Here take my hand." Eve felt his hands under her elbows, raising her to her feet and supporting her, walking her up the steps to the landing area.

"Right so… sit down here and I'll go and get your friend."

Eve tried to take stock of her situation, not understanding what was happening. There was a sense of unreality as if she was an observer in a play and someone else was in her body. She sat watching as the man descended the steps, undid the rope around the life ring, lifted it from Noah's shoulders and threw it spinning upwards where it landed on the concrete flat with a splat. Then he stepped down past

Dressing for God

Noah, waist deep in the water, picked him up in a fireman's lift over his right shoulder and made his way carefully up the steps, pausing at the top to speak.

"Are you OK to walk?" He indicated with his head in the direction of more steps leading to the pathway above them. Eve nodded yes—her speech was gone—raised herself up slowly and squelched after the man, her eyes down following his lead. 'I've never been so cold and tired in my life,' she thought. 'I feel like a vegetable.'

She followed him one step at a time, bent over with exhaustion, focused on his soaking leather shoes, his wet trouser legs—that was the extent of her view as she slowly climbed the steps.

Eve paused catching her breath, checked the time, twenty past five—looked to her left out to sea, the wind colder now than earlier and the visibility was closing in. She could just about make out Little Skellig through the mist, "Aw God—aw thank God." Took a deep breath and carried on slowly up the steps.

He had placed Noah in a sitting position against the rock on the right hand side of the pathway and was checking his pulse when Eve arrived and sat down wearily.

"How is he?"

"Alive but we need to get him warm. Wait here. I'll be back."

He stood and disappeared up the pathway. Eve put her arms around Noah, took his hand in hers and started rubbing him through his clothes trying to get some body heat moving, not knowing what else to do.

A squeaking sound out of the mist and the man appeared pushing a large wheelbarrow with some timber planks in it.

"It's a good walk up to the huts—this will make it easier for us."

He lifted Noah gently and placed him in the wheelbarrow with his head and shoulder forward, propped on the two planks, wedged underneath his torso, his legs sticking out the back between the handles. Satisfied, he helped Eve to her feet.

"Let's go." Picking up the handles he started pushing the wheelbarrow along the rough pathway, Eve following behind. The ground was jagged, stony and Eve was careful where she placed her step, glad now that she hadn't cast off her shoes in the water.

They entered the corrugated roofed section of pathway skirting Seal Cove, Eve remembering that she had aimed to swim into it for refuge. She peeked over the ledge into its depth and realized how futile that would have been. The swell was rising and crashing into the cliff face and there was only the cry of the birds to be heard above the sound of the swell heaving on the rocks far below.

The pathway meandered to the right, a tall chain link fence lay to her left between her and a helipad cantilevered over the sea—a helipad, rescue—her heart beat harder with excitement, "There's hope," she thought and pushed on following the squeak of the wheelbarrow.

They had reached the huts. He pushed the wheelbarrow through a small wooden gate set in a light timber fence, unhindered by the **Private—Keep Out** notice and beckoned Eve to him.

"Come on," he said, stopping outside the first hut. He looked around and stepped up to a firebox hanging on the wall, opened it, and removed a red five kilogram foam fire extinguisher, Eve wondering what the hell he was up to. He walked up to the door of the hut and leaning back, aimed the base of the cylinder like a battering ram and slammed it at the door. The lock popped open with a single blow.

Eve followed him inside. It was a two bunk cabin with a single clothes locker, a stove, sink and food presses. He tried the light switch, nothing. He rummaged in the locker over the sink and found a small camping light, shook it and yes there was fuel. He searched the other locker, some dry herbs, tea, sugar, powdered milk, flour, no matches. He opened the cutlery drawer, a cigarette lighter, he flicked it, "Yes," he said and fiddled with the lamp for a few seconds until a yellow flame gave light to the room. He then checked the oven, it was gas fired—he tried it, no supply. He stood surveying the room, made up is mind.

"OK then," he said and motioned Eve to stand clear as he pulled the bottom mattress off the bunk and placed it on the floor. "I'll get your friend in now."

Eve kicked off her wet jeans, shirt, and trainers and stood shivering in her wetsuit and body-glove. She was shuddering with the cold, her teeth chattering.

The man returned carrying Noah over his shoulder and lowered him gently on the mattress, examined the head wound in the lamp light.

"Can you get his clothes off and start rubbing him down?" He asked in a serious measured manner and then started rummaging in

Dressing for God

the clothes locker behind the door; he pulled out two grey blankets, a couple of pillows and a set of orange curtains which he tossed on the mattress.

"Here, use these as towels, I'll see if there's a first aid kit anywhere," he said and disappeared out the door.

Eve was silent, just doing as he asked, anxious to help. She unbuttoned Noah's dungarees and pulled them off. The mattress was already wet from his clothes but she put a blanket under him praying to God he'd recover. She heard the crash as another door was popped open and then the man was back in the room standing over her.

"Look, I found a first aid kit and some coveralls." He placed them on the countertop. "But we have to get some heat. I'm going up to the yard and see if there's fuel. Here, let me help you with his shirt."

He propped Noah up while Eve got his woollen top and T-shirt off. "Keep rubbing him, it keeps the circulation going—we need to get him warm, do your best."

She wrapped the blanket around him and trying to stop her teeth from chattering pulled on the smallest of the navy coveralls over her wetsuit and started rubbing Noah's chest with the curtains, working her hands over his heart area, hoping he'd regain consciousness. She felt hopeless, cold, and scared.

"Talk to me Noah—oh dear God, talk to me." She continued trying to revive him, willing him better.

She heard a clang of a canister being dropped outside and then he was back fussing at the stove. He switched on the top burner, pressed the piezzo starter and gave Eve a big smile as the gas jet burst into flame.

"OK, we're cooking on gas. Now let's get the oven going."

"Yes," he exclaimed, opening the oven door, "there, that'll heat us up in no time. Now then, the water." He found a kettle and filled it from a white twenty litre demijohn carried in from outside.

"Distilled water from the battery room above," he explained, setting the kettle on the stove then turning towards Eve he held up two fingers, "Two things—a hot drink for you—and I need the water boiling to clean the wound."

He opened the first aid kit and spread the contents out on the mattress: sterile wound dressings, scissors, antiseptic, paracetemol, Aspirin, antihistamine, plasters, bandages, antacid tablets, Vaseline, surgical gloves. He stood there looking pensive, scratched his chin. It was the first time Eve had a chance to really look at him. She felt as if she had been away somewhere and was just beginning to return to some sense of normality.

Eve continued to massage Noah who wasn't showing any signs of consciousness, though his breathing was regular now and there was some colour returning, as much as she could gauge in the soft light of the lamp. The window was boarded up on the outside and the light had a mirror effect in the room. The man was reflected in the glass, she didn't even know his name; he was putting tea bags into two mugs, adding sugar and powdered milk. She wanted to say, "I don't take sugar," when he spoke to her, "The sugar will give you energy," and handed her the mug. "Here try this, it'll warm you up."

He was about Noah's size. At least six foot, big shoulders, but he had a tight wiry strength like a finely tuned gymnast. fortyish, steel grey hair close cropped, dark complexion, weathered skin, could be a seaman, the navy Breton type cotton canvas smock, wide sleeves, high collar, trousers were the same colour and material. She looked down at his feet. He was barefoot. Of course his shoes were soaking wet. He was pulling a thread from the hem of his smock and used the scissors to cut off a length of about eighteen inches and placed it in a pot of water boiling on the stove. He then pulled down the lapel of his collar and extracted a small silver needle from the seam and placed it in the pot with the thread.

Feeling Eve's eyes on him, he smiled as he said, "Needs must."

Eve felt a strangeness sweep over her. This was the first time she had really seen his eyes—the blood was tingling in her cheeks, her skin felt electric—the reaction he invoked in her was unreal. Again she had a sense of being outside of herself, of being an observer looking on from the outside. His eyes were jet black with ice blue irises, they were unnerving. She sipped her tea feeling the warmth course through her veins, the taste of salt slowly clearing from her mouth as the sweet brew did its work.

She followed his movements in the mirror as he rolled up the sleeves of his smock above his elbows and started to lather his hands and arms in the sink with washing up liquid, sluicing them off with water from the plastic jeroboam.

He poured some hot water into another pot, tested the tempera-

Dressing for God

ture, added some cold, satisfied, he then pulled on the clear surgical gloves; wordlessly knelt on the floor beside Noah and using the damp cotton wool started cleaning his head wound. He gently wiped away the crusted blood from the hair line and forehead and used the scissors to trim back his eyebrow. Noah had an L-shaped scalp wound, about three inches by two inches, running from the eye up to the hairline and then across to a point in the centre of his forehead.

Eve watched intently, wondering why he was so quiet and yet hesitant of interrupting his concentration. He picked up the needle and thread out of the pot on the stove. Holding the needle close to the light he threaded the navy thread through the bottom centre of the needle. Eve had never seen a needle like it before. It was about an inch long, slightly convex and had a small groove at the top side. It was pointed at each end. He carefully put a small knot in the thread and pulled it secure, the knot recessed in the concave recess. He then put Vaseline on the thread, giving it a slight waxy finish. Starting at Noah's eyebrow he gathered the skin flaps together using two fingers of his left hand and with the needle in his right hand started sewing with the two pointed needle; pushing the needle fully through the folds of skin and then immediately back with the opposite pointed end of the needle making what looked like a hemming stitch. He finished with a double stitch and snipped off the thread. He handed Eve the needle then dabbed antiseptic lotion on the gash, applied a wound dressing and bandaged him, securing it with two plasters.

The man rose to his feet pulling off the gloves, "That will do until he gets to a hospital, now let's get him lying on his side."

Together they made Noah as comfortable as they could, head on the pillow, wrapped in double blankets, the room warm now from the heat of the stove.

He looked at Eve and asked, "Why don't you get yourself some shut eye, you must be exhausted," indicating the top bunk with the coveralls and other blankets. "I'll be next door if you need me." He gave Eve a soft smile and quietly left the cabin.

Eve stripped off the coverall and then her wetsuit, red circles on her wrists and neck, and wearing just her white Lycra bodysuit climbed onto the bunk, wrapped tight in the grey woollen blankets and was asleep within moments of her head touching the pillow. Adam on her mind, "What must he be thinking?"

Chapter 14

No Answer

Adam was sitting in the bar of Bonds Restaurant in the Threadneedle Hotel just around the corner from Lloyds in Lime Street, waiting for Giles Longman to join him for dinner. Giles was the actuary for the syndicate Adam had been contracted to and he'd promised a memorable dinner to celebrate the success of their claim rebuttal. It was his suggestion that Adam stay here instead of the London Bridge Hotel and Adam was glad of the choice. It had a refined, small hotel feeling to it and he'd read good reviews of the chef's cooking. However, he was beginning to get quite anxious that none of his calls to either Noah or Eve had been answered and he'd just sent another SMS to Eve again when Giles arrived.

They had finished a wonderful starter of Ravioli of Lobster and Armagnac Bisque when Adam asked to be excused to make an urgent call. It was past eight thirty and still no call back or message from Noah or Eve. Adam had called Sheila at her home outside Sneem and asked her to go to the house and check if the cars were still there. His main course had just been served when his phone vibrated in his pocket and again he excused himself to take the call in the bar.

"Mr. Adam, is that you?"

"Yes Sheila, go ahead."

"Both cars are here and no one's at home. The house and cottage are all locked up. I tried Mr. Noah's car; it was open and his phone is on the passenger seat and the fog is as thick as hay here. Oh my God, Mr. Adam, whatever can have happened to them?"

"Oh Jesus, Sheila; I don't know. Eve's phone doesn't answer either. Listen thanks for that, but I better go and call the garda and the Coast Guard."

Dressing for God

"OK then Mr. Adam, do you have their number?"

"I have Sheila, thanks. Look, I'll be in touch as soon as I know anything."

"Let me know if there's aught I can do, won't you? OK then, bye, bye, bye."

Adam sat quietly trying to get a plan together in his mind. He looked up the Sneem Garda Station in his mobile directory and rang through. The call was diverted to a different station.

"This is Cahersiveen Garda Station, Garda O'Sullivan speaking and what can I do for you this fine evening?"

Adam quickly explained that he was in London. His friend and his assistant had sailed from Sneem some time that morning to pick up a boat from McCarthy's in Valentia and there was no sign of them and they weren't replying to his calls. He was worried sick.

"If you can give me the details sir, I'll get on to the Coast Guard right away."

Adam gave him a brief description: red wooden hull, carvel built, twenty three foot boat, inboard diesel, small half cabin, no life raft but yes it had life vests and pyrotechnics and a life-ring. No, it didn't have a radio beacon as far as he knew. Yes it was surveyed and insured.

"Am I sure they had actually sailed from Sneem? Yes, I spoke with my assistant just before they set out."

"And when was that sir?"

"Around eight thirty this morning– I think they planned on leaving around ten."

"And did they notify anyone of their trip?"

"I don't know."

"Thank you for that sir. Now McCarthy Marine you say in Valentia?"

"Yes, he was picking up a new boat."

"OK then sir, leave it to me and I'll do some checking. 'Tis fierce foggy outside; maybe they got caught in it and are anchored up waiting for it to clear. Did they have radar?"

"No."

"Aw well, maybe that's it then. Did they have an anchor?"

"Yes, I'm sure they did."

"OK, you can be contacted on this number Mr. King?"

"Yes—it's my mobile."

"Grand—thanks—I'll get back to you. Take it easy now."

Adam returned to the table where Giles had finished his main course. "I sent yours back to keep warm, shall I ask for it now?"

"I'm really sorry, Giles, I just don't have an appetite any more. My friends are missing at sea and I'm waiting for the garda to get back to me. I'm really worried that something awful has happened to them," Adam took a deep draught of his wine.

"Oh dear me that's terrible Adam. I'm so sorry to hear that. Is there anything I can do to help?"

"Thanks Giles. I think I'd better go to my room and wait for the calls. I'm on the nine thirty flight to Cork in the morning."

"Isn't there an earlier one from Stansted to Kerry?"

"By God, you're right, there's the six forty-five. My car's in Cork but I can hire one in Kerry, listen forgive me." He rose from the table. "I have to get my act together. Giles I'm so sorry to ruin the dinner like this."

"Not at all Adam, away you go and I'll keep my fingers crossed for you."

Adam ordered a cab for three thirty in the morning and then logged on to Ryanair and booked a one-way ticket to Kerry with a hire car on arrival.

His phone rang as he finished his booking, "Mr. Adam King please."

"This is Adam King."

"Good evening Mr. King, this is the Irish Coast Guard here on Valentia Island. Officer Fitzgerald speaking sir, we understand you've reported a missing boat to Cahersiveen garda."

"Yes the *D'Ark Rosaleen*, with Noah Mahon and Eve McQueen on board."

Adam repeated all the details again and then asked if any contact had been made with McCarthy Marine.

"Yes sir. The garda spoke with Mr. McCarthy and he confirms that they were expecting a call from Mr. Mahon in the afternoon. Mr. McCarthy understood that Mr. Mahon would give him two hours notice of arrival."

"No sir, he never received any call. He thought maybe he hadn't set out due to the fog. I believe the fog set in early afternoon sir."

Dressing for God

"Yes sir, two hours at say eight knots would put the boat in a radius of around sixteen miles or so from Portmagee."

"Did the boat have VHF radio?"

"Yes a hand portable set; a VICOM, I believe."

"No, it didn't have a life raft."

"Right sir, well we must make sure we have all the information before we press the button."

"Yes sir, I will be contacting the local lifeboat co-ordinator in Knightstown directly and we will start transmitting a Securite PAN message to all shipping in the area."

"Are you the next of kin sir?"

"Well if you just stay on the line sir, my colleague will take some details from you and I will get the lifeboat alerted."

"Thank you sir, stand by please."

Chapter 15

The Play of Life

Eve swam effortlessly to the surface, the sunlight streaming through a crystal-pure sea that was a perfect temperature, bubbles of air streaming out behind her, she broke surface into the sunlight swallowing a big gulp of air and then feeling the woollen blankets rough against her face slowly opened her eyes. The oil lamp was flickering on the countertop, a gentle hiss of gas from the oven warming the room and Noah lying on his side on the floor was making small snoring noises. She closed her eyes reliving the experience of yesterday. It felt so very strange, the sinking of the boat, the long swim ashore pushing and pulling Noah, the cold and exhaustion and the man carrying Noah, and the damn fog and now I'm here, in this hut, "Oh Dear God above."

Eve blinked, "Bathroom—I need to go," she leant over the edge of the bunk, saw Noah quiet and breathing easily. "Ah thanks be to God, he seems OK." She lowered herself out of the bunk and stood there trying to make sense of her situation. Holding the blue coverall up against herself measuring its fit—way too big- but stepped into it anyway, rolled the cuffs up then slipped into her trainers, still soggy wet, she gathered up her wet clothes and went outside.

Eve could barely see six feet ahead of her. It was like being in the middle of a dense cloud; it was wet, dank, cold and scary. The flash of the lighthouse cut a dim orange yellow swathe in the fog above her, bouncing off the rock face and then flashing again every few seconds, it was so quiet. Not a bird call—just the shushing sea shoving against the cliffs, the sounds muffled in the dense fog. She checked her watch, ten after three, "What day is it?" she thought, "It must be Friday."

Dressing for God

Pushing open the door of the adjoining cabin, the lock hanging loose, another oil lamp flickering on the countertop, the oven door open, the gas hissing warmth into the room but no one there, the bunks empty. Eve dropped the wet clothes on the floor and turned to leave looking for the toilet when she heard the voice in the dark, "Are you all right?"

He was seated cross legged on the floor behind the door, hidden in its shadow. His hands were resting on his knees, palms up, forefingers and thumbs lightly touching.

Eve gave a small gasp, her hands up to her mouth, exhaled. "Oh I'm sorry I didn't see you there. You surprised me. Yeah I'm fine, thanks, just looking for a bathroom."

He nodded, "Yes, it's the last cabin down, the doors open, take the light with you." He pointed at the Tilley lamp.

Eve returned some minutes later. A kettle of water was coming to the boil on the stove, two mugs waiting on the counter; the man sitting cross-legged as before behind the door. Noah's and her clothes were draped over two chairs in front of the oven door, steam starting to rise from them already. Eve held the lamp up to see him better.

"I don't know your name," she said. "I'm Eve. How can I ever thank you for your help, I can't imagine what would have happened if you hadn't of turned up."

"I'm happy to help Eve. I just happened to be passing and heard your call. My name is A'Haon."

"Ahane?" she asked, "Is that how you pronounce it?"

"That's it, it's spelled A'Haon—it's Gaelic. Say, why don't you wet the tea there and join me? There's powdered milk if you want it. I'll have mine black, no sugar please."

Eve made the tea and passed him his mug then looked around for somewhere to sit. He reached up, took a pillow from the bunk and placed it on the floor beside him "Here take a pew."

Eve gratefully eased her body back against the wall and sat down.

"And how is your friend, still sleeping OK?" he asked.

"I'm really worried about his losing consciousness. Is there any way we can get him to a hospital? I saw the helipad on the way here; do you have a phone with you by any chance?"

"A phone? No I'm sorry." Eve noticed him smile at the question. "You'll have to wait until the fog clears I'm afraid. Sure there'll be all sorts of people out looking for you as soon as it's lifted—boats, helicopters, the lot."

She thought about this as she took a deep drink of the tea, grateful for the heat of the mug grasped in both hands.

"What are you doing here?" she asked, the question blurting out unconsciously.

"Well, truth to tell, I was here finishing off a small quest on the island when I heard you call." He gestured with his hand pointing upwards, "I'm staying up top."

"In the beehive huts?"

"Yes."

"But I thought they were all closed until the summer...what is it you do?" Eve asked directly.

"What is it I do?" he repeated, "I suppose you could call me..." he hesitated momentarily, "a spiritual archaeologist." His eyebrow raised, questioning her understanding.

"A spiritual archaeologist," She asked frowning. "What on earth is that?"

"What on earth indeed, I like that, a good turn of phrase." He let out a little laugh. "I suppose you could say that where archaeology deals with the study of the past through material remains—well my work is all about unearthing memories of the past and merging them with the present." He raised his eyes, head turned, watching for Eve's reaction to his answer.

Eve was sitting arms crossed tightly under her breast, a tight look on her face, a confused expression in her eyes. She shook her head irritably, "No, I don't get it, I'm sorry," a challenging tone in her voice. "What exactly are you doing here now?" she asked pointedly.

Her challenge did not go unnoticed. A'Haon replied in a gentle but firm voice. "The island is not as empty as you might think it is Eve. Skellig Michael is a sanctuary of memories from a host of special souls who lived here in other times. I work in uncovering these lost energies, getting them to surface. You could say that I'm a sort of mister in-between helping to dissolve them." He watched as she digested his explanation.

"Is this some sort of religious rite; are you a monk of some kind?" Her tone gentler now, as her belligerence faded.

Dressing for God

He gave Eve a glowing smile, eyes twinkling with humour. "Ah no Eve, I'm not a monk. I'm more of a spiritual archivist for my boss, who himself works for the main architect. So there you have it."

The note of finality in his explanation cut off further questions. Eve sat there mystified, her hands rubbing her thighs in the dim light as the blue hissing flame from the oven warmed the room.

"And" he paused, using the silence like a curtain being drawn back, "if I may also ask you the same question, just what exactly are *you* doing here on Skellig Michael?"

Eve was caught off guard by the question, her mouth working in embarrassment, she swallowed hard. She rubbed her eyes then drew her fingers down her face, held her hands palms together; chin resting on her fingertips looked up, "I'm sorry A'Haon, I must have sounded very rude, please forgive me, I'm still upset." Her breath was coming fast now and she stopped to take a drink of tea before continuing. "Our boat sank suddenly. It was around midday and I was in the water swimming here for, oh it must have been three or four hours when you found us. I can never thank you enough for what you did."

"That's quite all right Eve, you have absolutely nothing to apologise for. In fact you should be very proud for saving your friends life, for surely he would have drowned were it not for you getting him ashore. I was interested in where you were coming from and what were you doing here in the first place?"

Eve described working with a writer named Adam King who was in London on business or he'd have been with them yesterday. Told how she and Noah were en route to Valentia to get Noah's new boat and why they'd diverted for a close-up of Skelligs, "And that's it really." She shrugged, wondering if he was satisfied with the explanation.

He gave her an interested look, "And what is this book of yours about Eve?"

"Oh it's not my book A'Haon, It's Adam's book, I'm only the hired help; his sounding board as he calls me." Smiling cheekily, she added, "I just get to argue with him."

This drew a warm laugh. "OK then and what is it he's writing, or is that confidential?"

"No, I don't think it's confidential, I mean, he wants to share it with the public. It's about a character called Captain John who is sailing across the inner seas of life, or the "mind-field" as Adam calls it, and then he's to share all the lessons he's learned about how life works when he reaches the other side.... He wants to explain the meaning of life."

A'Haon had merriment in his eyes, "Well let's hope Captain John's boat doesn't sink under *him* before he gets into port." Eve straightened upright at the memory of Rosaleen sinking and shot a sharp look at Ahaon.

He continued, "Tell me this Eve," He folded his arms loosely, "Do you really believe Adam can sail his Captain John home safely in one piece?"

Without hesitation, she answered, "Oh yes, I have no doubt at all. He'll get there all right"

"So answer me this, if you can; has this Adam person actually mastered the unseen inner seas himself or is he relying only on what he has read in books? Can you tell me that?"

Eve felt a churning in her stomach, this was personal. Surely Adam's problems with Captain John were not hers to discuss with a stranger. "I think Adam still has a few details to sort out but he's a captain himself so I'm sure he knows what he's at." She answered, exuding a confidence she wasn't a hundred percent sure of.

He ruminated on this for several seconds then looking up he moved to within inches from her face, his jet black eyes studied her intensely. She felt him reading her deepest thoughts. She placed her hand over her breast feeling the blood pounding in her veins, her breath suddenly hurried, she gasped slightly and drew back from his stare.

Then his attitude changed visibly and he brightened up, "That's all right Eve, I think I have the picture now, thank you."

He beamed a smile at her. "Maybe we can help your Captain John navigate into the unknown, share a little local know-how with him; make sure he knows the ropes as the ancient mariner might say."

He straightened, ebony eyes shiny, a feeling of excitement bristling in the room as he got to his feet in a flowing effortless movement, like a cobra rising from a fakir's basket she thought. He opened the overhead cupboard and withdrew a pink A4 notebook and blue Biro pen.

"Here," he said, passing them over. "Take these; you might want to make some notes for later. Now if you'll excuse me for a few minutes, I have a small errand to see to and sure I'll check on our friend next door while I'm out. You just make yourself comfortable."

Dressing for God

He pulled the door shut behind him as Eve sat looking at the book, Printed by the Irish Stationery Office. Site Architect's Logbook.

It was brand new, no entries. She opened the book, looked at the empty page, recalled the old phrase, that "paper never refuses ink", then wrote the words that were still lingering in her mind, Let's hope Captain John's boat doesn't sink under him. She underlined it, visualised Adam's Captain John floundering in a small yellow life raft in the middle of an empty ocean, drifting aimlessly. Her thoughts on what this stranger just asked.

"Adam was in real difficulty getting *My Trust* cleared into port. He admitted there was something stopping him that he couldn't put his finger on. Did he really know enough to write about this inner journey or was he just winging it? Was he navigating on dead reckoning and trust, hoping for the best? Is this really happening?" Eve finished off the tea and sat thinking of Adam and his book.

"My list! What was on the list I started?" Eve put her head in her hands and tried to recall the points she'd wanted to explore with Adam. It was all so long ago. Then making a start, she wrote some bullet points on the page.

- Reincarnation
- Karma — where does it fit — past lives
- What else????

Wearily leaning back against the wall, Eve saw her reflection in the window; a bedraggled figure clad in a blue coverall that swamped her size ten frame, notebook propped on her knees. She was sitting like this watching, as A'Haon appeared standing beside her in the open doorway.

He looked down at her, sitting pen in hand, "Ah, you've been writing already?"

Eve nodded. "Yes it was what you said earlier, about the boat sinking under Captain John, it certainly got me thinking." She stood up and moved over to the stove, warming her hands, turning the clothes.

"Did you check on Noah? Is he all right?"

"Yes I checked on him, he looks OK. He's still sleeping and looks peaceful enough."

"Thank you for helping us A'Haon. Can I get you some more tea?"
"Tea? Yes please, that'll be nice."

They were sitting on the floor, mugs of tea before them, neither speaking for several minutes, sharing the silence easily. Eve was staring at the book in her lap. A'Haon was again sitting lotus fashion, hands folded lightly on his knees, eyes closed, breathing imperceptibly. It was Eve who eventually spoke, her voice quite.

"I was thinking of what you said about helping Adam, asking if he'd sailed across these seas before. Well to be honest A'Haon, I think maybe he is stuck in a fog bank or something and can't get John into port. I'm sure he'd love some help. That's really why he hired me, to try to find out." her voice trailed off.

A'Haon inclined his head, a look of kindness spreading across his face, "Eve, there is a big truth in life and it's called acceptance. One can *only* accept when one is ready to receive. Now do you believe Adam is ready to accept guidance because it sounds to me that the fog he's stuck in is of his own making and nobody else's."

Eve raised her head and looked him in the eye. "He'd welcome guidance A'Haon, I'm sure of it. He just wants to learn and share his lessons. He really does love learning about life."

"Aye a lot of folk seem to enjoy learning the hard way too. OK, so where do you think he may be caught; has he snagged some underwater obstacle without his knowing it? Is it dragging an anchor from his past that he hasn't identified yet? Did he give you any clues?"

"He asked me to make a list of things that I didn't fully understand. We were going to talk about them when he returned. I know past lives was a big subject for me—that and karma. But I'm pretty sure if Adam knew what was holding him up he'd do something about clearing it."

"Past lives indeed, what a great subject. Do you remember Shakespeare's *As you like it*?" Ahaon recited the words:

> All the world's a stage
> And all the men and women merely players;
> They have their exits and their entrances,
> And one man in his time plays many parts,
> His acts being seven ages.

Dressing for God

"Yes." Eve answered slowly, "I studied it in college."

A'Haon went to the small wardrobe in the corner of the hut, opened the door and picked out a wire coat hanger which he held in front of Eve.

"So let's imagine Eve that we hang your old past-life costumes all together in this wardrobe. Each past life in there hanging on its own hanger—and you could possibly have lived hundreds of lives—hundreds of old body costumes hanging in the wardrobe of your past."

"It'd need to be a bigger locker than that then, wouldn't it?"

"Well no, not really. You see you just need the one hanger for the latest body you're occupying. It's a bit like the rings in a tree stump. You've seen how each year's growth produces a ring—100 years of growth in a tree gives 100 rings from the centre of the trunk out to the bark. Well it's the same for the soul; each successive life builds on the previous life's experience. Soul is the centre of who you are being. Each time you leave life you get rid of the costume or body you were playing life in and next time back you get a new body costume for the new part you're acting in."

"So are my past lives not that important to remember?"

"Can I have your book for a moment please?" Eve handed it to him and he quickly sketched the hanger draped with a row of past life bodies suspended on it.

"OK, on the hanger we'll drape all the past lives, all the old body costumes we used, a sort of invisible trail of your past. Can you follow this?"

"Yes I see that, but what happens at the end of each life act?"

"As the actor exits stage left, into the wings, so to speak, its performance is appraised and in most cases it's given a chance to rest and recuperate and prepare itself ready for the next scene in the play of life."

A'Haon handed Eve the sketch. "I'm making it as simplistic as I can. Every soul is evolving—we each are the result of everything we ever thought, said or acted. We move in an intelligent energy field of life and as we exit we leave our impression on life and it leaves its impressions on us. We generate memories Eve and memories make us who we are today. It's really as simple as that."

Eve pointed to the sketch where he had sketched a balloon shape under the heading of Unconscious Feelings and asked "What are these?"

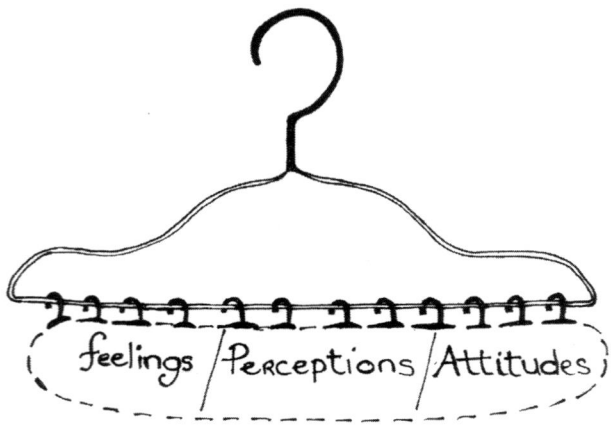

"They are the mix of who Eve is at any single moment—they are the aggregate of all your feelings, perceptions and attitudes."

He continued, "Every time you meet a situation in life, *several things happen almost simultaneously*. Firstly you ask yourself unconsciously, do I recognise this situation from anywhere—Yes or No?"

"And then you simultaneously ask the question—is my memory of this situation or event associated with pain or pleasure or is it neutral?"

"And then you asks the question, and just what does my memory have to say about this situation? And instantly your consciousness sends back its reaction by way of a chemical release from the brain and you experience this as feelings. This is your unconscious answer to your conscious mind from your very own memory bank."

Eve's face was bright with comprehension.

"It's how your consciousness operates; it's the shape of your own electromagnetic shell and it's transmitting away saying, I like this and I don't like that. It's you in your play of *As You like It.*"

"Are you saying that I bring old attitudes with me from one life to the next, is that it?"

"Yes, attitudes shape your life and beliefs shape your attitudes." A'Haon raised his hand up in a little twirling action as if he was swizzling the air.

"So when I incarnate I'm pre-selected to experience a life according to my past lives, is that it?" Eve asked quietly.

"Yes. Soul pre-agrees to the conditions of a coming life, and every soul's atmosphere resonates with the race, gender, country, town, and

Dressing for God

religion for its next life experience. However, once soul is delivered to earth, the memory of this agreement is gone and the journey resumes in the dark, as it were."

"But wouldn't it be easier if we all knew what we agreed to do here this time around instead of being in the dark?" Eve asked.

A'Haon smiled at the question. "But, Eve, we do know at one level, exactly what our mission is, the point of living is to break through the fog of mind and to remember who we truly are at source."

"And this soul atmosphere dictates to whom we are born, is that right?"

"Yes, incarnation is not a lottery of chance. Each soul arrives exactly where it deserves to be. Each lifetime is designed to give soul the best stepping-off point for its journey home. The circumstances of any life, allow soul to learn its own truth and evolve into its next state of consciousness."

"So what is it then, that makes this process work?"

"Beliefs Eve! Beliefs are what define behaviour. If soul has attachments to a limiting belief—say a man feels unworthy of wealth and robs and steals as a way of life—well, until that belief is changed to reflect the opposite, it will continue to attract more of what its resonating. Understand Eve, it's not the deed that draws karma to soul—it's the thought behind the deed."

"I never realized that life was so precise, so detailed."

He smiled. "Change your beliefs and you change what you are attracting into your experience and your soul atmosphere will reflect accordingly. Are you familiar with karma?" he asked kindly.

Eve sitting quietly composed replied, "Well there are lots of things I thought I understood before tonight and I've found out differently; so I'll say I know a teeny bit about karma but I'm open to learn more."

"Well a quick summary then of what it is and what it is not. There are many misconceptions about karma" he continued, of prime importance is to understand that God never made a rule to punish one and reward the other. And the law of karma is not about punishment, judgement, or failure and there's neither negative karma nor positive karma. There is only experience." He stressed the word *experience*.

Eve was surprised to see him get so animated. "Believe me, when I say that thought is the very basis of all creation. Yes Eve, how you think creates your own experience, are you clear on this?"

"Yes," she answered in a hushed voice.

"Then you understand," he continued quietly, "That thoughts are things and that thought precedes every single thing in life. Everything is born from thought. And just as the cart follows the horse, so energy follows thought. Everything you see in the world of matter is a result of thought. It's a world of cause and effect and if our thoughts result in causing suffering, then we'll experience suffering in return."

"I can go along with that, so tell me then, what is the best attitude to adopt, to stay clear of wrong thinking?"

"Embrace your own divinity Eve. Learn to love yourself first and then see the divinity in everyone else…You're using the law of attraction all of the time. It doesn't matter how many negative thoughts you've had in the past, it is the thoughts you're thinking now that have the power and *this is why living in the NOW moment is so important.*"

He looked enquiringly at her to see if his point had been made and then he continued softly.

"Every experience, every object, every person in your life is there because you, Eve, attracted them into your space. There are no exceptions to the rule. There are no fluke meetings, no coincidences, no accidents; nothing is stopping you from having what you want. You create ALL of your own experiences for YOU alone. You don't create just some of it, or most of it, but all of it—without exception. And you do this both consciously and unconsciously."

Eve looked up, "You said there are no coincidences in life?"

"Yes I did say that. There are no coincidences in life but yes, we have synchronicities. And isn't synchronicity about observing the interconnected universe we live in? Synchronicity is just another aspect of the law of cause and effect in action."

Eve's mind tried to recall the definition she'd looked up on the net, something about, 'when you ask a question the answer is there'.

A'Haon continued speaking. "The universe is totally neutral; it never judges your decisions. Does water make a judgement or refuse to assume a shape when it's poured into an ice cube mould? No, it does not and neither does the spirit of energy; it moulds to your thoughts regardless of whether it hurts you or pleases you. It all depends on what you think into it, what it gives back to you."

"So I should only think positive thoughts to get positive results—it's not that easy is it?"

Dressing for God

"It's a matter of practise. If you want something in your life and you do nothing but think of the LACK of that thing, then the universe will prove you right and deliver exactly that—more lack. That's the way the law works." He smiled in the dim light. "Isn't it ironic that this law proves everyone successful, think failure, achieve failure, thing success to achieve success; if only this simple truth were better understood." He exhaled deeply and gave Eve a resigned looking smile.

Eve replied, "I think I'm getting it, think lack, get lack."

"Yes, this universal energy force doesn't understand the difference between want and don't want or like and don't like; it only follows thought. I can see that you're flagging there Eve. I hope I haven't overdone it; why don't you try get some sleep."

"I am tired but I don't think I can sleep, there are too many things going on in my head."

He stood and padded in his bare feet to the open door. The fog was as dense as ever. He looked back at Eve, "See if your shoes are dry enough and we'll take a walk up to the lighthouse, help get the circulation going."

Chapter 16

Act As If

She slipped on her damp trainers and they walked slowly along the path hugging the wall towards the source of the flashing beacon: flash, one, two, three flash, one, two, three flash, counting the sequence with each pace forward—fifteen paces, fifteen seconds. The air was dank, redolent with seaweed, the only sound a low pulsing breaking of the sea rolling on the rocks below as they slowly made their way along the pathway. They passed a set of grey cabins on their right. She could just read the OPW stencilled on the door, "The huts for the guides," he said. "I've checked them out, no radio." The visibility was about twenty feet she reckoned, using Ahaon's height as a reference. He stopped and pointed up at a large battery of solar panels mounted on the cliff, fifty or so of them. "Power for the beacon," he said. "But they won't get much of a charge today."

The tall iron gates blocked their way into the lighthouse yard and bending down Eve saw where the padlock had been levered off its hasp. A'Haon with a wry smile pointed to a crowbar lying on the ground, "It just happened to be lying there when I came for the gas." Then he pushed the gate open wide and they entered the yard.

There was a single storey whitewashed storage shed on their left, a green painted window and door, then into a smaller yard where Eve saw a row of the water containers stacked against a wall with ten yellow Kosangas refills beside them.

The beacon was flashing atop the whitewashed circular lighthouse building, its green painted doors heavily padlocked; there was a small platform halfway up the outside wall with a ladder from there to the outside of the light itself. They explored the rest of the buildings in the courtyard, another set of bolted doors, "The lighthouse keeper's

Dressing for God

house," he said. "It's empty now. No one stays here anymore. Shall we go back and check on our friend?"

"Yeah, please, I'm getting really cold again."

They walked back to the huts and found Noah as they had left him. No change. Eve was beginning to fret about getting him to a hospital. A'Haon said he had to go up to his cell for an hour or so and would check back with her by and by.

"But surely you can't climb all the way up there in this fog."

"Ah, don't worry; I'm used to seeing in the dark," he said cryptically as he slipped out the door.

Eve returned to her bunk and gradually fell off to sleep wrapped tight in her blankets.

Waking up with a start, Eve slipped out of the bunk and checked the time, six forty.

"Is the bloody fog lifted yet?" Eve said out loud and stuck her head outside the door.

"No dammit, it's still as thick as ever." She filled the kettle, put it on to boil, wishing for a hit of coffee to kick-start her day. "I'll make do with the tea and be glad for it."

Eve stayed there warming her back to the oven, looking down at Noah lying supine, breathing easily. 'This is just too much. Shit, I must get help.'

Finishing her tea, she sat on the bunk with her eyes closed and started Adam's breathing exercise, visualising a big red SOS signal beaming out from the lighthouse—dit dit dit—dot dot dot—dit dit dit—the signal flashing out with each blip of the light, Help—Help—Help. She stayed like this, lost in thought for several minutes and then dropped down to the floor to tend to Noah.

Using a J Cloth and warm soapy water she gently washed his face and neck, speaking softly, hoping he could hear her calling him, a feeling of hopelessness beginning to gnaw at her, alone on this desolate island needing proper care. "This bloody fog… How can I get liquids into him, how long before we're found?" Questions were hitting her from all sides.

"How is he?" She hadn't heard him return. He was crouched down beside her, hands together, fingers entwined on his knees, a scent of the cold fog on his clothes, his tone cheery. Eve felt unable to answer, just shook her head in frustration, a deep sigh escaping her.

He took hold of Noah's wrist, counting silently, "Pulse is much better, I think he's coming round."

"Oh God I hope so, the fog looks as bad as ever."

"Well, actually it's not so thick at the top. The visibility is around 100 yards up there so with the grace of God, it'll clear when the sun has a chance to burn it off."

He placed his hand under her elbow, "Here let me help you up. I have a surprise for you."

"What? A helicopter?"

"No, food, let's go next door and I'll show you."

Eve, coverall discarded was now dressed in her almost dry jeans and shirt, watched A'Haon as he mixed flour, sugar, powdered milk and water, two small white eggs, added a pinch of salt then mixed it into a dough and kneaded it.

"What are those eggs?"

"Fulmars, they're the only birds that lay here this time of year."

He set the frying pan on the gas burner and added a drop of cooking oil then moulded the dough into the pan. "Griddle bread for breakfast."

He poked his finger into the soft dough.

"Do you see how malleable that is?"

"I do, I had forgotten all about food—I must say I'm hungry."

"What's the French word for pressure?" he asked from somewhere in left field.

"The French word for pressure?" She repeated, *"Pression."*

A'Haon picked up a fork and pressed in into the top of the dough cooking in the pan then removed it. "Do you see the impression that left on the bread mix?" Lifting the pan he held it under her nose.

"I do yes, so?"

"Well isn't that what we do when we form an idea; we make an *impression* on the mind and then when we keep a clear picture of what that idea is—then mind delivers its *expression* back to us." He seemed to be enjoying playing with the dough. "Pressure in, pressure back, impress, express; isn't life easy to understand?" he asked, shaking the pan to make sure the bread didn't stick to the bottom.

"Have you heard of thought-forms Eve?"

"Vaguely, aren't they those invisible shapes we make in the mind like the fork made in the dough?"

Dressing for God

The response elicited a laugh from A'Haon. "You're mostly right there. Yes they're invisible on the physical plane and yes they have shapes, so two out of three, well done."

"OK," he continued, "There are really three main types of thought-forms in our living space. Firstly we have the floating, vague kind. The leftover dross of a million other peoples old thoughts that we move through as we walk down the street and can pick up on, depending on our consciousness. And then there's the hovering ones attached to our subtle bodies which we create by our own thinking habits. And thirdly we have thought forms that we can send out to someone or something."

"So how do they actually take shape?" she enquired.

"Let's say you want to send love to a child. Once that thought is selected, the mind vibrates with it and because *like attracts like*—the elemental essence of the ethers form around it and shapes itself into a *live* cloud-like form of radiating energy. This thought-form can then be sent mentally to the child, where its vibrations pick up on it and the thought-form's energy merges with the child's own consciousness."

"I'm beginning to take my thoughts very seriously now."

"Indeed we are all shape shifters in our reality."

He placed a dinner plate on top of the pan, inverted it, and then slid the dough into the pan and set it back onto the heat. He turned to her saying,

"Have you heard the expression, there's that word expression again, to act as if?"

"Yes of course I have, but act as if what? Act as if there is no fog?"

"Precisely and how would that feel to you?"

"It would feel brilliant. There'd be lifeboats out looking for us, helicopters landing and we'd be rescued somehow."

"Exactly and how would YOU feel about that, if it happened now?"

"I'd feel grateful, relieved, really happy getting Noah to a hospital."

"So why not act as if it has already happened? If you can **know** it and **see** it and **be** it in your own mind—isn't that a de facto-done deal? So imagine that it has happened before it manifests; *feel* gratitude and *trust* that the rescue has happened. Energize that thought-form with feelings of deep thanks and relief. Banish your fears. Whenever a fear arises, look at it. Never be afraid to feel your fears because all fears evaporate in the light of love."

"Is it really that easy?" Eve asked, "To just sort of use my will and imagination to make it happen?"

"Use your will power *only* to stay focused on the direction of your desired end result Eve. It would be very presumptuous for any of us to think we could will a camel to pass through the eye of a needle, wouldn't it? Trust that your desired, perfect outcome is an undisputed reality. Imagine how the outcome really feels and avoid being prescriptive on how it should be delivered. Trust and faith Eve, they are the true carriers of miracles."

Eve ran her hand through her hair and then rubbed at her eyes feeling tiredness sap her attention. "There is just so much to take in," she thought, "And I am so tired."

"This bread smells done," he said sliding it onto a plate. "Let's get the kettle on for tea."

London 0600

Adam was in the departure lounge in Stansted—pacing endlessly up and down the waiting area; the 0645 Ryanair flight 703 to Kerry was boarding. His last call to the Coast Guard confirmed that the Valentia lifeboat was out doing a box search starting in Portmagee and was tracing back the probable route the Rosaleen might have taken from Oyster Bed Pier—staying as close inshore as possible—but the visibility was still bad and there was nothing to report so far. The Caherdaniel Inshore Rescue Boat was on standby waiting for first light to join the search. Coastal search parties would start walking the cliffs around Lambs Head as soon as daylight allowed—and he was assured that the helicopter from Shannon would be airborne as soon as the pilots had 500 metres of visibility. "Keep your fingers crossed," the Coast Guard said. Adam asked for a call as soon as they knew anything—good or bad.

"Will do sir, stay positive. Have a good flight sir."

Chapter 17

Me, Myself and I

They were sitting quietly together sipping tea and chewing on the doughy bread,

"Tell me then,' he leaned forward. "I spoke briefly earlier about acceptance, but tell me, what does self acceptance mean to you?"

"I haven't really thought about it." Eve pondered for a moment before asking "Self acceptance, is it looking in the mirror and liking what I see?"

"Yes," replied A'Haon. "It's about accepting gratefully everything in your life as it is—including everything about you, yourself."

"And I'm expected to say thank you in accepting where I am now? Our boat just sank in the middle of the Atlantic, my friend is comatose and I'm stuck here on this rock eating dry bread talking semantics with a stranger who appeared out of the blue. Is that right?"

"Well yes, actually that is right. You see, you can only change the outer conditions of life by changing the inner cause. The outer is the expressed effect from the inner so you must change the inner beliefs and then the outer conditions reflect that change."

"Yeah—that's not the first time I heard of that. My friend told me a story of someone who was looking in the mirror and she didn't like the look of her hair, so she tried to comb the hair in the mirror instead of on her head."

A'Haon chuckled with delight standing beside the window. He motioned for Eve to join him. "Watch this," he put his mouth close to the glass and hawed, causing a film of condensation to blur the reflection.

"You do it," he said. Eve hawed, causing more condensation.

"Have you ever considered how sacred your very breath is?"

"I know it's vital, I can't live without it and I suppose I do take it for granted."

"Your breath is your life force. When you stop breathing you leave this plane of existence, your body's shell reverts to dust and your light moves on. You remember that?"

"I'm not likely to forget it."

"You are a spiritual being of light living in a body. And just as the fog has closed in on the lighthouse and stopped its purpose temporarily, so does the mental plaque of old memories envelope the human body and shroud the light of soul. Can you see that now?"

"Yes, sort of, I suppose. I'm still a bit confused at who it is I really am. Am I soul or myself or something in between?"

"You are all of them. Here," he stretched out his hand to Eve, "let me draw it for you."

Eve flicked open the notebook and handed it to him.

"Thank you." He took the pen in hand and started drawing, "Look, here's the lighthouse with the beacon with all those millions of candela power shining brightly out into the universe." He quickly sketched a lighthouse perched on the cliffs on the island.

"And now let me surround the light house with a dense atmosphere of thick fog so the light becomes invisible." His pen drew concentric squiggles of lines totally encircling the lighthouse and extending all around. His face was etched in a humorous smile, "And here's the blinding foggy atmosphere where we can neither see in nor out. The light is still powering away but the fog has blinded it."

He looked at Eve and then wrote the word ME outside the fog and then the word My Self in the middle of the fog pattern and lastly wrote on the column of the lighthouse itself, the letter I.

Eve asked, "Is that a figure 1 or is it I?"

He let a small chuckle escape. "Well, let's just say for now, that it's I as in I Am, but your question is a most important one Eve."

A'Haon paused and fixed her with an intense look before he continued. "When you understand what is meant by the saying 'I am the whole of one' then indeed Eve, you will have cracked a mighty riddle of the universe."

Eve repeated, "I am the whole of one" and then asked, "Are you saying that I am my own lighthouse, is that it?"

Dressing for God

A look of satisfaction settled on his face. "Yes indeed. Very good, that's part of the picture, because when you say I am, you are saying, I am this spark of the one eternal light that's housed in the lighthouse of my body."

He pointed into the swirl of fog surrounding the light, "And when you talk of that part of you as my self, then you're in this foggy energy pattern created by your present and previous life experiences. That's the shape pattern of your unconscious memory box, all the accumulated attitudes that attract to you the experiences that form your present life conditions." He moved his pen outside the foggy atmosphere pointing at the word 'Me' – and this 'Me', is how you see yourself now and is the outer expression of the person you are being."

Eve took the proffered book in her hands and sat silently chewing gently on her lower lip, absorbing what he had explained.

"So how do I dissolve this fog?" she asked looking up. "How can I break down the patterns of my past lives, and well, see the light?"

A'Haon stretched out his hand for the book, "I left out one little detail." He took the book from Eve and drew a faint line through the centre of the lighthouse extending upwards into space, way above the fog pattern. "There, that will suffice," and handed it back to Eve who sat looking at it.

"And this is what?"

"That's the antenna link to home base in the fifth dimension. That's your link to the other side—to your higher self—that's your way out of the fog you have landed yourself in. You must break into the lighthouse of your own self and let your light shine true. Ask your higher self to be your messenger to the one from whom you evolved and ask for the blinds to be removed, for the windows to be cleaned, for the memory patterns to be erased. Forgiveness, repentance, gratitude and love, they're the only cleaning agents for the dirty windows of your own lighthouse."

Eve was looking nonplussed at the sketch, shaking her head trying to comprehend the full meaning of his words.

"So, what exactly should I do? How do I make it work for me?"

"Firstly, it is necessary that you desire to discover who it is you really are. You must want to realize your own spark of divinity hidden beneath the accumulations of the fears and doubts and pain of your past and current life experiences. Nobody can do this for you. No one can force you to do this. This is your own voyage of self discovery. This is why you come into existence, so you can realize your destiny and return home enlightened."

Eve contemplated on the sketch for several moments. A glimmer of realization occurred to her, "I'm beginning to see it now, I think. Is it, this little me on the outside—this outer personality who thinks it is separate from the 'I' of my inner self? And it's all my inherited beliefs and memory patterns that are blocking my ability to see the light of who it is 'I' really am... is that it?"

A'Haon held his hands out wide then clapped them together softly, "I believe you are seeing the light Eve. Well done."

She looked up and smiled at him. "There is one thing though; how do I get in touch with my higher self to get this window cleaning thing organized?"

"As soon as you consciously speak to your higher self, it will hear you. You can call it whatever name you want, my dear higher self, or my dear one within. It instantly hears your call, your antenna link is always tuned to the frequency of the divine; all you have to do is stop and connect. I Love You is my own call sign and you can try that as a failsafe."

"I love you?" Eve asked.

"Yes; unconditionally. Ask your higher self to bring your cleaning request upstairs to the Creator on your behalf. As I said, you have no idea what shape your unconscious self is in. You have no clear idea of what you were responsible for in all your many previous lifetimes, but one thing you can be sure of and that is that you have had interactions with many, many other souls. Each one of these souls is just like you, they each are experiencing new lifetimes here also. So try to accept total responsibility for everything that is present in your life now without any reservations. When you can fully understand this, then you can begin to apply it in your life and prove it for yourself, can't you?"

"Yes, yes, thank you. I'm beginning to see it."

"Good. The next step is to feel repentance. There is no way you could possibly understand the root cause of whatever memory pattern is causing your blocked vision and stopping your light from shining true, but as long as your desire is to face the truth, and you are genuinely sorry for whatever you may have caused, then this request will be processed and the energy patterns will begin to dissolve for you."

"And this is where the gratitude comes in?" Eve said. "The windows get cleaned and you sing with happiness and thanks for the... can I say enlightenment?"

"Exactly, which brings you back full circle, saying I love you again and again, and another round of window cleaning starts, and more blinds are removed as the consciousness responds to your actions, and instead of experiencing the rewind of old memories playing in your life, you can now access creative inspiration of a higher level of consciousness and you can start performing your own miracles."

"This is amazing." Eve said. "I don't know how to thank you."

"I am pleased to have been of assistance Eve and now it is very much up to you how you use this knowledge."

He walked towards the door, looked out and then turned back into the room.

"Eve, do try to remember that you are perfect. That was how you were created in the first instance. You are a magnificent child of God. Then try to remember that every other being on the planet is also a magnificent child of God. And then understand that whatever you may feel—whatever emotion may stir within you when you are in another's presence, that what you sense and feel about any other being is but a reflection of that condition within yourself. The trick of life is to see everyone as perfect but you necessarily must start with yourself. Love yourself for your own divinity and then acknowledge the perfection in everyone else."

Eve stood up, left arm crossed under her breasts, her right hand cupping her chin.

"Thank you A'Haon. I don't think I will ever be the same again."

"How true that is Eve," he replied. "We are continuously changing—it's just another aspect of the One Law, tell me what time have you got there?"

"It's just coming on seven thirty."

"I need to get back, but let me check on our friend first."

He checked the head wound, just a small seeping which he cleaned and applied a fresh dressing, fixed the bandage. "I'm sure Noah will be just fine. Do you want a hand getting his shirt back on?"

Together they dressed Noah in his dry clothes and laid him back on the mattress.

"And now I must get back up top. Are you feeling OK, besides being tired?"

"Thanks yeah, I'm really fine thanks. I can feel a rescue coming," she added, smiling.

"That's the spirit. Just before I go, may I ask a favour of you please?"

"But of course you can."

"Don't mention my presence to the rescue party when they get here please. It's important to me."

Eve's mouth dropped open in disbelief. "But I could never have done this on my own. No one would believe me."

He smiled at her. "Trust me, they will believe you Eve. You really did rescue Noah... here take this." He handed her the silver needle. "It's Egyptian, an artifact I found in the ruins above; it did a good job on the wound. We don't need to say whose hand guided it, do we?"

He rose, took her hands and looked into her eyes, "I've but two words of advice to offer," he said, his eyes penetrating yet gentle, "and they are: *grow faith*."

Dressing for God

He gave her hands a gentle squeeze before releasing his grip and then was out the door fading into the fog. Eve slowly sank to the floor beside Noah, wondering just what he meant by *'grow faith'*.

"Have faith that we will be rescued? What will that feel like?"

Eve stood up, went to the door and stepped outside, walked to the wall looking seawards, there seemed to be more movement of the fog, a definite feel of the air on her face.

'Oh please God let the weather clear. I must stay positive.' A puffin with three tiny sprats in its coloured beak perched on a rock beneath her, its big eyes clear and unblinking; it stayed there motionless watching her. She wondered, 'Was it lost, did it know where its chicks were? Why didn't it eat the little fish?'

Chapter 18

Breakthrough

Eve returned to the hut and sat beside Noah wondering what the effect of a coma might entail. She'd heard of people being in them for years and then having to try to slowly get their faculties back, some of them never fully recovering. 'Please God that Noah won't go through that,' she thought. As she looked at him in the dim light, he made a sniffle and licked his lips and momentarily his eyelids flickered, his breathing quickened. He moved his head slightly on the pillow. Eve took hold of his hand, clenched it tight, leant over him and whispered in his ear.

"Noah, Noah, wake up. Noah can you hear me? Oh God, Noah please speak to me."

Again the eyelids flickered as Eve massaged his hand, whispering in his ear, "Noah talk to me—blink if you can hear me please? Oh Noah please?"

His eyes blinked, once, twice, three times and then stayed open for about five seconds before closing again. Tears rolled down Eve's face, her control released, relief surging through her; the words tumbled out, "Oh sweet God above thank you. Oh Noah can you talk? Oh God I was so worried—can you speak?"

His mouth was trying to frame words; she put her ear close listening. He was breathing in fast gasps, the sounds forming at the back of his throat, "Watha."

"Water—he needs water."

She held the mug to his lips and fed him small sips, his tongue matted with a grey fungus, as he slowly opened and closed his mouth, letting the liquid slide down his throat. Eve taking her time; she dripped

Dressing for God

the water into his mouth, wiping the tears from her face with her forearm, leant over him and looked into his heavily bloodshot eyes.

"Noah can you hear me?"

He nodded his head, a guttural yes forming in his mouth. He reached up and touched his bandaged head, his eyes asking the question.

"You were knocked out when we hit a container. We're on Skellig Michael. You've been unconscious for….." she looked at her watch twelve minutes past eight, "For about eighteen hours. Oh Noah it's been foggy all night."

His eyes were wandering around the room; again a question in his eyes. Eve answered, "We're in the huts, in the workers huts near the lighthouse."

He nodded his head in understanding, then leant back on the pillow, closed his eyes once more. Eve remembered the paracetemol in the first aid kit.

"Noah can you swallow a tablet?" He opened his eyes, blinking yes. She crushed three in some water and fed them to him slowly. "These should help. Would you like some tea?"

His eyes opened wider in response, he gave a hushed, "Yeah… please" and a slight nod of his head.

It took about half an hour before he managed to drink the mug of strong, sweet tea, sitting up on the mattress. Eve assured him he was on the mend. "Take your time, relax you must be concussed. Everything will be OK. You'll see, the fog will clear soon."

"Fog," he whispered. "Lighthouse."

Eve sat beside him as he laboured to get his words out, "Its OK Noah relax. I've been up to the lighthouse—there's no one there."

His hand saying, no you don't understand, "Break in—break the window."

"Break in? But it's padlocked Noah, there's no one there."

He made a throwing motion with his hand, "Break the window."

"Break the window?" She asked a quizzical tone to her voice.

"Yes" he gasped "Alarm."

"There's an alarm if I break in?"

His hands saying, "Yes, go, go."

Eve ran out the door and up the pathway, stopping at the iron gate swinging open on its hinges, the fog was noticeably clearing. The visibility was at least 100 yards now. She picked up the crowbar and entered the lighthouse yard. "Which window would be alarmed?" Turning to her right, where the old living quarters were, she raised the crowbar and swung it at the kitchen window. The glass splintered inwards showering shards everywhere. There was no answering alarm so she went in search of another window to smash. All of the other windows were upper level and out of her reach but there was a green door marked Battery Room—Keep Out. Eve used the crowbar to jemmy open the door and saw inside. Rows of batteries lined the walls but again no alarm bells. "Noah must be mistaken. Anyway I've done what he asked," she dropped the crowbar on the floor and ran back to the hut.

Noah sat back on the mattress, an expectant look on his face. He gave her the thumbs up question.

"Yeah I did it and I broke into the battery room too," she said.

A big smile crossed his face and he leant back, saying, "Good, good and very good."

Chapter 19
Message Received

Derrick O'Hare was the duty Telemetry and Security Officer in the TSO command centre of the Commissioners of the Irish Lights Depot in Dun Laoire. He sat in front of the fully integrated command console showing the status of all of the eighty lighthouses dotted around the coast of Ireland. Routine status reports of all the functions were automatically transmitted by digital telemetry into the command centre. Derrick had come on watch at 0600 and was logging in the work load for the 'ILV Granuaile' maintenance and repair vessel, which was currently working in the Shannon estuary. It had been an uneventful morning for Derrick, sitting in his state of the art solar powered office in the heart of the port of Dun Laoire. A nice spring day with a touch of frost earlier, the 0820 sailing, 'Stena Adventurer' was just clearing the west pier to its right en route to Holyhead.

Derrick's attention was immediately brought back to the console. A red alarm light blinking up on his panel—intruder alarm on the Skelligs—he tapped in to see the precise location and confirmed it was the keeper's accommodation and then checked the visit rota and confirmed there were no maintenance visits scheduled. The last one was two weeks ago, so the island was deserted.

Maybe it was another false alarm, another electric glitch. He checked the records for spurious alarms on the Skelligs—nothing since November last and the local weather status in Valentia at 0600 was sea state Beaufort two to three, with thick fog, so it's not wave action at 175 feet. Better give a call to the keeper in Knightstown. He tapped on his monitor and the keeper's mobile phone number appeared and he was about to call him when another alarm went off on his screen. Skellig Michael again, this time it was in the battery room, the standby power source for the beacon. Someone had broken in to the lighthouse.

"Hello Paul, this is Derrick O'Hare here in Dun Laoire command centre."

"Hello Derrick, good morning to you, what can I do for you?"

"Paul it looks like you have unwanted company on the Skelligs. I had two alarms just now, the first one in the accommodation and now the intruder alarm in the battery room has just gone off."

"Jeepers Derrick, is that so? Well what do you know…Derrick we have a missing fishing boat situation here. The lifeboat has been out since seven doing a box search from Sneem to Portmagee. A small boat with two persons was reported missing since yesterday evening. The visibility is crap here just now, we couldn't get a chopper up but look, I'd best tell the *Cox'n* on the lifeboat and get him to head straight to Skelligs. Thanks Derrick, I'll call you back and let you know. It must be them on the island. Fingers crossed."

"*Valentia Lifeboat* this is Paul in Knightstown, come in please channel sixteen."

"Hello Paul, *Valentia Lifeboat*—go to forty two please."

"Hello Don—I just had a call from Dun Laoire control—it looks like we have visitors in the lighthouse, the intruder alarm has gone off in the accommodation and battery room, so it's a fair bet it could be our missing couple. Where are you now?"

"We're just coming out of the Kenmare Estuary Don. We could be at Skelligs in about thirty minutes. The visibility seems to be improving. Is the Coast Guard listening in? Hello Coast Guard, are you on this call?"

"Hello *Valentia Lifeboat*, yes this is the Coast Guard here monitoring—keep us posted please and good luck."

"OK, *Valentia Lifeboat* standing by channel sixteen."

Adam took the right turn at Faranfore village heading towards Killorglin and then onto the Ring of Kerry road through Glenbeigh and Cahersiveen, his mobile phone sitting on the centre console. The morning looked misty, the mountain tops wreathed in great sheets of low cloud, the sun making a weak effort to break through. He pressed on towards Valentia resisting the urge to stop for a coffee to keep his battery charged. He had hardly slept a wink all night, tossing

Dressing for God

and turning trying to keep his imagination from running away and trusting that Noah would be able to look after Eve; that they were both safe.

It was just on nine-thirty as he passed the Irish Meteorological Observatory outside Cahersiveen, shaping to make the right turn to Reenard Point and the Valentia car ferry when his phone rang. He pulled over to answer, "Hello yes?"

"Mr. King, this is Valentia Coast Guard. We have good news sir. The two persons have been located on Skellig Michael. The lifeboat crew are with them now and will be bringing them in directly."

"Oh glory be that's great news. Are they OK, are they injured?"

"Yes sir, they're both alive, though the male has a head wound and an ambulance is already arranged to bring them from Knightstown to Tralee General."

Adam gushed out his thanks, feeling a surge of relief race through his body.

"Thank you sir, you're very welcome. Yes sir, we're well pleased also. Thank you"

Adam spent the ten minute ferry ride from Reenard Point to Knightstown standing on the bridge with the ferry skipper listening to the radio traffic on the VHF.

"Aye they should be in about twenty minutes or so I hear. You can see the reception committee on the quayside there," the skipper said pointing to the garda car and the green and yellow ambulance parked outside the lifeboat shed by the jetty at Knightstown.

Adam was first off the ferry, parked his car beside the ambulance and hurried to the men gathered at the garda car. A tall man wearing the distinctive yellow sou'wester of the RNLI was speaking on a hand held VHF radio. He smiled at Adam as he approached. "Ok Don see you in ten. Cheers bye. Can I help you sir?" he asked.

"Yes please. I'm Adam King; it's my assistant Eve and our friend Noah Mahon who were on the Rosaleen. Are you the search coordinator?"

"Yes, I am." He extended his hand which Adam gratefully shook. "I'm Paul Reddan—that was the lifeboat *Cox'n* I was talking to, they'll be alongside here in a few minutes."

"The Coast Guard was saying Mr. Mahon was hurt. Have you any details?"

"Aye, apparently he has a nasty head wound and was unconscious for some time; he's a stretcher case and the lady I believe is fine. She must be quite a strong lassie by all accounts."

"Do we know what happened to them? Did their boat sink?"

"The *Cox'n* says they hit a submerged container off Skellig Michael yesterday and they managed to swim to the island and break into the OPW workers huts. We had an intruder alarm from the lighthouse this morning, picked up in Dun Laoire control, so we sent in the lifeboat to investigate. They found a life-ring from the Rosaleen on the boat landing at the top of the steps and the two survivors up in the huts reasonably safe and sound. That's them coming in now."

The *Severn class lifeboat*, 'John and Mary Doig', its number 17-07, painted in large white numerals on its navy coloured hull and the distinctive orange superstructure, had rounded Valentia Head, a huge wake veeing out behind her. It throttled back to slow speed, her bow wave reducing, as it squatted down in the water and lined up its approach through the floating pontoons of the half built marina flanking the port approach.

Adam watched in admiration as it stood off and then engines working against the rudders, with just a short burst of the bow thrusters, it pirouetted in a half circle and gently coasted in stern first alongside. Eve was standing at the stern doorway waving excitedly and was first off the boat. She ran up to Adam and leapt into his arms burying her face into his neck.

"Oh Adam, I am so happy to see you. Oh my God Adam, what a day."

"Oh Eve, I can't tell you how worried I was for you. I just thank God you're OK. You've no idea—tell me how is Noah, is it serious?"

"He's going to be OK—I'm sure. He's conscious again. I have to go to the hospital with him."

The two ambulance medics had gone aboard and now reappeared toting a yellow basket stretcher with Noah strapped in, his head swathed in a white bandage. The stretcher was manoeuvred up and along the steps into the open doors of the ambulance; Adam pressed close to the medics.

"Excuse me please but can I have a quick word with him?"

"I'm afraid not sir, we need to get him to the hospital soonest," and

Dressing for God

turning to Eve said, "Ma'am you'll need to come with us also, if you don't mind."

He smiled apologetically at Adam, "I'm sorry sir but we must be off straight away. Why don't you follow us to Tralee General?"

Adam thanked Paul and the lifeboat *Cox'n* for their help and was getting into his car when one of the boat crew handed him a notebook and Eve's wetsuit. "I think the lady left these aboard sir, can you give them to her?"

"Of course I can—many thanks." He put them on the back seat then drove to the jetty watching the ambulance disembark at the Point, worrying about Noah but feeling relief that Eve was safe and sound.

He caught up with the ambulance outside Kells and stayed in its shadow all the way to Tralee, losing it in the vast hospital car park as it stopped at the ambulance and emergency reception. Adam searched for a vacant spot, settling in the end for a grass verge, hoping the Avis sticker would discourage any wheel clamping.

Eyes closing with fatigue, he was sitting in the waiting area nursing a bottle of Lucozade wishing it was a double espresso when he spotted Eve escorted by a young doctor making her way over to him.

"I'm free to go Adam," she said taking his arm.

"Oh that's great Eve, I'm so happy to see you," he said giving her a gentle hug.

"And what news of Noah?" he asked facing the doctor, "How is Mr. Mahon doing? Is he going to be OK?"

"Yes he's OK. He's just had an MRI brain scan. The radiologist says it's mostly good news. There are no anomalies, though he has severe concussion, so we'll be keeping him in for a couple of day's observation at least. His head wound seems to be healing fine; there's no sign of infection which is pretty amazing considering the circumstances. The surgeon is still wondering what kind of suture process you used on the wound."

Eve looked a bit bemused, gave a small shrug of her shoulders said, "We used what tools we had, needs must," then reached into her shirt pocket and took out the silver needle with the remnant of thread still attached. "We sterilised the needle and thread first and then applied Vaseline to it before sewing him up."

Adam thinking to himself, "What 'we' is she talking about?"

"Can I see that please?" the doctor asked. "I've never seen anything like it before. Where did you get it?"

"In with the medical pack in the huts," Eve said, aware she was not telling a lie; "It *had* come with the medical pack in a sense."

"Amazing." he said, returning the needle. Adam picked it up looking from the needle to Eve and back again, but he chose to stay mute, thinking 'Where did I stay last night? In the Threadneedle Hotel in Threadneedle Street two minutes walk from Lloyds in Lime Street. This is all very strange. And what 'we' did she mean?'

"Is it possible to see Mr. Mahon?" Eve changing the subject put the needle back in her pocket.

"Well he's on his way to the ward just now; he's had a sedative so I suggest tomorrow morning might be a better time. You look like you could use some rest yourself ma'am, you too sir, if I may say so."

"OK thanks doctor", Adam said smiling gratefully. "C'mon young lady, let's head for home."

"Where's your car?" she asked, as he opened the door of the hired VW Passat.

"Its still at Cork Airport. I changed flights to Kerry to get here as quick as I could." He looked at her as she slumped into the passenger seat. He indicated behind her, "Your stuff is back there; your notebook and wetsuit."

"Oh heavens above I'd forgotten all about it." she said looking over shoulder.

"Uh Adam, there's so much to talk about. I've got so, so much to tell you but it'll have to keep for later and I'm absolutely bushed. Forgive me if I just close my eyes, I'm totally whacked."

Adam drove carefully, giving thanks for the amazing rescue. 'What a day,' he thought. He remembered something registering in his mind when he signed for the car this morning. The date—today was Friday March 13. 'Unlucky for some,' he thought, 'and very lucky for others and I won't forget this day for a long, long time. Thank you God,' he intoned quietly to himself. "Thank you God."

Chapter 20

Deliverance

It was Tuesday, March 17, St. Patrick's Day. and the three musketeers as Noah had taken to naming them, were celebrating Noah's release from hospital, seated around Noah's dining table enjoying an after dinner coffee. Noah was nursing a glass of mineral water. "I'm a caffeine free zone until I get the all clear from the doc," he said.

His wound had a clean dressing on it in lieu of the wrap-around, turban bandage he came ashore in and altogether he was very much back to his former vigour.

"I still have a memory gap though, from the time she drove us onto the container and sank poor Rosaleen, to when I came to, lying on the floor in the hut and me telling her to go break the windows in the lighthouse."

Eve almost choked on her drink, "The bloody cheek of the man. 'Give it some wellie', he said and then he fell overboard leaving me to fend for myself—men!" she said in mock exasperation.

"How are the stitches?" Eve enquired "Did they have to replace them?"

"Funny you should say that; the first doctor who saw them, the intern, he was going to take them out when the theatre sister it was, suggested that he wait until the surgeon saw them. She said it was the best hem stitch she'd ever seen. And the surgeon then decided that it would make a bigger scar to remove the thread so other than some new sterile dressings it's exactly as you stitched me."

Eve smiled, "That's excellent," and then held up her hand stopping further comment, "I've something to tell you about that, but later. OK?"

"There's something I want to show you both," Adam said. "If you'll just hang on there a minute." He placed his laptop on the table and logged on.

"Noah what was your bio-rhythm like when you had the accident on the twelfth? Do you know?"

"Sure I haven't a clue Adam. I suppose it wasn't too clever seeing as how I left the VHF battery on the table in the house."

"Aye and you left your phone in the car, and you weren't wearing your life vest, and you had the accident and nearly died on us. Well just look at this then; I checked it out as soon as I got back here on Friday. Your birthday is September 18, 1969 right?"

"You know it is, go on show me what you've got there."

Adam entered Noah's date of birth and the date of the accident March 12, 2009 into one of his bio-rhythm programmes and swivelled the screen around so both Noah and Eve could see it.

Biorhythm			
--Date--	**D O W N**	**0**	**U P**
3/10/9	P I E	I	
3/11/9	P I E	I	
3/12/9	P I	E	
3/13/9		*	E
3/14/9		I	I P E
3/15/9		I	I P E
3/16/9		I	I P E

"Look at this," Adam said. "See how all three cycles, the '**P**' for the physical, '**E**' for the emotional and the '**I**' for the intelligence bodies are all crossing over! You were triple critical Noah—sure you were an accident just waiting to happen!"

"Bloody hell," Noah exclaimed. "So it is—I was feeling a bit out of it all right; that's amazing."

Eve's eyes were open wide a look of astonishment on her face. "I don't believe it. Did you make that up Adam? I mean, it's just like that guy you told me about who lost his leg; it's a triple critical day."

Dressing for God

She faced Noah, "Did you know about this before we left Sneem?"

"Of course I didn't. Do you think I wouldn't have been more careful if I knew I was like that? Ah I knew about the rhythms all right, I just never used them really. But I'll tell you what, I will be using them from now on though."

"Isn't that a bit like going to the dentist with a problem and he telling you that you must floss your teeth and you saying, 'yeah I have the stuff in the bathroom at home but I always forget to use it."

"I suppose it is, now stop giving me a hard time. I'm giving me-self a hard enough time as it is." He turned facing Adam, looking him straight in the eye, "And for the love of God don't tell Hannah about this or I'll never hear the end of it. Please. Promise me now."

"All right, I won't tell her, but that's not to say she won't ask you and then you'll have to 'fess up."

"And I just might confide in her," chipped in Eve. "It appears to me that you need someone to give you a hard time, you big Irish lump."

"Oh God, I was waiting for this. Remember now, I'm in a delicate state of health. Don't go upsetting me and starting a trauma."

He took Eve's hands in his. "Listen seriously now Miss Eve, I can never thank you enough for saving my life." His eyes went all misty with tears, "I will never be able to repay you. Bless you."

Eve felt her eyes moisten, leaned over and rubbed noses with Noah, Eskimo fashion. "There," she said, "that's an Inuit kiss for you and you don't have to thank me. We were in this together and I can assure you it was a very strange experience for me as well as for you. I haven't told Adam much about it yet because I was waiting for all of us to be together first. Also I wanted to make as many notes about the experience as possible so as to remember everything he said to me."

"What *he* are you talking about?" asked Adam.

"Do you want to hear what actually happened?" she asked.

"We most certainly do." They both said, "Hasn't she told you anything then?" Noah asked Adam.

"No. Just about the accident and swimming to the steps and the rescue. She's been busy writing in her notebook there, said she didn't want to tell the story twice."

"Right then, gents. First off I need to ask a favour of each of you please. OK?"

"Yes, sure, go ahead."

"Well, listen while I share this in confidence with you please. That's the favour; please respect the confidence, OK?" They both agreed.

"You see we weren't alone on the island, we had help." She watched the looks of bewilderment spread across their faces.

"What do you mean we had 'help?" Noah asked.

"Just that, when you passed out completely at the steps, you were semi-comatose on the way in, swearing now and again to let me know you were still alive. You can apologise for that later—well, I was too exhausted to move you up the steps so I tied off the life-ring to the handrail with a scrap of rope to stop you floating away and I literally dropped off from utter exhaustion. I don't know how long I was like that, and then I felt this hand tapping me on the shoulder and helping me up the steps. Next he went down into the water and threw the life-ring up on the landing and then carried you up in a fireman's lift."

Noah exchanged a deep puzzled look with Adam who was transfixed at what Eve was saying. She continued the story.

"It was he who found the wheelbarrow and brought us to the huts. He it was who broke the doors down and got the heating going. He found the first aid kit and yes, he stitched Noah's wound not me. I couldn't stitch a wound. I can stitch a button on a shirt and I did first aid for my diving course but nothing like that."

"Well for God's sake who was he; where did he come from?" Adam asked.

"He said his name was A'Haon. He pronounced it Ahane, OK? He said he was on the island on private business and that he was a spiritual archaeologist, and that he was staying in the cells up at the summit. I had to give my word that I wouldn't tell anyone about him being on the island. I know it's OK to tell you two, but that's it. Agreed?"

They nodded their agreement.

"Was he one of the monks, was he dressed, you know in monks gear?" Noah asked, "How come I never saw him?"

"No, he wasn't a monk. He was dressed in a sort of fisherman's smock. It was like a cotton canvas, quite heavy. His pants were the same stuff and he wore some kind of soft leather espadrilles. And the reason you never saw him was because he had left by the time you came around. He said he had to get back up top to the beehive huts. His last words to me were 'Grow faith.'"

"Grow faith?"

Dressing for God

"Yes just that. He said, 'I have two words of advice for you and they are, 'Grow faith.'"

"Very strange," Adam said. Noah was silent, looking strangely at Eve.

"That's more than very strange, that's outright scary."

"I know," said Eve. "I've been thinking a lot about it since I got back. That's what I've been writing; my memories of everything he shared with me. It was all about how life works Adam. It was all about the answers I was looking for. I had made this list up on Wednesday after you left, so we could start getting your interview stuff ready and it was only when I got back here and started writing up what he said that I realized the... I was going to say coincidence, but I recognised the *synchronicity* of it all. I just about got all of the answers to all the questions that were on my mind."

"What did you say his name was again?" Adam asked "A'Haon?"

"Yes," she said. "A'Haon."

"A haon, a do, a tri, a ceathar—that's one, two, three, four in Gaelic!!" Adam said.

"A haon means ONE," said Noah.

Eve smiling replied, "Yes I figured that out for myself. I Googled it and guess what AON means in Gaelic also? It means *wise one*."

"But this," she said, "this is the kicker."

"Adam—Noah, look at this," Eve extracted a sheet of paper from her notebook and held it up, the large letters printed on it spelling out A'HAON.

"Isn't that Noah's name spelled backwards...now what do you make of that?" she asked.

Chapter 21

You Reap As You Sow

Adam had been writing tirelessly. He'd scrapped the first draft of his book and had started afresh using the insights Eve had captured in her notes. His daily routine started at five AM, sipping an eye-opening mug of tea while he read his emails. Then it was into action sailing with Captain John across the inner seas until around eight thirty he put the boat on auto-pilot and joined Eve for breakfast in the kitchen.

He was in his writing zone, as he called it and he stayed like that, quietly absorbed in his work, only occasionally surfacing to check with Eve on some point in her 'Skelligs Experience' notebook. Then it was back to his routine, tapping away on the computer, living in John's boat *My Trust*, until the early afternoon when he'd join Eve in a long walk along the coast, sharing what he'd written on Captain John's recent venture. Eve would listen and then offer critique. Adam would note her challenges and do some revision to his draft when they returned home. Then it was an early supper and into his bed and sleep before ten. It seemed to be working well. He felt that *My Trust* was close to getting full clearance into Port Abundance and he sensed that Captain John had sorted out his self steering problems using his new EFT tool box.

Noah had thankfully made a full recovery and sported a souvenir L-shape scar on his scalp and other than having a complete blackout on his 'missing day', he was in good spirits. The *D'Ark Rosaleen II* was now anchored safely off Oyster Bed Pier. McCarthy Marine had delivered it to Sneem, 'To save him the bother of sailing it home' as they had diplomatically put it. He was currently deeply immersed in a new series of paintings.

Dressing for God

"I'm exorcising a few ghosts of me own," was how he put it to Adam, and "Hopefully I can express what I'm feeling on a few canvases." He said he'd be in touch with them by and by.

They were sitting in Adam's Land Rover watching a glorious sunset over Kenmare Bay, the few small clouds above the horizon were glowing vividly in a moving palette of liquid colours—purple and indigo melding with streaks of gory, red splotches and then molten sheets of golden light seemed to pour from the heavens onto the sea stretching away from them.

"Sure you couldn't paint that if you tried," Eve said in wonder, more to break the silence between them than anything else.

Adam was sitting quietly, looking preoccupied. Eve couldn't help but notice that he had something on his mind. He turned sideways to face her, "Eve, I need to talk to you about something really personal," his voice trailed off as he let out a deep sigh of exasperation, and then moistened his lips with the tip of his tongue. Eve waited watching him, silent.

"I don't really know where to start." His voice was strained now. Eve thinking how out of character this was, she had never seen him so unsure of himself before.

"Well you could always try starting from now." she said quietly, leaning towards him in her seat, her voice full of understanding. "There really is nowhere else to be, is there?"

He allowed himself a small smile. "No, I suppose you're right at that." He straightened up in the seat, "I should have seen that myself. Now is the only place to work from isn't it? Thanks."

"You're welcome. Now then, what's bothering you?"

"Oh it's that old maxim of 'doctor heal yourself first, before you try healing anyone else'. Tell me, would you be surprised to know that I also had a boat sink on me?"

"You did? When was that? You never mentioned it before."

"No I didn't. I never really talked about it with anyone before. Do you remember the story I told you about the ghost?"

"Of course I do. Why, is there more to it than you told me?" He nodded yes. "Indeed there was. I honestly thought that I'd got the entire trauma of that episode out of my system. But is seems that I haven't. I only got rid of some of it and then I buried the rest deep within myself. I know the experience of bringing that wee soul home exposed me to a surfeit of psychic energy, it's is as good a way as any to describe it. It's a bit like being exposed to uranium and you can become radioactive. Well I got psychically over-exposed from that experience. But I told you about that didn't I?"

"Yeah, you did," she said in a soft voice.

"I've been noticing for a while now there was always something going astray in my life. It was as if some deep feeling or memory was locked solid in my unconscious and was sending out all these wrong messages and I couldn't for the life of me figure out what it was. It was like I'd be clear about what I was after and I'd do all the necessary steps but the opposite would happen."

"Is this your alter ego Captain John having this problem, or is it you?" she asked.

"I suppose it's both of us really. I began to think there was a stowaway in my steering gear with a mind of its own, and when I read about your lighthouse technique of going into the 'I am of myself' and asking for help from above, well I saw this as a great technique. I started the exercise a few weeks ago. I asked my higher self for some inner healing and last night I woke up with a real clear, deep prompt to clean on the sinking of this rig I'd been involved in way back. That sinking marked another critical turn point in my life. Basically because it carried huge pain memories and I had buried it as deep as I could to ensure it would never see the light of day again, which is where I wanted it to stay—until today that is."

"Do go on, please."

"It all started shortly after the ghost experience. I'd set myself up as a project consultant and got a start as a contract project manager with a would-be drilling company. They had a couple of scrap oil rigs and a colleague of mine, let's call him Dick, got a contract to convert two of them and he put the first one to work drilling in the Far East. I got involved getting the second rig ready for another contract to drill in Australia. It was great business for the guys who owned the rigs, as they never had to put their hands in their pockets for any of the conversion work, as Dick negotiated with the oil company to pay for the work up front as a forward payment against the rig day-rate. Talk about a sweetheart deal. It was amazing."

"We did really well and made good progress. We moved the rig to a shipyard in Singapore; the drilling contract was in place and we

Dressing for God

were about a month or so away from sail-away. I had finished my remit and asked to be paid my promised bonus. I didn't have my deal with the owner in writing you understand, I was naive enough then, to believe in a gentlemen's agreement and so when it came time for the rig owner to put his money where his mouth was, I found that his forgetfulness was stronger than his handshake. 'What bonus', he said?"

"I took this very badly as I had been budgeting the cash to make mortgage payments, and school fees, and taxes and when I knew that I'd been royally screwed by this guy, well I was more than annoyed, to say the least. It was a very costly lesson."

"What did you do?" Eve asked.

"Oh for a while I used my psychic energy to screw things up with them but I soon realized that this was playing with fire and the only one getting burnt was little me, so I stopped. I remember reading about a technique called 'Let go and let God' at the time and so I decided that I would hand the problem over to the big fella up top and see if he could maybe swing some bucks in my direction. Meantime, I tried not to put anymore energy into the drama."

"And what happened then? Did you get your results?"

"Ah, indeed I did and not the one I was after either. I managed to stay removed from feeling angry, but it wasn't easy as the home environment was crap and there were no more project prospects on the horizon. As far as I can honestly recall now, I managed to stay fairly philosophical about it and tried not to think of getting my own back. And then a few weeks later Dick and I were sitting in his garden in Singapore and he told me how he too had been screwed by Mr. Owner. He was really teed off and he started wondering how he could recover what was owed. I'd just started reading this book called *Three Magic Words* by U.S. Anderson and well I won't be spoiling the read for you when I say that those three magic word were 'I am God'! Yes, it was all about understanding the truth of self, being the spark of divinity as soul. It was the first time I had ever heard of the concept and I found it fascinating."

Eve said, "I saw the book in your bookcase."

"It's well worth a read, you'd enjoy it. Anyway I listened to Dick rant on about the owner owing him a bunch of money and I'm thinking about the $30,000 dollars I was owed, so I suggested we do this 'Let go and let God' exercise together."

"And," Eve asked, "what happened?"

"Well, Dick thought it was worth a try, so we agreed that we wouldn't influence the outcome with any preconceived thinking and we also agreed we wouldn't take the slightest pleasure from whatever result manifested."

Adam had a faraway look in his eyes, obviously very much back in the moment as he resumed his story. "So we shook hands and then did the exercise together. We silently contemplated on our grievances and handed over our gripe to God and waited to see what happened next. We opened a few Tiger beers and watched the geckos playing colour changes on the side of the veranda. We were completely caught off guard."

"I'm being very serious now and I know it sounds off the wall but it's completely true. Less than thirty minutes later Dick was called into the house to take a phone call. I heard him screaming for me to come in and listen. The drilling rig which had been working in the South China Sea, working in 400 metres of water, had just had a blowout. It had been drilling through what we call a BOP—a blow out preventer—when it hit this shallow pocket of $H2SO4$ and it ruptured the drill string and they had a massive blowout. As Dick was speaking on the phone all of the crew were doing an emergency evacuation—it was a real disaster. There were fifty or so guys on board. The phone call was from a pal of Dick's in the oil company head office, who knew Dick's involvement with the rig and he'd called him immediately after he'd heard the news."

"That's totally weird," Eve said.

"Weird maybe, but absolutely synchronous wouldn't you say? Honest, I'm not making this up."

"I believe you. It's unreal, what did you do then?"

"Dick's next phone call was to the rig owner. Dick was actually the first one to tell him of the blowout, which wasn't too nicely received either. So Dick asked him nice and polite, 'If maybe he could use our help in saving the rig' and ahem, obviously we'd like our debts paid up front please."

"But not surprisingly, he chose to ignore our offer and the rig sank twenty four hours later. The sea gets like a big bubble bath aerated with the gas and the rig just turned over and vanished beneath the waves. I don't really believe we could have got her out of there anyway, but we'll never know now will we? So that was the beginning of the end of that drilling company. And no, there was no loss of life or injuries to any of the crew, but I certainly suffered as a result; because it was the beginning of the end of a chapter in my life too."

"That's quite, quite scary," Eve said.

"Scary it was. I was scared shitless, if you will pardon the expression. I had so much conflict going on inside me and I just didn't know where to turn. I kept asking myself if I was responsible for causing the blowout and yet I knew I would never have dreamed of causing such havoc. But then I'd wonder if somehow maybe I had started it unknowingly. You know those three magic words and all that?"

"But you didn't cause it, did you? You and Dick both 'Let go and let God' and you said you didn't influence the outcome—wasn't that like an act of God—I mean a real act of God?"

"I wish I knew the answer to that. I've been spending most of the day trying to get my head around it. Did I consciously ask for a judgement from God, rationalising that I was really neutral in my request for a balance, while unconsciously I had already judged Mr. Rig Owner as being guilty? And when I look at it from that viewpoint, then yes, unconsciously I was pissed off at him and wanted justice. So on that basis yes, I probably was as much a part of the judgement as everyone else."

"Judge not lest ye be judged and all that," Eve offered.

"Precisely and I'm only beginning to see it now. I mean our attitudes are making our judgement calls for us every moment of our lives and we don't have to be consciously aware of them for them to be effective do we? So yeah, I'm just now beginning to accept that I was part of the judgement also. Cause and effect is life's balancing act—if you play with fire and *if you don't have protection in place* you get burned."

"And I suppose you don't have to be aware of what you are sowing in the subconscious for it to come back and hit you between the eyes. You reap as you sow. Oh Adam, you have been learning the hard way haven't you?"

"I can't even begin to tell you the relief I'm feeling right now in finding this out. I mean I can do something about it now. I have the tools; I can get at these buried pain memories and own them consciously. The hurt and guilt stuff surrounding this memory, well I just couldn't face them anymore and I never, ever, spoke again about what happened, to anybody, ever—to anyone but to you—until now that is."

Eve reached across and gently touched his hand.

"That's the memory that's been my stowaway in the self steering gear. That's the critter that's been trying to protect me from using myself realization and I'm the one who put it there in the first place. So today I got my window cleaners working with me on the other side of my unconscious self and I'm cleaning from the inside out. I can now accept full responsibility for causing this memory miasm in the first place. I ask forgiveness from everyone involved without exception, from Dick, from Mr. Owner, from my family and from anyone else involved and I ask for the memory window cleaners to get their squeegees out and start erasing please. I am so grateful and yes I know unconditional love is the currency that matters and there's another 'Yes Eve', your lighthouse technique is brilliant. Thank you."

"I am so pleased Adam, that's just beautiful. I am so happy for you, but it wasn't really my technique Adam. I was just the messenger."

"Well your message is well received here. It wouldn't have happened without you. I feel so good, so light getting that trauma off my chest—I had no idea I was so lumbered with my past—that it was messing me up so much."

Eve felt a surge of gratitude flood through her body and she leant over and gave Adam a hug, "I am just so," her words trailed off as she exhaled deeply, "There are no words can express just how good I feel. I'm just totally chuffed that I could help you." She sat back in her seat and held him at arm's length.

"Eve McQueen, dear Eve," she could feel his pulse quicken as he spoke. Then he gave a small shrug of his shoulders and continued, "I was wondering," he hesitated, his eyebrows wrinkling his brow. "I was wondering if you could eh, maybe stay on here a while longer until the draft copy of the manuscript has been accepted by my publisher. You know help me cross the t's and dot the i's. Would you be up for that? I'd really appreciate it if you could."

"Of course Adam—I always finish what's on my plate."

Chapter 22

Whole In One

Adam saved his draft and sat looking at the keyboard with mixed feelings. Captain John was home. He'd made it into Abundance and *My Trust* was tied up in the marina. Captain John was probably getting sluiced down in a hot shower in the clubhouse already, and then it'll be off to meet his old shipmate for dinner and a few beers. It had been some trip since he set out in The Prodigal all those years ago. So much water had passed under his bridge. He suddenly remembered something, shouted out.

"Eve, Eve are you there?" He arose from the desk and stood there looking down at the screen, a big truth dawning on him.

Eve hurried in from the kitchen, wiping her hands in a tea towel. "Yes Adam what is it?"

Adam pointed at the screen, "C'mere—take a look at this, he's in. *My Trust*'s moored at berth forty four in the marina and John's gone ashore to meet the harbour master. It's over. He's finally made it home."

Adam faced her, "And I couldn't have done it without you Eve. You really did make all the difference. I don't know how I can ever thank you enough."

Eve smiled and read the final paragraph on the screen, then laid her hand on Adam's shoulder.

"Actually Adam I'm the one who wants to thank you, for I too have grown in this experience."

She reached over to her desk and retrieved a sheet of paper from her journal and handed it to him.

"Here, my dear friend, this is for you. It's my way of thanking you Adam and saying, yes I also understand the How of Life. I do hope it pleases you."

J.F. Tallon

Adam opened the folded sheet of paper and silently read Eve's poem.

He was transfixed. He read it one more time and then holding the page close to his heart, he turned to Eve, feelings of gratitude and joy overwhelming him. He swallowed deeply and quietly said, "Oh dear God Eve, you got it in one, this is so beautiful. Thank you."

Dressing for God

Laundered in the wash of life's subconscious spin
The stains of blame and hurt and guilt resolved, dissolved and gone
My cloak of consciousness hangs
Freshly pressed
In Life's renewal dressing room.

So firstly
I assume the mantle of being Me
And in accepting Me
As whom I am being
I am mindful of all the other 'I Ams' I have been before
I look at each in all of it I was
And WHO it is I Aim to Be…
In this
It is
I Am

Soul thus draped and cloaked
Remembers not the who and where
Yet conscious all the while of why
It is
I am
Being Me

Dressing for God

I slip down a flight into our causal place
Where dwell the matchers and dispatchers into space
I'm checked for flight, my silver cord attached
I'm shown the plan and then it's wiped from sight

My targets picked and then it's curl up tight
Foetal first and head-first towards the light

I Am
Dear God
At last
Now

Dressed
For
Life

- Eve McQueen

EPILOGUE

20-01-2010

"*My Trust, My Trust,* this is Abundance Port Control, come in please *My Trust.*"

"Hello Port Control, this is My Trust—channel twenty four please."

"My Trust this is Port Control, Good morning Captain John; we have good news for you at last. Your inward clearance has been granted and you're assigned berth 44 in the small boat marina. The pilot cutter Deliverance is on its way in from seaward and will be at the fairway buoy in thirty minutes—can you follow it into port please? And also, the Harbour Master invites you to a welcome home reception this evening."

"Thank you Port Control; that is fantastic news, marvellous. I'll get under way immediately and yes thank Captain Magnusson for me and tell him I look forward to seeing him.... This is *My Trust* standing by on channel sixteen."

John weighed anchor immediately and headed over to the Eye of the Needle entrance channel awaiting the arrival of Deliverance to lead him through the narrows protecting the fabled harbour. He'd anticipated this moment for so long and now it was happening. His excitement was palpable, his mind was chocker block full of expectation; there was so much to look forward to... and then a sudden realisation stopped him in his tracks. Finity Muze will be waiting to see him at the reception. Darn it. He had nought ready for his showdown interview.

Deliverance was bearing down on him at a rate of knots—it cannot be more than five minutes away he reckoned; he had to get his act together in quick time.

Dressing for God

"What have I learned?" he asked inwardly. "What realisation can I share with Finity that is not already known?"

The answer was immediate and it was embodied in the word *realization*.

"I know what I'll do," he thought. "I'll share my own life voyage *realization* with her. The realization' *that it is a man's self-knowing mind that creates his own unique perception of reality. And that it is his unity with the whole of creation in the conscious side of Life that guarantees his oneness with the whole of God. Yes,*" he thought, "*I am a living pixel in the one big picture of the Creators expanding consciousness.*"

Deliverance drew abeam and he brought *My Trust* round and followed in her wake as she threaded her way through the Eye of the Needle channel into Port Abundance. He smiled broadly as he repeated his poem aloud—

"I am sailing in a boat named Trust, on an inner sea of being, knowing that my pilot has my aye to take me home, eye bring me home."

Acknowledgements

I have always held that ideas do not belong to anyone. All ideas derive from God, therefore no idea belongs to anyone, but we all have access to every idea in the divine providence. It is like the figure two. What intelligent mathematician would say, 'The figure two belongs to me'? The mathematician knows that it is impersonal; the concept belongs to the universe. It can be used many times and there is just as much left. We need to believe that reality is already delivered to us — reality as we see it, according to our awareness of it.

—Ernest Holmes

'My-Trust's on-board library did not contain the charts, pilot books, nautical almanacs and tide tables of the Earth's Oceans but instead housed the works of eminent Self-explorers of the Inner Seas of Life. Herein was the source of Captain John's inspiration and guidance that helped him navigate across the 'mind-field of consciousness' safely into Port Abundance.

Prominent amongst these explorers was Ernest Holmes. His work, 'The Science of Mind' was a source of enlightenment when the fog of the 'dark night of the Soul' descended and clouded Captain John's horizon. Mention must also be made of the valued insight gained from the exploratory journals of C.W Leadbetter and Annie Besant of the Theosophical Society. My thanks go to Mike Dooley for permission to use quotations from his wonderful book, "Notes from The Universe." Dr Joe Vitale's work with Dr Hew Len in "Zero Limits" also merits mention as does Rhonda Byrnes book 'The Secret'. I gratefully acknowledge the work of Brad Yates in EFT which provides a cornerstone of the narrative. I owe special thanks to Alison Dowling

Dressing for God

and Niall Wallace for their support and encouragement in getting this work finished.

References are made to "Three Magic Words" by U.S. Andersen and "The Ghost of Flight 401" by John G Fuller. The descriptions associated with these works in the storyline are factual.

I am most grateful to Richard Foran, the non-resident lighthouse keeper for Skellig Michael for his tour of the Skelligs Lighthouse. Richard is also the RNLI rescue co-ordinator based in Valentia Island and he and the staff of the Irish Coastguard Service provided valuable in depth colour for the rescue scene. And most importantly, I graciously acknowledge the synchronicity of the Universe in delivering Ed Cowan of Mosaic Press to my doorstep in answer to my prayer for editorial and publication assistance. Ed and his wife Nuala provided the means to the end for which I am so grateful. And indeed my special thanks are extended to Howard Aster who is the spiritual driver behind Mosaic Press and who thankfully persisted in getting this book out there.

And last but not least, my love and thanks are extended to my wife Vanessa who was an ever present 'sounding board' for Adam, during this voyage home.

Thank you one and all

Finbar Tallon
31st December 2010

J.F. Tallon

Portrait J F Tallon—painted by V Tallon

Finbar Tallon was born in Dublin. He went to sea with Irish Shipping Ltd. as an apprentice deck officer and graduated as a master mariner. On his thirtieth birthday he started a new career in project management in subsea engineering living in the Far East. In Singapore he had a major life changing experience when he was tasked to escort a 'lost Soul' home across the veil. The impact of this experience led him to study the complementary aspects of the hidden side of life and it is from this background that *Dressing for God* was written. Finbar lives with his wife Vanessa, in SW Kerry, Ireland, overlooking Valentia Island and the Atlantic Ocean.